"WHAT IN THE NAME OF . . ."

Geordi's voice trailed off as he stared through his VISOR at the screen.

The main viewer was filled with an image of a type of spacecraft none of them had ever seen before. It was Romulan in configuration, but it was *huge*, nearly twice the size of any Romulan ship they had ever encountered. It was unquestionably a warbird, possessing the same predatory birdlike lines that were the trademark of the Romulan shipwrights, but it was clearly an altogether different class of vessel. This was an advanced design, with larger, more powerful engine nacelles, and it was bristling with other innovations. Even at this range, they could see that it would dwarf the *Enterprise*.

"Red alert, Mr. Riker," said Picard.

Look for STAR TREK Fiction from Pocket Books

Star Trek: The Original Series

Star Trek: The Next Generation

Star Trek: Deep Space Nine

#26

STAR TREK®

THE NEXT GENERATION™

THE ROMULAN PRIZE

SIMON HAWKE

POCKET BOOKS

New York London Toronto Sydney Tokyo Singapore

An *Original* Publication of POCKET BOOKS

POCKET BOOKS, a division of Simon & Schuster Inc.
1230 Avenue of the Americas, New York, NY 10020

ISBN: 0-671-79746-8

First Pocket Books printing May 1993

10 9 8 7 6 5 4 3 2 1

POCKET and colophon are registered trademarks of Simon & Schuster Inc.

Printed in the U.S.A.

For Bruce and Peggy Wiley,
with grateful acknowledgment to
Pat Connors, Scott Glener, Seth Morris,
Henry Tyler and Rikki Winters

Prologue

DEANNA TROI wrenched herself free from the nightmare with an unaccustomed force of will, gasping for breath. She sat bolt upright in bed, disoriented and confused. She could feel the dampness on her skin and on the twisted sheets, but it wasn't her sweat, and the accelerated pulse rate she seemed to feel was not that of her heart. In fact, it hadn't even been her dream, and the force of will that had exerted its iron control to wrench her out of it was not her will.

Had she been fully human, Deanna Troi might have felt frightened and confused by such a strange and powerful experience, but she was half Betazoid, and Betazoids had a more profound understanding of the phenomenon of empathy than humans did. Humans were certainly capable of empathy, but not to the same extent as Betazoids, whose senses and levels of psychic awareness were much more developed and fine-tuned than those of humans. Being half human, however, Deanna experienced a brief moment of fear and disorientation. Then she realized what had happened and was up and running toward the door, pausing only long enough to pull on her robe.

As she ran barefoot down the deck's long, curving corridor, she quickly noted that it was still night watch, for the corridor was illuminated in a soft red glow. Beyond the night-watch lighting, Deanna had no clear idea of the time. She hadn't paused to check; she had simply reacted instantly to the profound empathic link she'd just experienced. She knew whose dream she had shared.

She was capable of forging an empathic link with any member of the *Enterprise* crew, but only one man had a force of will so strong that a link could be formed spontaneously, unconsciously, and with such force and intensity. She stopped at the door to the captain's quarters and pressed the small panel that activated the chime inside.

The door slid open, and from within she heard a weary yet strong and resonant voice say, "Come."

She entered, and the door automatically slid shut behind her. It was dark in the captain's quarters, but there was light coming from the bedroom. Deanna hesitated. "Captain?" she said uncertainly. "Captain, are you all right?"

"A moment, Counselor, and I shall be right with you," he replied, from the bedroom.

She stood and waited, moistening her lips nervously. The effects of the empathic link were now diminished, and her heart was no longer racing. She gathered her energies and centered her concentration, allowing a calm to descend upon her. She brushed her dark hair back away from her face and checked to see that her robe was properly belted. Then the light came on, and Captain Jean-Luc Picard entered the room.

He had put on a short robe, but his feet were bare. Otherwise, except for his somewhat haggard expression, he appeared every bit the commanding presence he always was on the bridge of the starship *Enterprise*.

"May I offer you something to drink, Counselor?" he said. "My throat feels a bit dry."

"Perhaps some water." Deanna sensed that the captain still felt some distress, but was trying to conceal it.

He got each of them a glass of water.

"You know why I am here, of course," she said.

He nodded. "Please, sit down, Deanna."

His unaccustomed use of her first name gave her some comfort. While not a stickler for military protocol, Picard usually addressed his crew members formally. His use of her first name indicated that he wished this to be an informal discussion. And a private one.

"It seems I have unwittingly alarmed you," he said. "Please accept my sincere apologies. It was merely a nightmare, nothing more."

"With all due respect, Captain," she replied, "it was much more than *merely* a nightmare. What I felt was far more profound."

He pursed his lips thoughtfully, then nodded. "Very well. How much did you feel, and exactly what did you sense?"

She paused a moment to consider her reply. "I sensed . . . fear. Profound anxiety. A sense of helplessness and loss of control. Almost . . . panic. All emotions I generally do not associate with you."

He nodded and took a sip of water. "A forced

empathic link," he said. "Unconscious on my part, of course. I would never do that consciously; I hope you realize that."

"I do," replied Deanna. She hesitated. "I also realize that what happened was very unusual and, in a way, constituted a subconscious call for help."

"Was it only my feelings that you shared, or did you experience the dream, itself?" Picard asked.

Deanna had to stop and think about that. It had all happened so quickly and she had reacted so instantaneously that there hadn't been time to analyze exactly what she had picked up. "Only the feelings," she said after a moment. "If I experienced any part of your dream, I cannot recall it now."

He nodded once again. "Just as well," he said. "However, everything is fine now. I appreciate your concern and your timely response, and I apologize once again for having unconsciously impinged upon your rest."

"Perhaps it would help if we discussed the dream." Deanna didn't like to push, and though she knew the captain valued her counsel, he was and always had been a very private person. She had never experienced a forced empathic link with him before, and the fact that it had happened argued strongly in favor of discussing what had prompted it, even if he was reluctant to do so.

"I really don't think that will be necessary," he replied with a smile that seemed to her forced. "I have disturbed you enough for one night. I am perfectly fine, I assure you."

He was not entirely convincing, however, and Deanna sensed that the dream was still bothering him. "Sir," she said uneasily, "I sense that your dream disturbed you greatly, and you are not generally disturbed by nightmares. I strongly suggest that we discuss it."

He seemed about to protest, then reconsidered. "Very well, Counselor," he said, reverting to formal address, a direct reaction to her reminding him of her role aboard the ship. He drank the remainder of his water and set the glass down. "I dreamed that I had lost control of this ship," he said. "The dream itself was somewhat disjointed, as dreams often are, so I cannot describe the exact circumstances. However, through some error or malfeasance on my part, I exposed the crew to grave danger, and I was utterly helpless to do anything about it."

"What sort of danger?" asked Deanna.

Picard compressed his lips into a tight grimace. "I cannot say," he replied. "I only know that through some action, or perhaps inaction, I lost control of the ship, and my crew. . . ." He frowned and shook his head. "Something terrible was happening to the crew, and there was absolutely nothing I could do to stop it. I felt a strong sense of impending disaster, and there seemed to be a heavy weight on my shoulders." He smiled suddenly. "Doubtless the symbolic burden of my responsibilities." He shrugged, attempting to min- imize the importance of the dream. "It was merely a stress reaction, nothing more. I imagine this sort of dream comes frequently to those in command."

"Perhaps, sir," she replied, "but it does not come frequently to you. I have seen how you react under stress. We have both been in situations where the stress was considerable, and you have never reacted with fear or panic."

"Well, Counselor, I am only human, after all," Picard said, with a self-deprecating smile.

"You are a human who has never been known to

panic in any situation," she replied. "Panic is simply not in your nature. Such a response is an anomaly. And you have never before had any dreams or feelings, either conscious or subconscious, strong enough to trigger a forced empathic link. It is a highly profound and unusual occurrence, even among Betazoids. With all due respect, Captain, this dream cannot be dismissed casually." She seemed to sense something, a brief impression, a guarded one, then just as suddenly it was gone. She decided to pursue it. "Tell me, sir, have you ever had a precognitive dream?"

Picard grimaced. "There is not much point in trying to keep anything from you, is there?" he replied.

"Sir, it is not my intention to be intrusive, but my role aboard this ship is—"

"Yes, yes, I know," Picard replied impatiently. "Forgive me, Counselor, I am annoyed with myself, not with you. There are some thingsss I am hesitant oo discuss with anyone, things of a private nature. However, where they may concern the safety of the ship and its crew, I should not shy away from them."

"So the answer is yes," she said.

Picard nodded. "Yes," he said. "I have had precognitive dreams, but only twice before."

"And in those rare occurrences, did the dreams come true?" she asked, pressing him in spite of her natural reluctance.

He hesitated, then nodded. "Yes, they did. One involved the death of my mother. I dreamed that she came to me to say good-bye. The next day I found out she had died during the night. She had been ill for quite some time. The other one . . . well, I would really rather not discuss that."

Deanna nodded. "The important thing is that you have had precognitive dreams."

"A coincidence," Picard said.

"The first dream concerned your mother, with whom you naturally had a strong empathic link. I am not so much concerned with the details of the second dream, but would I be correct in assuming that it also involved someone with whom you had a strong empathic link?"

"Yes," Picard said. "You would be correct in assuming that."

"You have a strong empathic link with the members of your crew," she continued. "Some more than others, but the welfare of everyone on board is of paramount concern to you."

"What are you suggesting, Counselor?"

"That it may be important for you to try to recall the details of tonight's dream," she said.

Picard took a deep breath and blew it out slowly, then shook his head. "I cannot. For a moment after I awoke, there was something . . ."

"What was it?" she asked. "Try to remember."

"Lightning," Picard said suddenly, a strange expression on his face.

Deanna frowned. "Lightning?"

Picard shook his head. "It was a fleeting image. . . . I'm afraid I have no idea what it means."

"This disturbs you," she said.

"Yes, it does," he admitted. "We have made a great many strides in science and technology, but we are only beginning to understand the human mind. I am tempted to dismiss this as merely a nightmare, something of no consequence, but the fact that it has happened before . . ."

"Perhaps if you try to remember . . . ?" she said.

"It's no use," Picard said. "Whatever it was, I can recall only what I told you."

"If it should happen again—"

"I will call you," said Picard. "And now you really should go back to bed and get some rest. We are both due to go on duty in another few hours, and I have disturbed you enough for one night."

She nodded and got to her feet. "With your permission, then, I will say good night."

"Good night, Deanna," he said. "Sleep well."

She looked at him curiously. "And you," she said.

Deanna Troi went back to her room and got back into bed, but sleep eluded her.

Chapter One

THE CENTURIONS AT THE DOOR did not move so much as a muscle as Valak approached, nor did they acknowledge his presence in any way. He did not speak to them or even look at them. They might as well have been statues. If Valak had no business being there, of course he would have had no hope of trying to get past them. Romulan security was strict, and protocol was complicated and explicit. He outranked them both, but they would have challenged him if they had not been instructed to expect him. And Valak would have known better than to try to see the Praetor of the Romulan Empire without a formal summons.

He did not bother to knock on the door but simply went inside. He had been commanded to appear before the Praetor at precisely this time, and he arrived not one moment early and not one second late. And that was as it should have been. In human society it was considered polite to knock before entering. Humans had such curious social customs, Valak often thought. It amused him to study them, but at the same time he took his research very seriously. He had made an exhaustive study of human cultures, especially of Starfleet personnel, protocol, strategy, and regulations. He was a warrior, and he believed it was part of a warrior's duty to know his enemy.

Many Romulans assumed their superiority to humans as a matter of course and dismissed humans as insignificant, but Valak believed it was important to know how the humans lived and how they thought. He often told his crew that no warrior, racial superiority notwithstanding, should ever take anything for granted. Even a superior intellect could make mistakes, and an inferior one could get lucky. Valak brought a hunter's sensibility to his military duties. He had grown up in the outer provinces of the Romulan Empire on one of the recently colonized worlds, a primitive planet that was still in the beginning stages of development. There had been no civilized indigenous culture to defeat and subjugate, but there were plenty of large, wild, and highly dangerous life-forms that were not at all impressed with the inherent superiority of Romulans.

Valak had learned to hunt almost as soon as he had learned to walk, and his father had instilled in him a hunter's respect for his prey. Valak's father still held to many of the old values and the old ways of Romulan culture, which were now considered out-moded on the civilized worlds of the empire. The old ways were mystical and profoundly philosophical. In some ways the old Romulan traditions were similar to the Vulcan belief systems, which was not surprising, for they sprang from common racial and cultural roots.

In an almost literal sense, Valak regarded humans as prey. In that, he was completely in line with Romulan thinking. He departed from it, however, in his respect for humans, and that made him something of an anomaly in Romulan culture. Most Romulans considered humans weak and decadent, an inferior species that would inevitably be subject to Romulan authority. Valak was not so sure.

He had studied humans, and concluded that they were simply different. They subscribed to a system of morality and social structure that was beyond the understanding of most Romulans because most Romulans did not make an effort to understand them. Valak had made that effort and through long and exhaustive studies of their history, their writings, and their social customs, had come to respect their culture and their way of thinking in the same way a hunter might respect the natural behavior of his prey.

He had even written several papers on the subject, which had won the approval of Romulan scholars, but his fellow officers considered his interest in humans a puzzling eccentricity. Early in his career, he was not taken seriously. However, though he was still young, and had only recently been promoted to command rank, his record spoke for itself. His summons to the presence of the Praetor was dramatic evidence of that.

He could think of only two reasons why the Praetor would wish to see him personally: either he had made some grave error that was cause for serious disciplinary measures—and he knew that was not the case—or his service record and qualifications had brought him to the notice of the Praetor. He was anxious to discover just what that reason was.

He stopped the required distance from the Praetor's command throne and waited, his posture erect yet relaxed, taking the formal stance of the Romulan warrior—legs slightly spread apart, back straight, shoulders squared, looking straight ahead, arms crossed in front of him at about belt level, right hand gripping left wrist.

The command throne was turned away from him, its high back obscuring the Praetor from Valak's sight. The throne faced a giant screen on which the face of a senior member of the Romulan High Council was visible. A conference was in progress, but Valak could not hear what was being said, which meant the Praetor was communicating over his remote security channel on a scrambled frequency. A moment later the face on the screen disappeared, and then the screen itself disappeared, quickly fading from black to opaque to transparent and becoming a floor-to-ceiling window looking out over the sprawling capital.

Without a sound the throne slowly swiveled around to face Valak, revealing the Praetor, his forearms resting lightly on the arms of his command throne, which had small consoles built into them. The secure channel comm set partly obscured the Praetor's face. The set consisted of a small metal arm containing the shielded mouthpiece and transmitter, which were attached to a headset receiver. As the throne came around to face Valak, the entire comm set assembly swung away from the Praetor's face, swiveling around its pivot and retracting into a panel in the back of the command throne.

"Commander Valak," the Praetor said. He made no mention of Valak's promptness—that was to be expected. Valak uncrossed his arms, allowing the left one to hang straight at his side while with the right he gave the Romulan salute, fist thumping the left side of the chest. The Praetor did not return the salute, which was simply his due and required no acknowledgment on his part. However, he did incline his head slightly, which surprised Valak and pleased him enormously. It was a small thing, perhaps, but it constituted a gesture of respect.

"I am deeply honored, my lord," said Valak. The Praetor was addressed not by his title, but by the honorific befitting his caste and rank.

As a young warrior, Lord Darok had achieved a record of military victories that remained unsurpassed. He had not traded on his high-caste birth to gain rank, but had chosen the warrior's way and achieved his current position purely on merit. He was no longer young and had not held a field command in years, but age had not diminished his powers to any visible extent. His face was lined, and his hair white, but the features were still strong and full of character, his eyes still clear, their gaze forceful. There was no trace of hesitation in his speech, and his posture was still that of the warrior he had been. Everything about Darok bespoke a shrewd alertness and, standing in his presence, Valak could feel his power. It was the first time they had ever met face to face, and Valak was impressed. This was a Romulan indeed!

There was no chair for Valak to sit on, and this, too, was to be expected. One did not sit in the presence of the Praetor. Valak simply stood and waited while Lord Darok gave him a long, appraising look. For what seemed like a long time, Darok did not speak, but merely gazed at Valak, as if measuring his worth. Valak calmly returned his gaze. Finally Lord Darok nodded, apparently satisfied with what he saw.

"You are no doubt curious as to why I sent for you, Commander," Darok said.

Valak made no reply. It was a statement rather than a question, and no reply was called for.

"You have been selected for a special mission," Darok continued. "A mission for which you are uniquely qualified. Your record of command, though relatively brief, speaks for itself, but that alone does not qualify you for the mission the council has in mind."

Valak's pulse quickened. A mission ordered by the high council itself had to be of great importance. Being chosen for such a mission was not only an honor but a tremendous opportunity as well.

"You are something of a scholar, I understand," said Darok, "with an expertise in human culture. In particular, you have made a study of Starfleet Command, its history, regulations, procedures, ordnance, and personnel. I am told the papers you presented on the subject before the Romulan Academy were very favorably received and regarded as models of scholarly research. I realize there are those who regard such academic pursuits as irrelevent preoccupations in a warrior of the empire. I, however, am not one of them. A warrior who has many interests is a warrior whose mind will always stay alert and sharp." He paused briefly. "You were born and raised on Abraxas Nine, were you not?"

"Yes, my lord."

"Have you ever hunted the syrinx?"

"Yes, my lord. I have taken three."

Darok raised his eyebrows. *"Three?* That is, indeed, an achievement. I have succeeded in taking only one myself, and that nearly at the cost of my own life. The syrinx is a most elusive and dangerous prey. To what do you attribute your success?"

"In part, my lord, to the training I was given by my

father, who taught me the way of the hunter," Valak said. "Also, to having been born and raised on Abraxas Nine. As a native, I had the advantage of knowing more about the habitat and behavior of the syrinx than those who came from off-world to hunt the creature for sport."

Darok smiled faintly. "A most diplomatic answer," he said. "However, it would be closer to the truth to say that you had made a thorough study of the behavior of the syrinx in preparation for your hunt, is that not so?"

"That is true, my lord. I was taught that proper preparation is a vital part of a successful hunt. My father believed a hunter must respect his prey, and that to respect it, he must know and understand it."

Darok nodded. "My father, too, believed in the old ways. Sadly, we have strayed from many of them in our march to progress and conquest. I was still young when I visited Abraxas Nine, and I sought merely a trophy and the excitement of the hunt. In my eagerness, and in the arrogant self-confidence of youth, I had failed to properly prepare myself. It was a mistake I was never to repeat. Early training as a hunter can be of great benefit to a warrior. Hunting teaches care, patience, and respect for one's quarry. I have read the papers you presented before the Romulan Academy. You seek to understand the humans, and you obviously respect them. Do you not consider them an inferior race?"

"With all due respect, my lord, I did not consider the question of inferiority relevant to my studies," Valak replied. "A scholar must strive for objectivity in order to gain true understanding of his subject."

"Once again you play the diplomat," said Darok. "You reply without answering the question."

"It is a question that defies a simple answer, my lord," Valak replied.

"I do not insist upon a simple answer," Darok said, sounding slightly annoyed, "merely an enlightening one."

"Then I shall do my best, my lord," said Valak. "Physically humans are inferior to us. We Romulans are stronger, our reflexes are quicker, our senses sharper, and our constitutions more resistant to disease. However, humans are clever, and they have found ways to overcome their shortcomings through training and technology. For example, I have studied their fighting arts, which are varied and many, and have found that, once mastered, they are at the very least equal to and in some cases even superior to the best training that we give our own warriors."

Darok raised his eyebrows. "Indeed?"

"My lord, you asked for my opinion, and I give it honestly."

Darok nodded. "Very well. Continue."

"Then there is the question of their morality and their philosophy," said Valak. "Most Romulans believe that human morality makes a virtue out of weakness, and that human philosophical beliefs are decadent and pointless. However, the fact is that their morality is often complex. It varies with their different cultures, as does their philosophy. We Romulans possess a greater unity of culture and cohesiveness of beliefs, but that does not make humans inferior to us. It merely makes them different from us, and there are some humans who would find our ways quite appealing and agreeable."

"Humans who think like Romulans?" Darok frowned. "I did not think such a thing was possible."

"Nevertheless, my lord, it is so," Valak said. "Not

surprisingly, perhaps, such humans often find themselves at odds with their fellow men. Shall I continue?"

"By all means. This is most interesting."

"Their scientific knowledge is in some ways inferior to ours. They do not, for example, possess the technology to produce a cloaking device. However, their ships and weapons are equal to ours in most other respects, and in some ways they are unquestionably superior. Their computers, for example, are marvels of sophisticated engineering and possess many advantages over ours. I could go on, but I do not wish to bore you with a tedious recitation. The point is that whether or not the humans are an inferior race depends upon how one defines 'inferiority.' The syrinx makes for an excellent analogy. I am smarter than the syrinx, and I can arm myself with weapons, while the syrinx cannot. Yet if I were to assume that these advantages would give me easy victory over the syrinx, then at best, I would have a disappointing hunt. And at worst, I would not survive it."

Darok nodded. "I am satisfied that I have chosen well in selecting you for this mission, Commander Valak. I believe that it will present a great opportunity, both for you and for the Romulan Empire. However, due to the mission's confidential nature, you will receive your orders and be fully briefed only after you are aboard your ship and under way. You will depart immediately. An escort has already been summoned."

"Forgive me, my lord," Valak said anxiously, "but I fear I must point out that my ship is not yet ready for active service. It is still being refitted, and the work will take at the very least four or five days, even if the engineers work without rest."

"You are being given a new ship," said Lord Darok. "You will assume command of the warbird *Syrinx*." He smiled at Valak's reaction. "I thought you would find the name appropriate. I chose it myself, just now. The *Syrinx* is the first of the new D'Kazanak class. Your crew is being transferred even as we speak."

A D'Kazanak-class warbird! Valak could scarcely conceal his excitement. His back stiffened with pride. This was a tremendous honor, especially for so young a commander. He had heard rumors about the new warbirds, but virtually nothing had been confirmed about the D'Kazanak class save for its existence. No one he knew had ever even seen one. The security measures surrounding the new design were so rigid that no one who had worked on it dared breathe a word about it, under penalty of death. No one even knew where the ships were being constructed.

Like all Romulan warbirds, and most Federation-class designs, the ship would have had to have been built in orbit. Rumor had it that the prototype of the new design had been constructed in secret in orbit above one of the remote colony worlds and that it represented a new age in Romulan warbird design. It was said to be larger, faster, and more heavily armed than the current D'Deridex-class warbirds. The D'Kazanaks were being specifically designed to compete with the new Federation Galaxy-class starships. However, in the absence of specific information, wild speculation about the nature of its superiority was rampant.

The Galaxy-class Federation starships had an advantage in speed over the D'Deridex-class warbirds: they were capable of sustained cruising at warp 9.6, which was 1,909 times the speed of light. Under extreme emergency conditions, their warp engines could be overstressed to achieve warp 9.9, though they could do so for only a few minutes before the dilithium crystals used to tune the harmonics of the antimatter reaction shattered. No matter-antimatter reactor, no matter how efficient, could drive engines to attain or exceed warp 10, which was the absolute speed limit of the universe. According to the relativy equations of the great Earth scientist, Einstein, a ship traveling at that speed would have to possess infinite mass, which was clearly impossible. However, within the physical limitations of the universe, the Federation Galaxy-class vessels were as efficient and powerful as a starship could be. The Romulan warbirds were almost as powerful and efficient, but the Federation starships always had an edge . . . until now.

The D'Kazanak-class design, it was said, could match the efficiency of the Federation warp drives. There were also rumors about a new generation cloaking device that could eliminate the "ghosting effect" which sometimes rendered a cloaked ship visible to Federation scanners. There was also talk about more powerful photon disruptors. Some rumors even hinted at the possibility that these weapons could be employed while the cloaking device was engaged, something the D'Deridex-class warbirds had been unable to do. This had always been the single greatest limitation of the cloaking device, and Romulan engineers had labored for decades to find a way to overcome it. Had they succeeded at last? Valak would soon know.

As he left the Praetor's chambers and marched down the wide and crowded corridor with an escort before and behind him, his heart raced with excitement. They moved quickly, at a martial step, and everyone hastened to get out of their way. Lord Darok had done more than merely provide an escort. He had summoned an honor guard of Praetorians, the elite of the Romulan warrior class. In their crested helmets and black anodized battle armor, they made an impressive sight as they marched in perfect synchrony down the corridor, their bootheels echoing as one. Everyone they passed turned to stare at them as they went by. The more observant noted the new, never-before-seen insignia Valak wore over his breast—a badge in the shape of a shield, bearing the image of twin black lightning bolts against a white background and the stylized red letters spelling out "D'Kazanak." Lord Darok himself had pinned the insignia on, and Valak wore it proudly.

The guards conducted him to a transport and boarded it with him. They skimmed out to the shuttle launch pad, where the guard formed up by the hatch and saluted smartly as Valak boarded the shuttle. Moments later the craft was airborne, gathering speed until it reached escape velocity.

Valak sat in the copilot's chair, staring out the viewport as the pilot flew the shuttle toward the point where Valak's next command awaited him. They passed the space station orbital control base above the capital and flew on, escaping orbit after being cleared and heading out into the blackness of space. Nothing was visible ahead of them. Valak glanced at the pilot briefly, and saw that he was intent on his instruments. How far out was the *Syrinx?* They would soon reach the point beyond which the shuttle could not safely turn back; there would not be enough fuel.

The pilot saw Valak's questioning stare and said, "The shuttle will not be returning, Commander. It has been my honor and privilege to be assigned permanently to your crew. Forgive my failure to formally present myself for orders, but there was no opportunity to follow proper protocol."

Valak nodded. "What is your name, Centurion?"

"Atalan, Commander."

"And what was your previous station?"

"I had the honor to serve as pilot and navigator aboard the warbird *Kazar.*"

Valak nodded once more. "Commander Gorak's ship. I know it well. However, I already have a pilot and navigator, and cannot offer you the same post."

"I am aware of that, Commander," Atalan replied. "I had requested the honor of being assigned to your crew in whatever capacity I could serve in. I have been assigned to your engineering section, as second engineering officer."

Valak raised his eyebrows. "That constitutes a demotion from your previous station," he said, with some surprise.

"Yes, Commander. However, the privilege of serving under your command aboard the first D'Kazanak-class warbird will more than compensate for that."

Valak nodded with approval. He glanced at the instruments. "We are reaching the limit of our fuel supply. Are you certain you have computed the correct course?"

"Quite certain, Commander," Atalan replied. "With your permission I shall hail the *Syrinx* now."

"Permission granted."

"Base shuttle to *Syrinx,*" Atalan said, speaking into the transmitter arm on his helmet. "Base shuttle to *Syrinx.* I have Commander Valak on board. Request permission to dock."

The reply came back, "Permission granted." And

suddenly the black space ahead of them in the viewport seemed to shimmer and the D'Kazanak-class warbird *Syrinx* faded into view as it decloaked.

Valak's eyes grew wide and he swore softly, invoking the gods of his forefathers. The ship was huge, almost twice the size of the D'Deridex-class warbirds, and the lines of its design possessed a predatory magnificence that was awesome to behold. But what took his breath away was the way it had uncloaked.

There had been absolutely no hint of its presence before them. The cloaking device used on the D'Deridex-class warbirds rendered the ships completely invisible, but an experienced eye, especially that of a Romulan ship's captain, could detect certain telltale signs of its presence—very minor spatial fluctuations in close-range scanner readings, which would be unnoticed by all but the most experienced scanner operators, and a slight distortion in space, a sort of faint visual echo that constituted a barely perceptible ghost image of the ship, undetectable at long range and difficult to detect even at close range. With the *Syrinx,* however, there had been no trace of ghosting. The ship had suddenly appeared as if from nowhere; there had been no sign of its presence whatsoever. The rumors were true. There *was* a new generation cloaking device, and Valak had just witnessed dramatic evidence of its effectiveness. Not even the most experienced Federation starship captains would be able to detect it.

The shuttle entered the docking bay, and the hatch closed behind it. Moments later Valak exited the shuttle as the shrill tritone of the watch pipes heralded his arrival. The crew marched out in dress formation into the docking area and formed in parade phalanx before the shuttle. His bridge crew came marching out to meet him in wedge formation, led by his first officer, with the rest of the senior officers formed up behind him in descending order—the pilot and navigator behind the first officer and to the left, the chief weapons officer behind the first officer and to the right, followed by the communications and engineering officers, the security and science officers, the medical and tactics officers, and so on. They came to a smart halt in front of the shuttle hatch and snapped to as one, giving him the Romulan salute.

"Welcome aboard, Commander," said his first officer, Korak, with obvious pride. "The D'Kazanak-class warbird *Syrinx* is yours. The crew stands ready for your orders."

Valak stood in the shuttle hatchway gazing out at his crew. They were as fine a body of warriors as any ship's commander could hope for. Most of them had served with him aboard his old ship, but he saw some new additions. He would have to check their service records at once and meet with all of them, but he was confident that only the cream of the Romulan space fleet had been assigned to duty aboard the *Syrinx*. Lord Darok would have seen to that.

There was much to do. He would have to familiarize himself thoroughly with the workings of his new ship, run tests and diagnostics on all its systems; he was sure the chief design engineers had already done so, but a good commander always made sure of everything himself. He had a mission before him, and he would have to conduct his own shakedown cruise while en route to that mission, whatever it was, so there was no time to waste. All of the members of his crew knew they would be working around the clock until Valak and all the rest of them were so intimately familiar with their new ship that it would seem almost like a part of them.

Valak noticed a figure approaching from the entrance to the docking area. He was young and did not march like a warrior, but walked in a casual manner that Valak would never have tolerated in a member of his crew. He was not wearing a uniform, either, but a black tunic and breeches, unadorned by any decorations or insignia of rank or caste. A civilian. Valak frowned. What was a civilian doing aboard his ship? Had Lord Darok saddled him with some glorified bureaucrat representing the Romulan High Council?

"Allow me the honor to welcome you aboard my ship, Commander," the civilian said as he approached.

Valak gazed at him coldly. "*Your* ship?"

The civilian bowed respectfully. "My apologies. It is, of course, *your* ship to command. I had fallen into the habit of referring to it as mine, as I was the one who designed it. I am Lord Kazanak."

Valak was taken aback. "Forgive me. Perhaps I did not hear you correctly. Did you say . . . *Lord* Kazanak?"

"That is correct, Commander."

Valak assumed the formal stance and, as Lord Kazanak was a civilian and not a warrior, gave him the proper respectful bow from the waist rather than the Romulan salute.

"If my lord will permit a question?" Valak said, using the deferential form of address required by Lord Kazanak's high caste.

"Ask," Lord Kazanak replied.

Valak inclined his head toward him. "I was under the impression, my lord, that the D'Kazanak design was named after Lord Kazanak, who presides over the high council. Have I the honor of addressing his son?"

"The president of the high council is my esteemed father," Kazanak replied. "I have the honor of bearing the family name and title, for which I have named this ship's design. Because it is the crowning achievement of my life's work, I have asked the high council to allow me to go along on this mission so that I can familiarize you with this ship and its improvements. I shall also evaluate its performance."

Valak tried to hide his disappointment and maintained a carefully neutral expression as he said, "I see. Am I to understand, then, that the purpose of this secret mission is merely to test the capabilities of this ship and submit formal evaluations to the high council?"

Kazanak smiled. "In part, Commander, only in part. As this mission has been conceived and planned by the council under the authority of my esteemed father and Lord Darok, I have been entrusted with the task of briefing you as to its purpose. However, rest assured that I shall act only in an advisory capacity regarding this ship's design and capabilities. As to the mission itself, I am prepared to brief you fully, at your convenience and discretion."

Valak nodded. "Very well. We shall see to that at once, then, in my quarters, if you will be so kind as to show me the way." He turned to his first officer. "Dismiss the ship's company, Korak," he said. "Make ready to get under way."

Chapter Two

ENSIGN RO LAREN frowned at her scanner consoles. The watch had just changed and she had come onto the bridge to start her shift. She did everything by the book when she was on duty, even though that was not her nature. Far from it, in fact. Had she been a stickler for following regulations and procedure, she never would have wound up in prison, from where she had been plucked for a special mission that eventually led to her becoming a permanent member of the crew of the starship *Enterprise.*

Since joining the crew at the personal invitation of Captain Picard, an invitation she might well have refused had he not put it to her as a challenge, Ro had become accepted by the other personnel aboard the ship, though she had never quite meshed with them. Most of the crew members were human, though other races were represented, most notably by Lieutenant Commander Worf, a Klingon, and Counselor Deanna

Troi, who was half Betazoid. However, Ro was the only Bajoran, and that, combined with the persecution suffered by her race throughout the years, made her feel like an outsider.

Though no one on board the *Enterprise* regarded her that way, or treated her differently from any other member of the crew, Ro still possessed the defensive mechanisms she had been forced to develop from early childhood. There was an aggressive stand-offishness about her, a sense of separateness she wore like a chip on her shoulder. She was Bajoran and proud of it, and she had a tendency to display her disputatious individuality as if it were a badge of honor or even, on occasion, an offensive weapon.

She had still not grown accustomed to the fact that her being Bajoran made no difference to the crew. She kept expecting someone to make an issue of her race, and so she had a tendency to make an issue of it first, even when there was no call for it.

Her fellow crew members did their best to make allowances for her behavior on such occasions, which served only to make her even angrier, not so much at them as at herself. She knew they all tried to make her feel like one of them, but she still did not fit in. For that matter, she wasn't really sure she wanted to fit in. Deanna Troi would probably have told her that she feared being vulnerable—something most humans understood and accepted as the risk one took in allowing others to get close—and that this fear had kept her from abandoning the psychological defense mechanisms she had built up over the years, but Ro had never asked Deanna for her counsel, and Deanna would not offer it unsolicited.

Time, perhaps, would ease Ro's defensive posture, but meanwhile, she continued to coexist in a state of nervous tension with her fellow crew members. Always half expecting someone to make an issue of her being an outsider, a Bajoran who, by virtue of her race, did not belong, Ro made a point of performing all her duties in an exemplary manner, completely by the book, as if daring someone to find fault with her work. So, as she took her seat behind the scanning consoles, she followed strict procedure and even went beyond it, to the point of running a quick auto-diagnostic to check on all the sensors and then testing them by running a multiband frequency check.

She did not really expect to find anything out of the ordinary, for the members of the engineering staff were nothing if not completely thorough in their maintenance procedures; Geordi La Forge would stand for nothing less. She was surprised, therefore, to find a blip on her console, indicating the reception of a faint transmission on a frequency that was normally not used by Federation vessels.

"Sir, I am picking up traces of a subspace frequency transmission," Ro told Commander William Riker.

"Identify," said Riker, speaking in the clipped, formal tone he used whenever he was in command on the bridge. Under most other circumstances, Ro thought, Riker's manner with his subordinates was so informal that some might have found it too casual, but such a snap analysis would have been inaccurate. The crew of the *Enterprise* functioned as a tightly knit unit, and there was a closeness in their relationship that outsiders might have found too familiar to be conducive to good discipline. However, both Riker and Picard had their own unique leadership styles, and if Riker's seemed a bit too casual and informal most of the time, it served to offset the crisp, no-

nonsense manner he adopted whenever there was call for it. When necessary, he knew how to crack the whip, and because his subordinates knew he cared about them, they cared about him and never gave him less than peak performance. In any case, one could not argue with results. The *Enterprise* was the tightest ship in all of Starfleet, and no crew could boast a higher overall efficiency rating.

Ro stared at the signal blip, then fine-tuned the sensors to focus in on it. The blip came in stronger and data started appearing on the screen, identifying the frequency as the receptors automatically filtered out subspace interference. She shook her head, frowning. "It's distant, sir . . . and reception is intermittent, but it is not on any of the normal Federation frequency bands."

"Mr. Worf, run a data-base cross-check with the ship's computer," Riker replied.

"I have already done so, sir," the Klingon replied, having anticipated Riker's order. "It should be coming up any second now. . . ." He stiffened as he stared at his screen, then looked up at Riker. "Sir, it is a Romulan frequency."

Riker sat forward in his chair. "Ensign, can you boost reception of the signal?"

"Working. . . . It seems to be a distress beacon, sir." Ro seemed surprised.

"Can you get me coordinates for its source?" Riker said tensely.

"Working. . . ." She shook her head. "That doesn't seem right."

"What is it?"

"I'm getting a reading for source coordinates near the border of the Neutral Zone," she said. "But, sir . . . it's coming from Federation space."

Riker tapped the duranium casing of his personal communicator, shaped like the Starfleet emblem and worn on his breast. "Riker to Captain Picard," he said. "Please report to the bridge immediately."

The reply came back almost at once. "I'm on my way, Number One."

Riker tapped the emblem once more, switching off. "Mr. Data, I want precise coordinates for the source of that transmission," he said.

"Understood, sir," the android replied, rapidly tapping in commands on his console.

Moments later, Captain Jean-Luc Picard stepped off the turbolift and came onto the bridge. Tall and leanly muscled, he walked with fluid grace as he moved quickly to the captain's chair and took his seat. "Report, Number One," he said.

"Sir, we're picking up a signal from a Romulan distress beacon, emanating from Federation space on our side of the Neutral Zone," said Riker.

"Have you plotted coordinates for intercept?" asked Picard.

"Plotted and locked in, sir," replied Data.

"Good. Set course for intercept, warp factor three."

Data's fingers flew over the control panel. "Course set, sir, warp factor three," he replied.

"Engage," said Picard, punctuating the command with a gesture.

As the ship's engines engaged warp drive, Picard glanced at his first officer. "What do you make of it, Number One?" he asked.

Riker shook his head. "I don't know, sir," he replied. "On the one hand, it *could* be a legitimate distress signal, in which case the incursion into Federation space could well be accidental. A disabled ship might easily have drifted across our border of the Neutral Zone, especially if it was engaged in patrolling the Romulan border. On the other hand, it might be some sort of trap."

Picard nodded. "Indeed," he said. "In either case, caution is definitely called for. If it truly is a disabled vessel, then we are bound to offer our assistance."

"Assuming the Romulans will accept it," Riker said dryly.

"I think we may safely assume that they will not," Picard said, "but if this distress call is legitimate, then we shall make the offer."

"Assuming it *is* on the level," Riker said, "we may find, when we get there, that another Romulan ship has already responded."

"Indeed we may, Number One," said Picard. "In which case a light but firm hand will be called for."

"You think we should notify Starfleet Command?"

"Not yet," Picard replied. "At this point that would be premature. They will want a complete report, and we do not yet possess enough information to provide one. Let's tread softly on this one, Number One. There's no telling what we may be getting ourselves into." Anything involving the Romulans could be dicey.

As the ship sped toward its destination, the officers of the bridge crew carefully checked all their systems. Throughout the *Enterprise,* there was a bustle of activity as the crew members took their stations and prepared for whatever might develop. Soon they were approaching the source of the transmission they had intercepted.

"Sir," said Data, "we should be within visual scanner range in a few moments."

"Thank you, Mr. Data," said Picard. "Slow to impulse power. Prepare to activate main viewer. Yellow alert."

As the *Enterprise* slowed from warp speed to impulse power, Deanna Troi and several other crew members came onto the bridge to fill out the full bridge crew complement for alert conditions, which could result in an order for red alert and battle stations. Deanna Troi took her seat on the captain's left, with Worf manning the tactical station, Data and Ro at the forward stations, Riker sitting at the captain's right, and other crew members manning the science stations, mission ops, and engineering, the latter manned by Lieutenant Commander Geordi La Forge, who had come up from the main engineering section in response to the yellow alert. Quietly, but quickly and efficiently, the bridge stations had shifted into full enable mode, ready to deal with anything that came up. No one spoke. All of them went about their tasks, taking up their stations with a practiced assurance that would have seemed almost casual but for the atmosphere of controlled tension on the bridge.

"We are within visual range, sir," Data said. "Scanners show an unidentified craft, bearing zero three six, mark two five."

"On screen, Mr. Data," said Picard.

The main viewscreen came on, like a window opening onto the star-filled blackness of space. In the distance, barely visible, was a faint object—the source of the distress beacon.

"Distress signal coming through loud and clear, Captain," Ensign Ro said.

"Confirmed," Worf said from the tactical station. "It appears to be a nonverbal automated distress signal, sir, broadcast on a coded frequency."

"Increase to maximum magnification, Mr. Data," said Picard.

"Maximum magnification, sir," Data replied, echoing the order.

The image on the screen grew larger as the sensors zoomed in, boosted to their maximum range. Picard slowly leaned forward in his seat, his eyes intent upon the screen. All eyes were riveted to the main viewer. Riker slowly got to his feet, his expression astonished.

"What in the name of . . ." Geordi's voice trailed off as he stared through his VISOR at the screen.

The main viewer was filled with an image of a type of spacecraft none of them had ever seen before, though its lines were vaguely familiar. It was unmistakably Romulan in configuration, but it was *huge,* nearly twice the size of any Romulan ship they had ever encountered. Its design configuration marked it unquestionably as a warbird. It possessed the same predatory, birdlike lines that were the trademark of the Romulan shipwrights, but it was clearly an altogether different class of vessel. This was an advanced design, with larger, more powerful engine nacelles, and it was bristling with other innovations. Even at this range, they could see that it would dwarf the *Enterprise.*

"Damn, it's big!" said La Forge.

"As you were, Mr. La Forge," snapped Riker, his gaze intent upon the screen.

"Red alert, Mr. Riker," Picard said tensely.

"Red alert! Battle stations!" Riker repeated, and as the signal alarm sounded throughout the ship, it triggered a flurry of activity on every deck as crew members hustled to their posts.

Picard got to his feet and moved forward, approaching the screen, coming up behind the forward stations. He could not take his eyes off the image on the main viewer.

"Mr. Worf, what do you make of that?" he asked.

Lieutenant Commander Worf shook his head. "It is not a standard D'Deridex-class warbird, Captain," he replied. "It appears to be an entirely new design." He consulted his scanner console. "I am not picking up any activity in reponse to our approach, sir. Their shields are still down."

"Mr. Data, status report, please," Picard said.

The android quickly checked his readouts, assimilating the information faster than any human could. "The ship appears to be completely powered down, Captain," he replied. He frowned slightly, a response unnatural for an android, but one he had cultivated in his attempt to learn more about humans and to adopt as many of their natural behavior patterns as possible. "I am not picking up any signs of life aboard the ship, sir. The distress beacon is broadcasting on an automated frequency. Scanner readings show all life-support systems aboard the Romulan ship to be inoperative." He glanced up toward Picard. "They are all dead, sir."

"*Dead?*" Picard said.

"It could be a trick," said Riker.

"Mr. Worf?" Picard said without taking his eyes off the main viewer.

Worf shook his head. "I am showing no power, sir. At this range they cannot possibly be unaware of our approach, yet their shields are still down. I am showing no power to their weapons; readings are negative on life-support systems, and we are now within visual range and have not yet been scanned. The ship is drifting, sir. All readings indicate a derelict, with no life aboard."

"Mr. Data, do long-range scanner readings indicate the presence of any other Romulan vessels?"

"Negative, sir," Data replied, his gaze intent upon his readout screens.

"Maintain red alert," Picard said. "Slow to half impulse."

"Half-impulse power," Data acknowledged.

"Mr. La Forge, what do you make of it?" Picard asked.

"I've never seen anything like it, sir," Geordi La Forge replied. "So far as we know, the Romulans don't have any ships like this. It's a completely new design, a brand-new class of warbird. It makes their D'Deridex-class ships look as obsolete as our old Constitution-class starships. I think we may be looking at a prototype of a new generation Romulan warbird design, one that we know absolutely nothing about. Sir, this could be an incredible opportunity. If the ship truly is a derelict, we could beam over a boarding party and—"

"Delay that suggestion for the moment, Mr. La Forge," Picard said, still keeping a wary eye on the main viewscreen. Every muscle in his body felt taut. Something wasn't right. He could *feel* it. All eyes on the bridge were upon him. No one spoke. They all watched him and awaited his orders.

"Status report, Mr. Worf?" he said, his eyes intent upon the screen, as if he were trying to bore holes through it with the force of his gaze.

"No change, sir."

"Mr. Data?"

"No change, sir. Scanners indicate no life-form readings," Data replied. "Life-support functions aboard the Romulan ship are inoperative."

"They may have experienced a catastrophic failure

of their life-support systems," Riker said. "If the ship's a prototype, it may have contained a design flaw that remained undetected until it triggered a massive systems failure. If so, they never had a chance. They suffocated even as they were trying to evacuate."

"But surely they had backup systems?" said Deanna. "Life-support suits they could have worn in an emergency?"

"Not necessarily," said Riker. "The Romulans have never given as much priority to the safety of their crews as we do. They may well have had a backup system, but if it crashed at the same time as their main system, then that's all she wrote."

"Excuse me, sir," said Data. "That's all *who* wrote?"

"It's merely an expression, Mr. Data," said Picard. "It means that was the end of it. There was nothing they could do."

"That's all she wrote," repeated Data. He nodded. "Yes, I see. She, in this case, doubtless referring to the human conceptualization of Fate, writing a final chapter, as it were, and putting a period to the—"

"Please, Mr. Data," Picard said impatiently.

"Yes, sir. Sorry, sir."

"Counselor, your opinion?" said Picard.

Deanna shook her head. "I am sorry, Captain, but lacking any individuals on whom to base an intuitive reading, I can give no relevant response. I can only advise caution."

"Indeed," Picard said, his lips tightening into a grimace.

"Sir," said La Forge, "this could be an amazing windfall for us. A chance to examine firsthand a new generation Romulan warbird, to say nothing of the opportunity this represents to gain valuable intelligence. . . . All their codes, their computer files —it's all there, ripe for the taking!"

"Yes, Mr. La Forge, I am aware of that," Picard said. "If, indeed, this situation is what it appears to be."

"Sir, there *are* no life-form readings aboard that vessel," said Worf. "All systems are powered down. Even if it were some sort of clever ruse, at this range they could never power up in time to constitute a threat. The ship is completely at our mercy."

"I know, Mr. Worf, I know," Picard replied. "But it just seems too easy."

"Why would they send a prototype design out on a shakedown cruise without an escort?" Ro asked. "It seems illogical."

"Yes, to us it does," said Riker, "but maybe not to the Romulans. They have an obsession with secrecy. If there were any flaws in the design of a new generation warbird, they would not want them revealed. Typical Romulan pride and arrogance. They never admit to making a mistake."

"Well, it looks like they made one hell of a big one this time," Geordi said. "Captain, it'll be only a matter of time before some Romulan ship responds to that distress beacon, and then we're going to be up to our ears in warbirds. We've got a window of opportunity here, but it's not a real big one. With all due respect, sir, we can't afford to pass it up."

"Geordi's right, Captain," Riker said. "What's more, the law is on our side. That warbird is in violation of Federation space, even if there is no living crew aboard. Technically we'd be within our rights to claim it as a prize."

Picard shook his head. "No, Number One, that would never do. We will have to return that ship to the

Romulans. Otherwise we risk creating an incident that could threaten the truce, which is already fragile at best. However, that does not mean we cannot take advantage of the opportunity to learn as much as we can about that vessel before the Romulans respond to its distress beacon."

"Prepare an away team, sir?" asked Riker, anxiously.

"Yes," Picard replied. "Stand down from red alert, but maintain yellow alert. I want protective suits for the away team, Number One. There may be contamination. Also, a full complement of security, Mr. Worf."

"I shall see to it, Captain," Worf replied.

"Ensign Ro, maintain long-range scanner sweeps for any sign at all of Romulan vessels responding to that distress signal."

"Understood, sir."

"Number One, I want you to head the away team," said Picard.

"Yes, sir. I'll take La Forge and Data in addition to the security detail," Riker said.

"Dr. Crusher will be standing by, ready to beam over as soon as you've established that it's safe," Picard said. "I shall want a full medical report on conditions aboard that ship before we send anyone else over."

"Understood, sir. I'm on my way."

"And, Number One . . . be careful."

When the away team materialized on the bridge of the Romulan warbird, the security personnel had their weapons ready and each member of the away team carried a Type II phaser set on heavy stun. Regardless of what the scanner readings said, Riker saw that Worf wasn't taking any chances. Prior to transporting to the ship, the security personnel had taken up position around the rest of the away team in tight perimeter formation, their phasers held ready so that, if necessary, they could fire the moment they materialized aboard the Romulan ship. However, there was no reason to fire. For almost a full thirty seconds after they materialized, no one moved or said a word.

The scene on the bridge of the warbird was not pretty. It was a graphic reminder of what could happen to any of them if there was ever a similar catastrophic failure aboard the *Enterprise*. The bodies of the Romulan bridge crew were slumped in their seats and over the consoles. Some were simply sprawled out on the floor.

"Riker to *Enterprise*." The first officer spoke over the comm circuit inside the helmet of his protective suit.

Picard's voice came back over the speaker in his helmet. "Go ahead, Number One."

"We're on the bridge of the warbird," Riker said, looking around him. "The entire bridge crew is dead, apparently of suffocation."

He glanced around at the bodies sprawled all over the bridge of the Romulan warbird, then began taking tricorder readings as the rest of the personnel carefully spread out.

"There is no sign of life aboard the ship," he continued. "Repeat: no sign of life. Whatever happened must have happened very quickly. Judging by the positioning of the bodies, my guess is that the life-support system not only underwent catastrophic failure but set off a purging cycle that was evacuated through the exhaust ducts and failed to properly cycle in new air. We don't have a vacuum, but there simply wasn't enough air for the crew to breathe. They were literally choked to death by their own ship."

"Any sign of radiation?" asked Picard.

"Negative," Riker replied. "La Forge is checking out the bridge engineering consoles right now, but it doesn't look as if there was any leakage. We can beam Dr. Crusher over and have her check for possible viral contamination, but that isn't what killed them. The bodies are all displaying signs of cyanosis. My guess is that this happened a very short time ago. Dr. Crusher should be able to confirm that."

"Have you checked out any of the other decks?" asked Picard.

"Worf is on his way to do that right now with a security detail," Riker replied, "but if there were any life aboard this ship at all, we would have picked it up by now."

"Shall I have Dr. Crusher beam over with her medical team?" Picard asked.

"Affirmative," said Riker. "Just make sure they're wearing suits."

"Commander, there's a chance I may be able to get us some air," La Forge said. He was standing by one of the consoles on the bridge and gazing down at it intently. "I've found their engineering bridge consoles. The configuration is different from ours, but with Data's help I think I can figure this thing out."

"Can you get the life-support systems back on line?" asked Riker.

"There's a good chance of that," said Geordi. "I'm still showing residual power to these instruments, which means that as soon as Data can help me decipher these Romulan controls, I can run some diagnostics, maybe even adapt some of our instrumentation from the *Enterprise,* and figure out exactly what went wrong here. Maybe the ship powered down as a by-product of the systems failure. Maybe the crew powered down by accident while they were dying, or the disaster could be a result of some sort of fail-safe program they built in. I don't know for sure yet, but if I can get a crew down into the main engineering section, I should be able to find some answers for you pretty quick."

Riker activated his communicator. "Mr. Worf, report please."

"It appears to be the same all over the ship, Commander," Worf replied. "The Romulans are all lying dead where they fell when the life-support system purged itself. The systems failure must have occurred at the same time all over the ship."

"Which means it must have been a failure in the central control in main engineering," La Forge said. "We might be able to jury-rig a repair from our own engineering stores."

"Okay, Geordi, get on it," Riker said.

As La Forge left the bridge, heading for the engineering section with Data, Dr. Crusher materialized behind Riker with her medical team. They were all dressed in protective suits with self-contained life support. They began at once to examine the dead Romulans.

"Riker to *Enterprise.*"

"Go ahead, Number One," Picard replied.

"Dr. Crusher and her team have arrived," said Riker. "La Forge is on his way down to the main engineering section with Data. He thinks he can effect repairs and get the life-support systems back on line. There doesn't seem to be any immediate danger here. Any sign of Romulan ships responding to that distress signal?"

"Negative, Number One," Picard replied. "We are picking up nothing on our long-range scanners."

"Sir, I'd like to request permission to deactivate the distress beacon," Riker said. "If the Romulans haven't picked up the signal yet, there's no point in inviting trouble, is there? And it would buy us a lot more time."

Picard did not respond immediately.

"Sir?" said Riker.

"I heard you, Number One," Picard said. "Very well, make it so. Secure the ship and report back to the bridge as soon as possible."

"Understood, sir," Riker replied.

He turned to Dr. Crusher. "I'm beaming back to the ship," he said. "Geordi's going to see if he can get the life-support systems functioning again. He'll need help from Engineering, and probably some equipment, too. The captain's going to want a full medical report."

"I should have one for him shortly," she replied. "It seems fairly obvious what happened here. They all suffocated. The cyanosis, the attitudes of the bodies, the superficial injuries where they clawed at themselves and at their clothing, it all bears out your initial assessment. Should we do anything about the bodies?"

"No, not for the moment," Riker replied. "In fact, it might be best to leave everything the way we found it. The Romulans may claim that we had something to do with this. I want the evidence to speak for itself. We should probably get a visual record of what we found here." He spoke to Geordi over his comm circuit. "Riker to La Forge."

"La Forge here. Go ahead, Commander."

"First things first, Geordi. Switch off that signal

beacon. Then see if you can restore life-support functions. I'm heading back to the ship. I'll assemble an engineering crew to beam over and assist you."

"I've already taken care of that, Commander," La Forge replied. "We're making headway in translating some of these Romulan schematics down here, thanks to Data's help, and I think we can probably restore life-support functions within the hour."

"So soon?"

"It looks as if they had a breakdown in their central bioprocessing unit," La Forge replied. "They don't seem to have the same multiple redundancy in their systems that we do. They have only the central system and a reserve utilities-distribution network. You're not going to believe this, but as near as I can tell, their main reserve utilities-distribution processor was never hooked up properly. I'm looking at it right here, and the wiring is all wrong. Whoever hooked this up just slapped it together and didn't even bother to test it."

"You mean they departed on their shakedown cruise without properly installing their reserve life-support backups?" Riker said with disbelief.

"The backup system was properly installed, all right," said Geordi, "but the main processor wasn't connected properly. It was just a sloppy mistake, but the sort of mistake that would never show up unless they were specifically looking for it. The way this is hooked up, if their engineers had run a full diagnostics on the backup system, they would have obtained a false positive reading. Without actually going into the control panels, as we're doing, they would have had no way of knowing the reserve system was dysfunctional unless the main system broke down, and by then it would have been too late."

"What would have been the odds of a main system breakdown?" asked Riker.

"A thousand to one, maybe?" La Forge said. "I don't know. This ship could have put in years of active service without anyone ever noticing the problem unless somebody actually opened up the panels. It's the kind of thing that would have shown up in a second during a routine maintenance overhaul, but if they just relied on diagnostic scans, they would have gotten a green light every time and never known that it was just a short."

"Several thousand lives lost because of a simple mistake in wiring," said Riker, shaking his head. "Geordi, remind me of this the next time I get on your case for being too obsessive about routine maintenance overhauls."

He could almost hear the grin in La Forge's voice. "Yes, sir."

"Commander," Dr. Crusher said, "I hate to break in, but we've done just about all there is to do here for the moment. With your permission, I'd like to check out the sickbay. We know almost nothing about their medical facilities."

"Go ahead," Riker said. "But be careful. I'm heading back to the ship. . . . Riker to *Enterprise.* One to beam up."

As soon as he beamed back aboard the ship, Riker hurried to the bridge to make his report. Captain Picard nodded when he was finished telling him everything they'd learned so far.

"Excellent, Number One," he said. "Long-range scanners still show no approaching Romulan vessels. I think we may have stolen a march on them. However, I have my doubts about deactivating their signal beacon."

"We picked up their distress signal and responded to it," Riker said. "There wasn't anything we could do to help the crew, but Geordi should have the life-support systems functioning again before too long, and if the Romulans still haven't shown up by then, we can always send our own signal and let them know what happened. Meanwhile, they can hardly complain about our examining their ship. It's in Federation space, and it's a derelict. From a legal standpoint, we'd be fully within our rights to confiscate it and consider it a prize."

"Yes, I am aware of that, but we are in a gray area here," Picard said, frowning. "You know as well as I how the Romulans would react to such a decision."

"We could send a message to Starfleet Command," Riker suggested. "That would put the ball in their court."

"And I am almost certain what Starfleet's decision would be," Picard replied. "They would undoubtedly order us to confiscate the ship, place a prize crew on board, and take it to the nearest starbase."

"What would be so wrong with that?" asked Riker.

"The Romulans would never stand still for it," said Picard. "They would almost certainly accuse us of seizing their ship and causing the death of its crew, and they would claim our actions constituted an act of war. I am simply not prepared to delegate responsibility in a decision of such magnitude, Number One."

"Yes, I see your point," said Riker. "There's too much at stake here to allow some glorified desk jockey at Starfleet to call the shots on this one. But headquarters will still have to be notified."

"Indeed," Picard replied, "but not until I have carefully weighed all of the potential consequences."

"Sir, if I may play devil's advocate, have you

considered the potential consequences of our turning the ship back over to the Romulans *without* consulting Starfleet?" asked Riker.

"I have been doing exactly that, Number One," said Picard. "However, if we can provide Starfleet with a full report concerning the design and capabilities of this new warbird, that would certainly mitigate in favor of our decision to return the ship. But I feel strongly that if we wish to avoid a major incident that could well destroy the truce, the vessel will have to be returned, and the sooner the better. If the Romulans picked up the distress signal, they are bound to send out rescue missions. Even if we send a message to Starfleet right now, chances are the Romulans will still arrive before we can receive a response."

"So we notify Starfleet, maintain alert status, and scramble to find out as much as we can about the warbird in the meantime," Riker said.

"I think, under the circumstances, we should call a briefing and discuss our options," said Picard.

"Sir, I am receiving a message from Commander La Forge, aboard the warbird," said Ensign Ro.

Picard tapped his communicator. "Picard here. Report, Mr. La Forge."

"Captain, we're ready to attempt restoring life-support functions aboard this ship," said Geordi. "We've repaired the main bioprocessor, reinstalled the reserve utilities distributor, and rigged a backup with one of our own units, just in case. We've also run a preliminary diagnostics check, and the setup should work. If we don't run into any other problems, we should be able to get this bird fully powered up in no time."

"Have your engineering crew proceed, Mr. La Forge," Picard said. "In the meantime, I want you,

Dr. Crusher, Mr. Worf, and Mr. Data back here for a situation briefing right away."

"Understood, sir. I'll contact the others and we'll beam right over."

"Very good, Mr. La Forge," Picard replied. "I shall see you in the briefing room. Picard out." He tapped his communicator, switching off. "I want a look aboard that ship, Number One."

Riker smiled. "I figured you would, sir."

"It will have to wait until after the briefing." Picard turned to Deanna Troi. "Counselor, I would like you to be present at the briefing as well. In the meantime, we will stand down from red alert, but maintain yellow alert and keep an eye on those long-range scanners. Ensign Ro, you have the conn. Let me know the moment there is any change in the situation."

"Understood, sir."

"We will have to send a message to Starfleet," Picard said as he headed for the turbolift with Riker. "I want a complete report ready for them, and that means accessing the warbird's data files and the captain's log. Get that information transferred to our own ship's computer as soon as possible."

"Geordi should be able to handle that as soon as he gets the warbird powered up," said Riker. "And if the Romulans have built any safeguards into their computer system, Data should be able to defeat them."

They entered the turbolift and proceeded to the briefing room. Within moments the others all arrived and they took their places around the conference table.

"Report, Mr. La Forge," Picard said.

"Life-support functions aboard the warbird are now restored and fully operative," said Geordi. "Our people should be able to get out of those suits in about five minutes. Meanwhile I've ordered my engineering crew to run a complete systems check before we attempt to restore full power."

Picard nodded. "Excellent. Mr. Data, as soon as we are finished here, I would like you to accompany me to the bridge of the warbird and assist me in the transfer of the information from their ship's computer to ours."

"Understood, sir."

"Number One, have Ensign Ro prepare to receive the download as soon as we can effect a link. Make certain you filter the transmission through our safeguard programs, just in case. I'll want you to coordinate things from this end. We can't waste any time, but I want that ship gone over with a fine-tooth comb."

"Understood, sir," Riker replied. "We've already got engineering and medical teams aboard; I'll organize several intelligence survey teams to fill out the security detail and go over the warbird deck by deck."

"Excellent," Picard said. "Now I would like to hear discussion concerning our options. This ship is the most advanced warbird we have ever seen, which means the Romulans will value it very highly indeed. They will not take kindly to Federation personnel poking around inside it and downloading all the files from the ship's computer. The Romulans could never allow us to get away with all that information. If they arrive before we complete our work aboard the ship, I do not see any way we can avoid a confrontation. This entire situation is, in effect, a time bomb that could explode at any moment. Therefore, I would like to hear some opinions."

"Well, there is no immediate threat," Dr. Crusher said. "The crew members are all dead, all suffocated due to the failure of the life-support system. There was no contamination aboard the ship—no radiation, no virus. All the evidence clearly indicates that the situation is exactly what it appears to be—a catastrophic accident aboard a prototype Romulan warbird on a shakedown cruise."

"An accident that has resulted in an intelligence windfall for the Federation," added La Forge.

Picard nodded. "I'm wary of windfalls, Mr. La Forge. They are often not what they appear."

"Still, we shouldn't look a gift horse in the mouth," said Riker. "The difficult part will come when we finish our job and have to decide what to do with the ship."

"Starfleet authorities would be within their legal rights to order the vessel taken as salvage," Data said. "It is a derelict, and it is in violation of Federation space."

"Their eyes will get big at the idea of a captured Romulan warbird, and a brand-new superior design at that," said Dr. Crusher. "They won't see any further than the prize being dangled before them."

"We, on the other hand, *have* to see further," said Picard. He held a field command out in "the Big Empty," as the desk jockeys at Starfleet Command liked to call it, never mind that space was not only far from empty, but full of more complications than most bureaucrats could dream of. "We have to consider all the implications of such an act. A wrong decision on our part could easily result in war."

"Too easily," said Riker. "In my opinion, if we take the warbird as a prize, the Romulans will go absolutely berserk, never mind the legality of the situation. Starfleet can claim, truthfully, that the warbird is a derelict that drifted over the border of the Neutral

Zone into Federation space and, as such, is subject to confiscation and the laws of salvage. From a legal standpoint, it's a clear-cut case of finders keepers. The only problem is that the Romulans have their own way of looking at things."

Worf nodded. "I agree. They will never believe it happened that way. Perhaps they will accept that an accident aboard the warbird caused it to drift across the Neutral Zone, because that would absolve them of any direct responsibility for the violation of Federation space. However, they will still believe that we seized their ship illegally, and they will suspect that we caused the death of its crew. If the situation were reversed, they would undoubtedly have done that very thing themselves."

"There is no basis for trust between the Federation and the Romulan Empire," said Troi, "and there never has been. Each is far too ready to believe the worst of the other. From a logical standpoint, we must assume that they will react with the same distrust as we would if the situation were reversed."

Picard nodded. "I agree. The situation is volatile enough as it is. The warbird will have to be returned to avoid precipitating an incident that could break the truce."

"Starfleet might not see it that way, sir," Riker said, "but if we can supply them with an exhaustive intelligence report concerning the design and capabilities of this new class of warbird, they won't scream too loud."

"My feelings exactly, Number One," Picard said. "However, we must go about this very carefully, and we may not have enough time. If the Romulans arrive before we complete our work, I see no way to avoid an armed confrontation. They will not allow the *Enter-*

prise to get away with information about the design of their new prototype, and with all the coded and classified files contained within their data banks."

"We've repaired the warbird's life-support systems and are now preparing to power it up. If this comes down to a fight, that works in our favor," said La Forge. "If the Romulans show up now, two ships will be much better than one. If we can figure out their cloaking device, we might even be able to hide the warbird under their very noses."

"Or we could finish our survey of the warbird," said Riker, "and then download the information from its data banks, including all the schematics from its engineering section. That would be as good as actually having the ship itself, and it should satisfy Starfleet. Then all we'd have to do is tow the warbird back to the Neutral Zone by tractor beam or power it up and lock in a course to take it back across the Neutral Zone and into Romulan space."

"They'd find their warbird with its crew all dead," said La Forge, "and they would also find the repairs we made to their life-support system. That would allow them to deduce what happened, but with no Federation starship on the spot to trigger them off, cooler heads might prevail."

"They would realize, of course, that Federation personnel had been aboard their ship," added Troi, "and had access to all their classified systems and computer files, but they could do absolutely nothing about it. They could, of course, protest, but what would be the point?"

"Exactly," Riker said. "They'll still have their warbird, but we'd have all the specs, and all their codes and classified files. The trick will be to pull it off just right, if we have enough time to do it."

"Then we are all agreed," Picard said. "Regardless of how the situation develops, the warbird will have to be returned to the Romulans. If we can complete our survey of the ship and download its data files, so much the better, but if they arrive before we can complete our work, then we must be very accommodating and withdraw rather than risk a confrontation that could violate the truce."

The others all nodded in assent.

"In that case," said Picard, "let us proceed with all possible urgency. This meeting is over."

As the others filed out, Picard said, "A moment, Number One."

Riker stopped and turned around. "Sir?"

"I shall leave you in command while I go aboard that ship. For the present, maintain yellow alert. However, Romulan long-range scanners may pick us up before we can detect their approach. In that event, they will undoubtedly come in cloaked. They must uncloak before they can open fire, however, so be prepared to go to battle stations and raise shields at a moment's notice. If pressed, do not take the time to beam us back aboard. The safety of the *Enterprise* must remain your chief priority."

"Understood, sir."

They took the turbolift together, and Picard stepped out on Deck 6 while Riker continued on to the bridge. The captain moved briskly down the corridor toward the transporter room. As he entered, he nodded at Chief O'Brien, who immediately snapped to attention. "As you were, Chief," Picard said. "Lock in coordinates to transport me to the bridge of the warbird."

"Yes, sir."

He switched on his communicator. "Picard to La Forge."

"La Forge here, Captain. I just arrived. Are you coming aboard?"

"Yes, I am preparing to beam over to the bridge of the warbird," Picard said. "What is the status of the life-support system?"

"Fully restored, Captain," Geordi said. "We're out of our suits and getting ready to power this baby up."

"Excellent. Picard out." He switched off his communicator and stepped up on the transport platform. "Ready to transport, Chief O'Brien."

"Coordinates locked in, sir."

"Energize."

Chapter Three

DATA WAS WAITING for Picard when he materialized on the bridge of the warbird. As usual, the android's facial expression was neutral, yet at the same time it somehow managed to convey an impression of both alert expectation and an almost childlike inquisitiveness.

Lieutenant Commander Data was the creation of the late Professor Noonian Soong, an enigmatic and reclusive genius whose work even the most brilliant minds of Starfleet were still struggling to understand. Except for his pale alabaster skin, which was synthetic, and his yellow eyes, which were sophisticated cybernetic optic units, Data was entirely human in appearance. He was, however, completely inorganic and, as such, he did not age. His positronic brain was a sentient, self-aware computer, capable of learning and processing information with incredible speed and efficiency.

After he was discovered in Soong's abandoned laboratory on a remote colony world, eminent Starfleet scientists started competing with one another, trying to lay claim to him. However, Data resisted becoming a laboratory specimen. He wanted to remain with the crew of the *Enterprise,* and Picard supported him in his decision. When Picard was overruled, Data threatened to resign from Starfleet. A court of inquiry was assembled to determine whether or not he, as an android, had any civil rights.

The key to the case was the question of Data's sentience. He was highly adept at mimicking human behavior and responses, but more than that, he sought to understand and assimilate them. The android had an insatiable desire to learn, and more than anything, he wanted to be human. From a logical standpoint, he understood that this was a dream he could never hope to realize, but on a metaphysical level, it was, perhaps, a more attainable goal.

A human being, ultimately, was more than merely the sum of his or her parts. Data's sophisticated positronic brain performed essentially the same functions as an organic human brain. In fact, it performed most of those functions in a superior manner, allowing him to breeze through the courses at the Starfleet Academy. Science answered for him many questions about the fascinating puzzle of human existence, but it had yet to determine exactly what constituted the human soul. If intelligence and self-awareness were used as criteria, then Data more than met those qualifications. If it was a question of animating force, then an argument could be made that Data met the criteria there as well, for the electrical impulses of the human brain were essentially the same, in principle, as those that powered Data's positronic circuits. If it was a question of the genetic templates of DNA, then Data failed on that count, but to resort to DNA as a definition of the concept of humanity was to open up a controversy no system of theology or philosophy could adequately deal with, for it would imply that cloning could essentially produce a soul.

Picard had avoided the metaphysical issues and based his argument purely on the question of sentience and self-awareness. He had pointed out to the court that if Data was sentient and self-aware, something that was easily demonstrable, and if the judges disregarded his will, they risked setting a dangerous precedent that could ultimately result in the creation of a slave race, something that voilated everything the Federation stood for. Given Picard's persuasive moral argument, the court had no choice but to rule in Data's favor.

The court had thus validated Data's right to self-determination, and the android became a permanent and highly valued member of the *Enterprise* crew. Legally he could not be considered human, but the court had recognized Data's civil rights—a decision that had highly controversial implications. The time would come, Picard was certain, when the decision of the court would raise some fascinating legal and philosophical issues, but for the present, Data was the first and only inorganic being to have been granted civil rights, and the android considered it a great personal victory. The decision didn't mean that he was human, but it was perhaps the next best thing. And if people wondered whether or not a computer-brained inorganic being was capable of loyalty, then they had to look no further than Lieutenant Commander Data.

"Sir," the android said, "I have deduced the operating principles of the Romulan ship's computer, and I have entered the appropriate instructions to prepare a download of its central data files. I am ready to proceed at your instructions."

"Excellent, Mr. Data," said Picard, as he glanced uneasily around the bridge of the warbird. It was larger than that of the *Enterprise,* and everything about it felt alien and disturbingly malevolent, especially with the bodies of the bridge crew still lying where they had fallen.

It was, Picard realized, partially his own reaction to the unsettling sight of death. The body of the warbird's young captain lay twisted at the foot of the elevated command throne with its built-in operating consoles. His hands were frozen in an attitude of clawing at his throat, and his eyes and mouth were open wide in a horrible grimace. The bodies of the other crew members were either draped over their duty stations or lying on the deck where they had fallen, vainly gasping for breath. It was, Picard thought, an awful way to die.

The bridge of the warbird was laid out with an almost Byzantine devotion to form, less like a military command center than a place of ritual. The command post where the captain sat, looking down over the bridge, vaguely brought to mind the throne of an Egyptian pharaoh, and the tandem consoles where the pilot, navigator, and weapons officer had their posts— raised on a platform higher than the other duty stations, but lower than that of the captain—were reminiscent of an altar on which sacrifices could be made to the Romulan deities of war. And in this case, thought Picard, those sacrifices had been terrible.

Ships had their own distinctive personalities, Picard thought, and this ship was no different. Somehow it simply felt *wrong,* and it wasn't just the aura of death brought about by the terrible disaster its crew had experienced. Picard wondered if any of the other personnel on the away teams felt it, then quickly dismissed the matter from his mind. Doubtless, he told himself, it was merely the tension of the situation. He was anxious to have a look around this formidable new warbird, but the sooner the work was done, the better he would like it. He did not enjoy being aboard a death ship. He glanced at the body of the fallen Romulan commander and quickly looked away. Then he frowned and looked back again. Was there something different in the attitude of the body?

He moved closer to the corpse of the Romulan commander and stared down at it intently. Perhaps it had merely been a trick of peripheral vision, but for a moment he almost could have sworn he saw the Romulan take a breath. But no, that was clearly impossible. Doubtless, he told himself again, it was merely the tension of the situation and his anxiety to get on with their business here.

"Captain?" said Data. "Should I proceed?"

Picard frowned and shook his head, thinking it must have been merely his imagination. Scanners had picked up no signs of life aboard this ship. He forced his attention away from the body of the Romulan, back to the task at hand.

"Have you checked the warbird's computer for any safeguard programs?" he asked Data, concerned about the possible loss of information due to the detection of unauthorized access. The *Enterprise* computer was equipped with such safeguards, designed to prevent access if the proper coded commands were not entered.

"As far as I have been able to determine, sir, there

seem to be no programs to guard against unauthorized entry," Data replied, as he sat behind the console at the science officer's station. "I have deciphered the language of their software, and while their files do contain coded entries, their codes seem to be based on a simple mathematical progression. It should be a relatively simple matter to download them to our own data banks and translate them at our leisure. Curiously, I find a singular lack of sophistication in their computer technology."

"Perhaps it isn't so curious, Mr. Data," said Picard. "Romulan captains are trained as warriors, not as engineers. It follows that their systems would have been designed to be easily accessible to any of the bridge crew. The possibility of a Romulan warbird falling into enemy hands was probably unthinkable to them. They would destroy their ships before surrendering them."

"That would seem wasteful and illogical," said Data.

"Not to a Romulan, Mr. Data," replied Picard. "To a Romulan warrior, surrender means dishonor and disgrace. On Earth there is an old military saying, 'Death before dishonor.' The Romulans have their own version: 'Death before defeat.'"

He turned and glanced around at the bridge of the warbird again. In this case, he thought, it was the Romulans' own ship that had defeated them. He heard a faint, unintelligible sound, rather like a moan, and turned back to Data with a frown.

"What was that, Mr. Data?"

The android looked up at him. "I said nothing, Captain."

"I thought I heard—"

And then he heard it once again, this time accompanied by a rustling sound of movement. This time Data heard it too, and he glanced up from the screen, looking for the source of it. Picard's first thought was that it might be someone from the away team, but as he looked up toward the warbird's communications station, he distinctly saw the arm of the communications officer move.

At once he reached for his phaser, but even as his fingers closed around it, a voice behind him said, "If you draw that phaser, Captain, it will be the last thing you ever do."

Picard spun around, eyes wide, to see the Romulan captain standing behind him with his disruptor drawn and aimed squarely at his chest. Data reached quickly for his phaser, but the "corpse" of the Romulan science officer suddenly rose from the deck beside him and pressed the emitting cone of his disruptor against the android's head.

"Lieutenant Commander Data, is it not?" said Valak. "I would advise against resistance. It would be a shame to destroy Starfleet's only android officer."

Picard stared with utter disbelief as the bodies of the Romulan bridge crew suddenly came to life around him. "But . . . this is *impossible!*" he said, his senses reeling in the face of the unacceptable reality. *"You were dead!"*

"In the words of your human philosopher, Mark Twain," said Valak with a smile, " 'The reports of my death are greatly exaggerated.' Korak, relieve Captain Picard of his phaser before he succumbs to temptation and does something foolish."

As the Romulan first officer stepped up to Picard and took his weapon, Picard twisted away from him and slapped his communicator. "Picard to *Enterprise:* red alert! Battle stations—"

Korak clubbed him down with the butt of his disruptor, and Picard fell to the deck, stunned.

"That was admirable, Captain," Valak said, "but pointless and not entirely unexpected. Even as we speak, my warriors are transporting to your ship. Korak, open a channel to the *Enterprise*."

The Romulan first officer quickly moved to the communications console. "Hailing frequency is open, Commander," he said.

"This is Commander Valak of the Romulan warbird, *Syrinx*. Your ship has been boarded, and your captain is my prisoner. I wish to speak with First Officer William Riker."

As Picard slowly got to his feet, his head still aching from the blow, he heard Riker reply to the Romulan commander. "This is Commander William Riker of the starship *Enterprise*."

Valak glanced at Picard and smiled. "Put him on the viewer, Korak."

As Picard stared at the viewscreen on the warbird's bridge, he saw an image that made his heart sink. Riker stood on the bridge of the *Enterprise* flanked by two Romulan warriors, their disruptors drawn. Other warriors were covering the remainder of the *Enterprise* bridge crew, and Riker's face bore a taut and grim expression.

"Captain," he said tensely, "are you all right?"

"For the moment, Number One," Picard replied, rubbing his head. He glanced at Valak. "May I ask my first officer for a report?"

"As you wish," Valak replied.

"Status report, Number One."

Riker took a deep breath. "The ship has been boarded, sir. The bridge and the engineering section have been seized." He moistened his lips. "Our scanners detected power surges aboard the warbird, but I assumed it was La Forge getting the ship powered up. Instead, it must have been their transporter activating and beaming their boarding parties to our ship. I'm sorry, sir."

Riker looked shaken. He's blaming himself for this, Picard thought. "You couldn't possibly have known, Number One," he said. "Considering the circumstances, I would undoubtedly have made the same mistake. What about the crew? Damage report? Casualties?"

He could see Riker's jaw muscles clench as he replied. "I have been prevented from communicating with the away teams aboard the warbird or with other sections of our ship, sir, but it seems there have been casualties. I have also been informed that hostages have been taken on Decks Five, Seven, Twelve, Fourteen, and Thirty-six." He swallowed hard and continued. "They moved very fast, sir, and they knew exactly what they were doing."

They did indeed, Picard thought grimly. The Romulans must have simultaneously beamed boarding parties to the bridge, the engineering section, and the family housing decks. The whole thing had been an elaborate trap, flawlessly planned and executed. His eyes were hard as he gazed at Valak. "You seem quite well informed about the layout of my ship, Commander."

"I have studied the construction of Federation starships in great detail, Captain," Valak replied smoothly. "To quote one of your Earth sayings, I know your ship 'like the back of my hand.' I have also made a study of key Starfleet personnel, and I might add that it is both a pleasure and a privilege to meet face-to-face with the famous Captain Jean-Luc Picard of the starship *Enterprise.*"

"I am sorry to say I cannot share your sentiment," Picard replied, a hard edge to his voice. "My compliments, Commander Valak. You have executed your plan brilliantly. However, if you expect to use your hostages to force my unconditional surrender—"

Valak held up his hand. "I would never expect *you* to surrender, Captain. Quite the contrary. I fully expect you to resist to the utmost of your ability. However, you will see that I have taken steps to ensure that your ability to resist has effectively been neutralized." He signaled his first officer to close the channel to the *Enterprise,* then activated his communicator. "This is Commander Valak. All units, report."

Picard listened with a sinking feeling to the litany of Romulan boarding parties reporting in. The Romulans were in control of the battle bridge, the shuttle bays, and key environmental systems in addition to the family housing decks, the bridge, and the engineering sections. He would not have thought it possible to execute so complex an operation with such incredible speed and efficiency.

There was, he realized, only one way it could have been done. The entire warbird, in a sense, had been a loaded gun, a booby trap set to go off and trigger the ambush the moment the ship was powered back up. The Romulan commander must have had his boarding parties distributed throughout the warbird, with their coordinates fixed and locked in to the transporter. He also must have had his transporter programmed with the coordinates of the assault points aboard the *Enterprise*—but Picard could not see how on earth Valak could have done that. It seemed utterly impossible.

His train of thought was interrupted when Data spoke to Valak. "Commander," Data said, gazing curiously at the Romulan commander, "a question, if I may be permitted?"

Valak turned to face him. "Ask."

"In order to beam your boarding parties so quickly to key positions on the *Enterprise,* your transporter would have to have been preprogrammed with the appropriate coordinates. I am puzzled as to how you anticipated the position of the *Enterprise* in relation to that of your own ship at the time of your assault."

Valak smiled. "An excellent question, Mr. Data, and an astute observation. Let us see if your reasoning capabilities are equally as excellent. You already possess all the information you need to allow you to deduce the answer, if you consider that there is only one way we could have accomplished that goal."

Data frowned slightly. "You have already demonstrated your familiarity with the layout of Federation ships," he replied. "And since your entire assault plan depended on programmed coordinates and settings on your transporter, sequenced for automatic engagement the moment the ship was powered up, the only unknown variable would have been the position of the *Enterprise* in relation to that of your ship." He cocked his head in a curiously birdlike movement.

Valak was watching him intently, confident that Picard was covered by his other officers. He actually seems to be enjoying this, Picard thought. This was a very different sort of Romulan from those he had encountered in the past.

"There is no way you could have determined the position of the *Enterprise* when we arrived," Data continued, "for you were, to all appearances, quite dead. The logical assumption is that you employed some sort of drug to induce a state of suspended animation so deep that tricorder readings would detect no life functions. In that state you could not possibly have ascertained the position of the *Enterprise* in relation to that of your own ship. Therefore you must have devised some method for your scanners to automatically compute our ship's position and communicate it to your ship's computer, which would initiate the preprogrammed transporter functions." Data frowned again. "However, that still does not explain how so many varied coordinates could have been anticipated and plotted so quickly and so accurately. There would not have been adequate time for you to—" Data stopped suddenly and cocked his head in the opposite direction, raising his chin slightly.

Valak watched him almost as if he were a teacher listening to the recitation of a gifted student, or a scientist observing the object of his research.

"Of course," said Data. "You programmed your scanners ahead of time to fix on the emissions of our dilithium crystals. Once your scanners had ascertained the precise position of our matter-antimatter reaction chamber, your ship's computer initiated a preprogrammed sequence that allowed it to rapidly compute the necessary transport coordinates aboard our ship, based on your knowledge of the layout of Federation vessels. It was all planned and carefully programmed in advance, for automatic initiation once your ship was powered back up." Data nodded. "Most impressive, Commander. A brilliant and audacious scheme."

"Thank you, Mr. Data," Valak replied. He turned

to Picard. "Your android is every bit as sophisticated as I had expected, Captain. It must be quite an asset to your command."

"We prefer to think of Lieutenant Commander Data as a 'he,' rather than an 'it,'" Picard replied dryly.

Valak gave him a slight bow. "I stand corrected. No offense intended, Mr. Data."

"None taken, Commander," Data replied.

Picard's mind was racing. The Romulan was toying with them, confident that he had the upper hand. Unfortunately, so far as Picard could see, he *did* have the upper hand. There had to be some way to get out of this desperate situation, but for the moment, Picard could only stall for time and await an opportunity—assuming Valak would allow them one.

The doors to the turbolift slid open, and Picard heard a roar of rage as five Romulans dragged a struggling Worf onto the bridge. His arms were bound behind him, but it still took all five of them to hold him. They threw him down onto the deck and stood over him, breathing heavily.

"Commander, this Klingon filth killed five of our warriors before we could subdue him," one of the Romulans said through gritted teeth.

"He did no less than his duty," Valak replied evenly. "You were warned to expect severe physical resistance from the Klingon, were you not?"

"Yes, Commander, but—"

"Then the men who died paid the penalty for not having properly prepared themselves. Lieutenant Commander Worf is now our prisoner, and he will be treated with the respect due to a Federation officer of his rank."

"But, Commander, surely you do not intend to allow this Klingon filth to live!"

Valak turned a steely gaze on his subordinate. "Do you question my authority?"

The Romulan warrior quickly averted his gaze. "No, Commander, of course not."

Picard watched this interchange with interest. In battle, Romulans were always merciless and utterly ruthless. This Romulan, however, was different. This Romulan has studied us, he thought, and studied not only our behavior but also our social and military customs. This was a Romulan who believed in knowing his enemy, a Romulan who *respected* his enemy. Valak was a Romulan who believed in exhaustive preparation and who took nothing for granted. And that, Picard thought, made him exceedingly dangerous.

"Forgive me, Captain," Worf said heavily, as he got up from the deck. "I have failed you."

"You did not fail me, Mr. Worf," Picard replied. "The fault is mine. I fear I was simply out-generaled."

"That is high praise indeed, considering the source," said Valak, inclining his head toward Picard.

"It was said as a statement of fact, not praise," Picard said. "You have seized my ship, Commander, and that constitutes an open act of war."

"Quite the contrary, Captain," countered Valak. "You had boarded my ship and were attempting to pirate classified information from our data banks. I have acted entirely in self-defense."

"Nonsense," said Picard. "Your ship was in Federation space, and you had gone to considerable trouble to disguise it as a derelict. We merely responded to your distress beacon."

"Which was operating on a Romulan frequency," said Valak.

"Let us dispense with this pointless charade, Commander Valak," said Picard. "We both know what has occurred here. You set a trap to capture a Federation starship, and for the present, you appear to have succeeded. Now precisely what do you intend?"

"Refreshingly direct, as I expected," Valak replied. "Very well, Captain, I shall tell you what I intend. I intend to hold your ship and your crew. Resistance will be dealt with harshly, but as I expect you to resist, I have made preparations for it. I control your engineering sections, your bridge, and all of your ship's vital functions. Any attempt at resistance will result in the execution of hostages. And I shall start with the children."

"And to think I was just beginning to respect you," Picard said with disgust.

"I do not require your respect, Captain Picard," Valak said flatly, "merely your compliance. Personally I find the prospect of executing children loathsome, even if they are merely human children. However, I can think of no better threat to compel your cooperation. And if you hope to engage your emergency autodestruct sequence, let me assure you that my engineers will have deactivated it by now, as that was their first priority once they had seized your main engineering section."

Picard compressed his lips into a tight grimace. It seemed the bastard had anticipated everything. But no plan, no matter no carefully conceived or brilliantly executed, was without a flaw. Somewhere the Romulan had overlooked something. The trick was to find out what it was.

The doors to the turbolift slid open once again and three Romulans came onto the bridge, one of them an officer. "Commander, I regret to report that nine of our warriors did not awake from their cryptobiotic sleep; they are now dead."

"Only nine?" said Valak. He nodded. "Acceptable losses, considering the experimental nature of the drug. Note in your report that it functioned within acceptable parameters, though I would not care to repeat the experience." He turned to Picard. "You see, Captain, it was essential to the plan to convince you that we had all died, so we could not resort to cosmetic subterfuges, as I quite expected your medical personnel to conduct examinations of our 'corpses.' Therefore it was necessary to administer the cryptobiotic drug and then purge the ship's life-support system so that we would all literally suffocate as the drug was taking effect. It was altogether a rather unpleasant way to die."

"You gambled that your drug would take effect within seconds of the time you would have actually died," said Data.

"Correct, Mr. Data."

"You risked losing your entire crew," said Data.

"Correct again," said Valak. "As you humans say, 'Nothing ventured, nothing gained.' We also risked reviving too early, before life-support functions aboard our ship had been fully restored by your engineering crew. I was confident in their ability to diagnose the problem, however, and I took care not to make it too difficult for them. Fortunately the risk paid off."

"You still have not told me what you want," Picard said.

"Ah, yes, forgive me," Valak replied. "To begin with, I want certain information from the classified data banks of your ship's computer."

"Then you are doomed to disappointment," Picard said harshly. "Nothing you can do will compel me to surrender classified information."

"Not even the execution of the hostages?" said Valak. But then he held up his hand before Picard could reply. "No, of course not. To safeguard the hostages, you would comply with my demands only to a certain point, where they would not conflict directly with your sworn oath as a Federation officer. Beyond that point, you would do your duty, even to the point of destroying your own ship and all aboard it. Such is the responsibility of a Federation starship captain, and you would carry it out unfailingly, whatever your personal feelings might be. Perhaps not every starship captain would, if faced with such a choice, but Jean-Luc Picard would never hesitate." Valak smiled. "You see, Picard, I know you. Even though we never before met face-to-face, I know you. I could recite your distinguished service record down to the last minute detail."

"Indeed? What have I done to inspire such scrutiny?" Picard asked, his voice laced with irony.

"In short, Captain Picard, you have excelled at what you do," Valak replied. "You see, I am considered something of an anomaly among Romulan commanders in that I also happen to be a scholar, and my chosen field of study is human culture and behavior, especially where it applies to Starfleet. I have focused my research on those officers whose records indicate that they are among the very best in Starfleet. The elite, if you will. And your name, Captain Picard, heads the list."

"I suppose I should feel flattered," Picard replied sarcastically.

"No, Captain, you should feel proud," said Valak. "Proud of your accomplishments and those of your crew. Your ship is considered the finest in all of Starfleet, and I regard it as a most fortuitous circumstance that it was the *Enterprise* that took the bait I offered. This situation affords me the rare opportunity to test my mettle against yours. The finest Starfleet has to offer, tested against the elite of the Romulan Command. I find the challenge stimulating."

"You seem already to have won the test," Picard replied wryly.

"If you seek to find a weakness by appealing to my ego, Captain, you are, as you humans say, barking up the wrong tree. My ego is strong and healthy, but it is tempered with a fine edge of pragmatism. This contest is only just beginning. To use a metaphor from your human game of chess, I have opened boldly and taken control of the board, but the match is only just begun. Even now, as we speak, you plan strategies and gambits, with a mind to dislodging me from my dominant position and gaining the advantage. I am most anxious to see how the play develops."

"You certainly seem to have done your homework, Commander," said Picard. "Romulan intelligence is clearly much better than we had supposed. However, if you know that nothing you can do will compel me to surrender classified information from my ship's data banks, then you must also know that any attempt to bypass the safeguards of those data banks will result in the data being wiped."

"Indeed, the information I require would be erased," Valak agreed, "if I were to make any attempt at 'hacking,' as I believe you call it. However, thanks to our Romulan intelligence, and to one agent in particular, whom you were so kind as to return to us, that will not be necessary."

Picard frowned in puzzlement. "An agent whom *I* returned to you?"

"Sir," said Data, "I believe Commander Valak is referring to Subcommander Selok, the Romulan spy who posed as an ambassador to Starfleet from the planet Vulcan. If you will recall, we did not discover the deception until a transporter accident was staged, designed to make us believe the so-called ambassador had died. It turned out to be a clever ruse to cover up their agent being transported to a Romulan warbird in the vicinity."

"Yes," Picard said, "I remember now. It was quite a coup for Romulan intelligence."

"Perhaps more of a coup than you might think, Captain," Valak said. "Our agent was able to glean from Starfleet certain coded references to Hermeticus Two."

Picard was aware that Valak was watching him carefully for a reaction. "Hermeticus Two?" He frowned. "That means nothing to me."

"Indeed?" said Valak. "Well, we shall soon see. Korak, escort Captain Picard to the transporter room. We are going to pay a visit to the *Enterprise.*"

Chapter Four

CHIEF O'BRIEN STOOD AT the controls of the transporter, his expression tense. Two Romulan warriors stood on either side of him, keeping him covered with their weapons. Picard and O'Brien exchanged quick glances as the party beaming aboard stepped off the pads beneath the primary energizing coils.

"Captain," said O'Brien.

"Chief," said Picard.

A great deal went unspoken in the terse exchange. Their glances said it all: Romulans in control of the *Enterprise.* This was more than a mere skirmish along the border of the Neutral Zone. This was an open act of war in Federation space. The Romulans had gone way over the line this time. Picard wondered what had made them take such a risk. Was this merely a first step, a prelude to invasion and all-out war? Were they trying to gain some early advantage by seizing a

Federation starship and trying to break into its data banks? But Valak had said that breaking in would not be necessary. What did he mean? Was there something else aboard the *Enterprise* they really wanted? Or did they believe they could somehow bypass the computer's safeguard programs? Picard thought furiously as they made their way to the bridge.

"Still weighing strategies and gambits, Captain?" Valak said as they entered the turbolift.

"You may have stopped me from resisting for the moment, Commander Valak," Picard replied brusquely, "but you cannot stop me from thinking."

"Even if I could, I would not dream of it," said Valak with a smile. "That would only spoil the game."

"Is that what this is to you, a *game?*"

"Some games are more serious than others," Valak said. "And those are the ones I find the most stimulating."

Picard grunted. The turbolift stopped and the doors slid open. They stepped out onto the bridge. Picard quickly glanced around. His bridge officers were all at their posts, but every one of them was covered by at least two Romulan warriors. The tension on the bridge made the air seem electric. Riker stood before him, flanked by two Romulan warriors.

"I'm truly sorry about this, Captain," he said.

"So am I, Number One," Picard replied. "Anything further to report?"

"No, sir. I have been denied communication with other sections of the ship. The Romulans are in complete control." He gave Commander Valak a hard look.

"Watch them both," Valak told his warriors as he crossed the bridge and headed for the main computer console.

Picard was shepherded to stand next to Riker, where the warriors could keep an eye on both of them. "They've got to be out of their minds to try something like this," Riker whispered savagely. "Do you have any idea what they're after?"

"Something in our ship's computer files, apparently," Picard replied, in a soft voice.

"They'll never get past the safeguards," Riker said.

"Oh, but we shall, Mr. Riker," Valak said. He pointed to his ear. "My hearing is excellent, by the way. There is no point in whispering. If I had intended to prevent you from communicating with each other, rest assured I would have done so." He reached out toward his first officer and snapped his fingers. The man took something out of his jacket pocket and handed it to him. It was an isolinear chip. Picard frowned.

"Observe, Captain," Valak said. He slipped the chip into the computer.

"What the—" Riker began, but Picard shook his head, motioning him to be quiet. They both watched the Romulan commander intently as he began punching commands into the console.

"He's not using voice command," said Riker. He shook his head. "If he thinks that will enable him to bypass the safeguard codes—"

Suddenly the computer voice responded: "Security access code validated. Priority One-A. Subject: Hermeticus Two."

"Good God!" Riker said. *"He's in!"*

"Class-H planet, located Delta Quadrant, Sector Thirteen, coordinates four-nine-four-five—"

Picard suddenly called out, *"Computer: priority override! Picard, alpha alpha one zero!"*

One of the warriors clubbed him down with his

disruptor, but he was too late. As Picard fell, Valak stared intently at the screen, saw it go blank, and stabbed vainly at the buttons on the console.

"Priority override," said the computer voice, "alpha alpha one zero; authorization confirmed. Command executed."

Valak glanced sharply at Riker, who had started to move when Picard was struck but was immediately grabbed from both sides and a disruptor pressed up beneath his chin. Valak tried to punch in instructions on the console once again, but to no avail. He looked up at Riker, his eyes hard. "I locked out voice command. What did he do?"

Riker stared at him with cold fury. "Priority one, alpha alpha one zero overrides all other instructions, and the computer is programmed to recognize the captain's voice and receive it even during voice command lockout."

Valak stared at him. "Very clever," he said. "I did not know about that. Well, I shall simply have to find another way to retrieve the file."

"You can't," said Riker. "The command has been executed. That file has been erased."

"So." Valak nodded. "Well done. Well done indeed. Fortunately I managed to note the last four digits of the planet coordinates on the screen before it went blank. I did not obtain the full file on Hermeticus Two, Mr. Riker, but at least I now know something I did not know before. I know exactly where the planet is."

Riker glanced down at the captain, who was still lying on the floor. "Captain Picard needs medical attention," he said. "I demand to be allowed to take him to sickbay."

Valak made a dismissive gesture with his hand.

"You are in no position to demand anything, Mr. Riker," he said as he stared contemplatively at the blank screen.

"Then I *respectfully request* that I be allowed to take the captain to sickbay," Riker said through gritted teeth.

Valak glanced up at him, then smiled. "Very well, Mr. Riker. Since you respectfully request it, your request is granted." He gestured to several of his warriors. "Accompany him. And keep a close watch in case he attempts any heroics." He turned back to Riker. "If you try anything foolish, Mr. Riker . . ." He turned and glanced around at the bridge crew. His gaze fell on Deanna Troi, and he saw Riker stiffen. "Need I say more?"

"I get the message," Riker said tersely.

"Take him," Valak said. "I hope the injury is not serious. I still have need of him."

Riker bent down and lifted Picard, then carried him to the turbolift, accompanied by the Romulan guards. "Sickbay," he said. The turbolift activated. The guards watched him carefully but did not say a word. Picard moaned softly.

The doors to the sickbay opened, and Riker entered carrying the captain, followed by the guards. Dr. Beverly Crusher's eyes went wide with alarm when she saw them. "Put him on the table," she said. "What happened?"

Riker quickly filled her in. The Romulans remained by the door, watching them carefully, their weapons held ready.

"Are you all right?" asked Riker, as Dr. Crusher bent over the captain.

"Yes," she replied, "but I've been kept prisoner in here. They wouldn't let me leave."

"I know," said Riker. "I saw those two centurions in the companionway."

"He'll be all right," she said after a moment. "He was just knocked unconscious. There are no fractures, but there may be a slight concussion."

Picard groaned again. His eyes flickered open. The first words he said were "Did it work?"

"It worked," said Riker. "The file was erased, but not before Valak got the final digits of the planet's coordinates." He frowned. "Hermeticus Two. I've never even heard of it. And what the hell is a class-H planet?"

Picard slowly sat up, rubbing his head and wincing. He glanced at the Romulans by the door and spoke softly. "Class H stands for Hermeticus, an old classification no longer in use. It was once employed as a file designation to signify quarantined planets."

"It's the first I've heard of it," said Riker, puzzled.

"As I said, Number One, the classification is no longer in use. Most of the old reasons for imposing quarantines on planets no longer apply. The class H–Hermeticus designation was dropped about twenty years ago."

"But it was still active in the files," said Riker, looking confused.

"Yes, it was," Picard replied, as Dr. Crusher sprayed sealant on the wound. "And that can only mean the quarantine is still fully in effect."

"Priority One-A is top secret, Captain's eyes only," Riker said. "How in hell did Valak gain access?"

"That chip he had must have contained coded and classified command instructions," said Picard. "And there is only one place where he could have obtained it."

"Starfleet Headquarters?" said Riker, with astonishment.

Picard nodded. "Such chips are kept on file to enable specially cleared computer maintenance engineers to gain access in order to effect repairs, under strict clearance and supervision, of course. The chips are used to test and debug priority command instructions in the software. Supposedly they are kept in vaults under top security conditions."

"So how did Valak get his hands on one?" asked Riker.

"Good question, Number One. You recall that spy the Romulans planted at Starfleet Headquarters under cover as a Vulcan ambassador?"

Riker frowned. "Yes, I remember. But even a Vulcan ambassador wouldn't have had access to top secret coded and programmed instruction chips."

"Perhaps not," Picard said, "unless some fool bureaucrat at Starfleet was showing off security procedures in order to impress a high-ranking foreign dignitary. At any rate, that chip is useless to Valak now."

"But he did get the planet coordinates," Riker said grimly. "What *is* Hermeticus Two?"

"I haven't the faintest idea, Number One," replied Picard. "The fact that it was designated Hermeticus Two means that it was only the second planet to be placed under quarantine. That means no Federation vessel has visited there in over thirty years."

"You mean you don't know *anything* about it?" said Dr. Crusher.

Picard shook his head. "No, and I never would have, unless we happened to be in that vicinity and I specifically requested the information. However, that would have been extremely unlikely, as those location coordinates place it squarely in the middle of the Neutral Zone."

"Great," said Riker. "And now the file's been erased, so no information is available. The Romulans don't have it, but neither do we. The question is, why did Valak want it?"

"Your guess is as good as mine, Number One," Picard said.

"Bridge to sickbay." It was Ensign Ro.

Riker touched his communicator. "Riker here."

"Ah, Mr. Riker," Valak's voice came on. "I trust Captain Picard has sustained no serious injury?"

Riker glanced back at the Romulan guards. It was pointless to lie with them standing right there, watching and listening to every word. "He's all right, no thanks to you."

"In that case, would you both be so kind as to rejoin me on the bridge? We shall be getting under way shortly."

Picard touched his communicator. "This is Picard. What do you mean, we shall be getting under way?"

"Call it a tandem mission, Captain," Valak said. "Your ship and mine. A sort of cooperative venture. I admit that the cooperation is somewhat forced on your part, but it should be an interesting experience just the same."

"Where do you intend to take my ship?" Picard demanded.

"Why, I should think that would be obvious, Captain," Valak replied. "We are going to Hermeticus Two."

"Hermeticus Two is located at coordinates that place it squarely in the middle of the Neutral Zone," Picard replied.

"On its outer edge, to be exact," said Valak, "in a remote sector that, according to our charts, has no habitable planet. I would be most curious to see why the Federation has an interest in an uninhabited planet that lies so close to Romulan space."

"The Federation has not visited that planet in over thirty years," Picard replied. "It is a quarantined world."

"So you say," said Valak. "We shall see. Valak out."

Picard shut off his own communicator. "So that's it," he said tensely. "Romulan paranoia. Their agent somehow stumbled upon Federation references to a classified planet in the Neutral Zone, and they are convinced that we are hiding something there."

"*Are* we?" Riker asked.

Picard glanced at him sharply. "I hope you know better than that, Will."

"I know that Starfleet has its share of intelligence officers who just love planning secret missions from the safety of their office desks," Riker said.

Picard frowned. "I suppose that's possible," he said, "but it seems unlikely. Why use a coded designation that has not been current for some twenty years?"

"That could be the reason," Riker said "It could make for a good way to hide something."

Picard shook his head. "Perhaps, but I simply don't believe it."

"I don't believe it, either," Dr. Crusher said. "Setting aside the danger and the foolhardiness of putting a secret base in the Neutral Zone, the logistics involved in supplying it would risk giving it away."

Riker nodded. "Maybe. But somehow I don't think Valak is going to buy that."

"No, nor would I expect him to," Picard agreed. "If the Romulans thought there was a chance they could

81

get away with it, it is precisely the sort of thing that they would do themselves, and so they attribute the same motivations to us. I fear that no amount of reasoning will convince them. But it's worth a try."

"The question is, what will happen when they find out there *isn't* a secret Federation base on Hermeticus Two?" asked Dr. Crusher.

"No, that is not the question, Beverly," Picard said. "The question is, what *will* we find there? The Federation considers planetary quarantine only as a last resort. Somehow we have got to take back control of the ship before we arrive there."

They were speaking in very low voices, and the Romulan guards had become suspicious. *"Enough!"* one of them said, gesturing with his weapon. "The commander wants you on the bridge. *Now!"*

Picard rubbed his sore head and winced. "That's twice I've been hit in the head," he said in a surly tone. "I intend to return the compliment to Commander Valak personally."

Picard and Riker were hustled out into the companionway. As they moved down the corridor toward the turbolifts, they saw a number of Romulan warriors herding a group of crew members in the opposite direction.

"Where are you taking those people?" Picard demanded.

"Move on!" said one of the Romulan escorts, giving Picard a shove.

"You push him once again and I'm going to feed you that disruptor," Riker warned him.

The Romulan sneered at him. "Move!"

"They're heading for the shuttle bays," said Riker. Picard's face was grim. "Valak is transferring his hostages to the warbird and depriving us of our shuttles at the same time."

"What are we going to do?" asked Riker.

Picard shook his head. "For the moment, Number One, I am afraid there is nothing we *can* do. Valak is rapidly closing off all of our options."

They entered the turbolift, which took them to the bridge.

"Ah, Captain Picard," said Valak, "and Mr. Riker. I trust that you are feeling better, Captain?"

"Spare me the false pleasantries, Valak," Picard said tersely. "Where are you taking my people?"

"A portion of the *Enterprise* crew is being transferred to the *Syrinx,*" Valak said, "where they will be well treated as long as they behave themselves. You have my word on that."

"Your word?" Riker said scornfully. "You can't even trust a dead Romulan."

Valak smiled. "Very good, Mr. Riker. I like that. You can't even trust a dead Romulan. I must remember that."

"What assurance do I have that you will keep your word?" Picard asked.

"You are hardly in a position to demand any assurances," Valak replied. "However, I can understand your concern for your crew. You will be going with them. We shall leave the *Enterprise* in Mr. Riker's capable hands, under Romulan supervision, of course."

"This is still my ship, Valak," said Picard, "and I demand—"

"Demand all you like," Valak interrupted him impatiently, "but you will do as you are told. You can be delivered to the *Syrinx* conscious or unconscious.

The choice is yours. I have already instructed your navigator to plot a course for Hermeticus Two. And I have advised your bridge crew that my men have been trained to anticipate any tricks. For each instruction not explicitly complied with, a hostage will be executed, so I would advise you, Captain, to urge your bridge crew to cooperate fully."

Picard scowled. "Do as he says, Number One."

"Understood, sir."

"We shall get under way in a moment," Valak said. "For the record, Captain, slightly better than half of your engineering crew is already aboard the *Syrinx,* as well as half of your security crew and other essential personnel, in addition to hostages taken from your family quarters. Dr. Crusher will be allowed to assemble a medical kit, under careful supervision, and join them. Your communications system has been modified to allow only ship-to-ship communications, so you can forget about attempting to send out any distress calls to Starfleet. As you can see, I have taken everything into account."

"Apparently so," Picard said grudgingly.

"Good. Then we understand each other."

"I understand you only too well, Commander Valak," said Picard. "You have asked me to take your word that my crew will not be mistreated. Perhaps you will accept mine when I assure you that there is no Federation base on Hermeticus Two or anywhere else in the Neutral Zone. I swear it on my honor as an officer and a gentleman."

"I believe you, Captain," Valak said.

Picard frowned. "Then why—"

Valak held up his hand. "I should say I believe that *you* believe there is no Federation base hidden in the Neutral Zone. However, I have my orders. And even if there is no Federation base on Hermeticus Two, I have been instructed to discover exactly why the Federation is so anxious to conceal any information about that planet. It is a matter of Romulan security, Captain. As an officer, I am sure you can appreciate that. We simply cannot afford not to know."

"Valak, listen to me," Picard said. "The designation Class H–Hermeticus signifies a quarantined world. I do not know why Hermeticus Two was placed under quarantine, but the fact that it was can mean only one thing: there is grave danger there, either from indigenous life-forms or from the environment. Leaving aside any considerations for the *Enterprise,* if you care for the safety of your own crew, then I urge you in the strongest possible terms—"

"Save your breath, Captain," Valak said. "My orders are explicit. If you place yourself in my shoes, as you humans say, then you will appreciate that I have no alternative but to complete my mission. My warriors will escort you to the transporter room. I shall join you presently."

After Picard was beamed over to the *Syrinx,* Valak permitted him to visit the hostages. They were all gathered together in one of the warbird's shuttle bays, where they could easily be guarded. Bedding and other comforts had been provided for them. As Picard entered the shuttle bay, the Romulans allowed him to go forward and speak with his crew members while they remained behind, watching and guarding the doors with their weapons drawn. As his crew members surrounded him, Picard quickly filled them in on what he knew.

"What happens after we get to Hermeticus Two, Captain?" Deanna Troi asked.

"I have no idea, Counselor," Picard replied. "Regrettably, by erasing the file to deny the Romulans access to the information we denied ourselves access to it as well. We have no way of knowing what we may be getting into."

"Captain," Worf said, "I have organized some of the men. I believe that if we create a distraction, we can rush the guards and—"

"Negative, Mr. Worf," Picard said. "I cannot risk it. Even if you managed to surprise the guards, it would take Valak but a moment to open the outer bay doors and cancel the forcefield. You would all be killed. I am certain he allowed me to come here so that I could see for myself the dispositions he has made to secure his hostages. It would seem that he has thought this all out very carefully."

"But we must do *something,* sir!" protested Worf.

"Indeed, we must, Mr. Worf," Picard agreed, "but now is not the time. We must await the right opportunity."

"Captain," said Deanna, "I sense in Commander Valak a strong desire to compete with you and to impress you. He wishes to win your respect. He seems to regard this situation as a challenge—in a way, almost as a sporting proposition."

Picard nodded. "Yes, Counselor, that is consistent with my own observations. Valak is highly intelligent and very capable, but his ego is his weakness. He never should have allowed me to be present on the bridge when he attempted to access the classified files in our ship's computer, but he wanted to show off. His constant quoting of human aphorisms is another way of flaunting his knowledge about us and our culture, as if to prove that he has done his homework and is fully prepared for anything we might attempt to do."

"It may be something that we can use against him," said Deanna.

"Perhaps," Picard said. "He is young and seems eager to prove himself. His arrogance is tempered by insecurity and an ambition that seems to drive him. There may be a way to turn that to our advantage."

"What would you have us do, Captain?" Worf asked.

"For the moment, Mr. Worf, nothing. Keep your eyes and your ears open, and see what you can learn. We know little about this new class of warbird. There may be a design weakness we can exploit, or something in the crew's routine . . ." He shook his head. "For the present, Valak has left us with no viable options. However, this isn't over yet."

"It is *maddening* to feel so powerless!" Worf said furiously.

"We are not powerless, Mr. Worf," Picard said. "We are merely at a disadvantage for the present. Have patience."

"There is one thing that we have not yet admitted to ourselves," said Dr. Crusher. "What Valak has done is a flagrant violation of the treaty and constitutes an act of war. He cannot allow the Federation to find out about it."

"Which means that he cannot allow any of us to live," Deanna said grimly.

"We are not dead yet, Counselor," Picard replied.

"The ship is getting under way," Worf said as the sound of the drives filtered through the walls of the shuttle bay.

"Have courage, all of you," Picard said. "Valak is smart, but he is not infallible. We shall all get out of this somehow, I promise you."

When he rejoined Valak on the bridge of the warbird, the Romulan commander said, "I trust you have assured yourself that your crew members are being well treated, Captain?"

"If being confined within a shuttle bay like animals in a corral is what you consider being treated well," Picard replied.

"A regrettable necessity," said Valak. "We have no brigs aboard our ships because we do not take prisoners, and disciplinary measures aboard Romulan vessels are too draconian to allow for mere incarceration. However, at least I can provide comfortable accommodations for you, Captain. You will occupy my first officer's quarters while he remains aboard the *Enterprise.* You will find them somewhat Spartan, as humans say, but reasonably comfortable."

"I would prefer to remain with my own people," said Picard.

"I am sure you would, Captain," Valak replied, "but I cannot allow that. It would not be prudent, if that is the appropriate word. Your people will be managed more easily if they are deprived of your leadership skills."

"You seem to have thought of everything," Picard said, playing to the Romulan commander's ego.

"I have tried to anticipate all possibilities," Valak said smoothly.

"You cannot anticipate what may happen when we reach Hermeticus Two," Picard said.

"True," admitted Valak. "However, I have planned what we shall do if we find—as I suspect we will—a Federation base there."

"And if you do not?"

"Then, as you humans say, I shall play it by ear," said Valak.

"You seem fond of quoting our expressions," said Picard. "That is a most un-Romulan trait."

"True," Valak said again. "Few Romulans have made the effort to learn as much about human culture as I have. Few consider the subject worthy of serious attention."

"But you do," Picard replied. "I am curious to know why."

"In part, because I believe in knowing my enemy," said Valak. "However, there is also another reason, Captain. Your Federation will someday be a part of the Romulan Empire, and humans will be governed more easily by those who understand them."

Picard raised his eyebrows. "So you have political ambitions. And rather lofty ones, it would seem."

"I do, indeed, Captain. And you will help me realize them."

"Yes, I suppose the successful completion of your mission would provide quite a feather in your cap . . . as we humans say."

Valak seemed amused. "It will indeed," he said, "but more than that, Captain, you and your crew will provide a valuable asset to me when we return to Romulus."

Picard frowned. "What do you mean?"

"You are surprised?" said Valak. He seemed pleased. "You thought I planned to kill you all when this was over?"

"Do you expect me to believe otherwise?"

"I cannot be held responsible for what you choose to believe, Picard," Valak replied, "but while disposing of you all would certainly be one way to prevent the Federation from discovering what we have done, it would also be a grievous waste of an invaluable resource. I do not plan to execute any of your crew unless I am forced to do so. I intend to take you all back to Romulus as prisoners. That will, as you put it, provide an even finer feather in my cap, not only for all the valuable intelligence your people can provide, but also for the opportunity it will present our scholars to make a firsthand, intimate study of human behavior and of the behavior of the nonhuman members of your crew. I intend to claim the right of possession by conquest. Your crew, Captain, and your ship will be my war trophies. That alone should win me a position as a prefect on the council."

"I see," Picard said, looking at him with a respect he did not truly feel. "You plan to use us as a tool for your political advancement. And we shall live out the remainder of our lives as slaves to the Romulan Empire."

"To a large extent, Captain, that will depend on you," said Valak. "Those of you who choose not to cooperate will be forced to do so. Those who survive will be sent to the slave markets. However, if you cooperate, I shall have considerable influence over your fate. As you humans say, you scratch my back, and I shall scratch yours."

"If you expect me or any of my crew to voluntarily turn traitor to the Federation, then you know far less about us than you think," Picard said harshly.

"We shall see," said Valak. "You have not yet been exposed to Romulan methods of interrogation. Allow me to assure you, Captain, that you can be broken. Anyone can be broken. Why subject yourself and the members of your crew, some of whom are merely children, to needless pain and suffering when the end result will be the same no matter what you do?"

"I see that I have underestimated you," Picard said coldly.

"If it provides any consolation, Captain, you are not the first to underestimate my ability," said Valak.

"It is your savagery, not your ability that I underestimated," said Picard. "Now unless you require my presence on the bridge, I would just as soon retire to the quarters you have set aside for me."

"Very well, Captain. I have no use for you at the moment. You may go." Valak turned to the warriors guarding Picard. "Take Captain Picard to First Officer Korak's quarters," he said, "and keep a close watch on him."

Riker stood on the bridge of the *Enterprise,* trying to settle himself and keep his anxiety from mounting. Inside, he was seething. The captain, Deanna, Worf, Dr. Crusher, and a large complement of the *Enterprise* crew were being held aboard the warbird as hostages, while on the *Enterprise* itself, Romulans were in key positions everywhere. And he could do nothing.

As soon as the ships had engaged their warp engines, the *Syrinx* had cloaked itself so that any Federation ships that happened to be in their vicinity and picked them up on their scanners would detect only another Federation ship. By the time they discovered their error, it would be much too late, and there was no way for Riker to warn them. Fortunately they had not encountered any other vessels, so Riker was thankful, at least, for small blessings.

Valak's warriors were watching every move he made. They questioned even the slightest unfamiliar action, in case it was an attempt to trick them. And it was the same all over the ship. The strain was building.

Although Commander Valak was well versed in the finer points of Federation vessel design and Starfleet procedures, his warriors were unaccustomed to the *Enterprise* and its routines; they were suspicious of everyone and everything. Riker was faced with the unenviable task of trying to run a ship while almost every single thing he did had to be cleared by the Romulan first officer Valak had left in command on the bridge of the *Enterprise*. At one point, Subcommander Korak had allowed Riker to communicate with La Forge when a call came in to the bridge that they were having trouble down in engineering.

"Commander, I just can't run engineering like this!" La Forge had said, with exasperation. "They've taken away half my crew, and I can't make a move down here without somebody looking over my shoulder and demanding to know what I'm doing!"

"I know, Geordi, I know," Riker had said, trying to calm him down. "We've got to put up with the same sort of thing up here. Just do the best you can. Riker out."

"Do your people always complain so?" Korak asked him.

"No, not really," Riker replied tensely. "Just when we've got Romulans underfoot everywhere we turn."

"On my ship, my subordinates never complain," said Korak. "They simply do their duty. You humans are weak."

"We're strong enough that you Romulans couldn't simply run right over us, as you did with the other races you've subjugated."

"When the time is right, said Korak, "your Federation will be swept away, and you will be able to offer no more resistance than your crew did when we took your ship."

"We *chose* not to resist," Riker said, "so that lives

would not be risked needlessly. Unlike you Romulans, Federation officers value the lives of the people under their command."

"You merely play with words," the Romulan replied with a sneer. "There was nothing you could do. No human could ever be a match for a Romulan warrior in combat."

Riker gave Korak a hard look. "Care to put your money where your mouth is?" he asked the Romulan.

Korak frowned. "I do not understand. Why should I wish to put money in my mouth?"

"It's an old human expression, Korak," Riker said. "Translated loosely, it means would you care to wager on it, to prove your assertions through action?"

Korak stared at him. Data and Ro watched the interchange with interest, as did the other Romulans on the bridge. "Are you *seriously* challenging me to physical combat?" Korak was obviously astonished.

"Why not?" Riker said. "You said no human could ever be a match for a Romulan warrior in combat. I stand ready to prove you wrong. Unless you are afraid to have your nose rubbed in the dirt by a mere human."

"That expression I understand!" Korak said angrily. He looked ready to launch himself at Riker right then and there, but then he hesitated, taking control of himself with an obvious effort. "I could show you whose nose would be rubbed in the dirt, human," he said, "but you will not so easily distract me from my duty."

Korak had almost lost his temper, Riker realized. Follow up on that weakness, he told himself. Exploit it. "What is there to be distracted from?" he asked in a mocking tone. "The course has already been locked in. No new command functions will be required until we're ready to come out of warp speed. We've got plenty of time to go down to the holodeck and put your empty boasting to a test."

Korak gazed at him intently. "If you seek to try some sort of trick, human, it will never work. My warriors will watch each and every move your bridge crew makes in our absence."

Data glanced at Riker. "Sir," he said, "with all due respect for your abilities, I feel I really should point out that, according to all known studies, the average Romulan is physically far stronger than the average human of equal weight and size, owing to such factors as greater muscular density and bone mass, in addition to the genetic—"

"That'll do, Mr. Data," Riker said.

"Your android is correct, Riker," Korak said with a smug, superior look. "I could crush you like a slime beetle!"

"Talk is cheap," Riker said.

"Very well, human. I accept your challenge. You will soon wish that you had never issued it."

"After you, Korak." Riker indicated the doors to the turbolift.

Korak turned to the other warriors on the bridge. "Watch them! If any of them try anything, you know what to do!" He glanced at Riker with contempt. "This will not take long."

"I hope Commander Riker knows what he is doing," Data said to Ro uncertainly as he watched the door of the turbolift slide closed behind them. "The odds against him prevailing over Korak in a contest of physical strength are—"

"Don't tell me what the odds are, Data," Ro

replied, keeping her eyes on the scanners. "If we are ever going to get out of this, it will have to be against the odds. Knowing what they are won't make it any easier."

"Perhaps not," said Data, "but having Commander Riker seriously injured or even killed will certainly not improve our situation."

"Riker knows what he's doing," Ro replied, then added uncertainly, "I hope."

The corridor was clear as Riker and Korak headed toward the holodeck. All nonessential personnel had either been taken hostage aboard the warbird or were being confined in Ten-Forward, where small numbers of Romulans could easily keep large groups under guard. Riker found it strange to see no activity at all in the companionways of the *Enterprise*.

They obviously want to keep us all alive for some reason, Riker thought. Why? Valak had planned everything with excruciating care. Picard would have blown up the ship before surrendering it to the Romulans, but Valak had anticipated that and had quickly taken steps to prevent the captain from exercising that option. Picard would probably have died before surrendering his ship, but Valak had realized that, too, and had seized the *Enterprise* without ever formally demanding its surrender. In fact, he had seemed to take great satisfaction in telling Picard that he *expected* him to resist, as if challenging him to do exactly that. It was as if he were daring Picard to find some flaw, some weakness in his strategy.

Yes, thought Riker, that's their weakness: their arrogance in believing themselves superior to all other races, especially humans. It had to be galling to be challenged by someone you considered your inferior.

Riker had baited Korak into a fight, and the Romulan was anxious to put him in his place. Unfortunately the odds were excellent that he could do precisely that. There had been no need for Data to remind him that Romulans were physically stronger than humans. Riker knew it perfectly well. That wasn't the point. The point was, how far could Korak be pushed?

Riker was almost certain that he had one advantage: the Romulans wanted to keep the crew alive. If all they wanted was the *Enterprise* itself, the Romulans would have killed off the crew immediately and seized the ship as a prize. They could have put a prize crew aboard, powered up the impulse engines, and followed the warbird back into Romulan space, or the *Syrinx* could have towed the *Enterprise* with tractor beams. But no, they wanted the humans alive. That much was clear, and that was why Captain Picard had not fought them to the last man. Picard never went to extremes until he had exhausted all other options. He valued the lives of his crew members, and he refrained from violence except when he was left with no other choice.

Valak had closed off a lot of their options, but they were still alive. The Romulan captain had not harmed any of the hostages—at least, so far—and as long as they were still alive, they still had a chance to get out of this. In the past, whenever they were faced with a crisis, Captain Picard always said, "I want options!" And somehow the crew always managed to come up with them.

Riker's job was to look for those options, and pressing Korak for weaknesses was a beginning. It would give him a way of gauging how far Korak could be pushed. Push a man far enough, thought Riker, and he will start to make mistakes. One way or another, he was going to force Korak to start making mistakes—assuming, of course, that he survived this challenge. He thought there was a good chance of that; since Valak obviously wanted them alive, Korak would not go so far as to kill him. At least, that was what Riker hoped. It was a gamble. But then, nothing ventured, nothing gained.

They reached the holodeck doors, and Riker stopped by the control console mounted on the bulkhead. There were four main holodecks here on Deck 11, in addition to smaller simulation rooms on Decks 12 and 33. Riker chose Holodeck 1, the simulation chamber he normally used for his workouts.

"Ever use a holodeck before?" he asked Korak.

"It is a holographic environment simulation chamber, is it not?" said Korak. "We have no such luxuries aboard our warbirds. We consider them decadent and wasteful."

"Perhaps because your 'superior Romulan culture' doesn't have the computer technology to make a holodeck work right," Riker replied, needling him. "You may think differently after you've experienced it. We've found holodecks useful not only for recreation, but for training as well. The holographic imagery subsystem creates the illusion of realistic environmental backgrounds while the matter conversion subsystem creates physical props through transporter-based replicators. The system cannot create actual living beings, of course, but it can create simulations that are manipulated by highly articulated computer-controlled tractor beams, rather like very sophisticated puppets. What you'll see in there isn't real, but it will certainly *feel* real."

Riker reached out toward the control console, but Korak grabbed his hand before he could hit any of the selector buttons. "Wait," he said.

Riker looked at him questioningly. Korak picked up his communicator. "Korak to Engineering," he said.

"La Forge here," Geordi replied. "What is it now?"

"I wish to speak to Atalan," Korak replied.

"Anything you say," said La Forge dryly. A moment later the Romulan came on, and Korak instructed him to release Holodeck 1 for function, but to stand by to shut down power to it immediately if Riker attempted any tricks.

"Now," said Korak, when he was finished, "you issued the challenge. By our custom, I am allowed to choose the weapons for the contest."

Riker tensed. "We have a similar custom."

Korak smiled. "Very well, then. You will program your chamber exactly as I tell you. I shall be watching closely. Any tricks, and you will pay for your deception."

"It's your call," Riker said.

"I shall not attempt to make you fight with unfamiliar Romulan weapons, so you will not be able to claim the contest was unfair," said Korak. "Likewise, I shall not fight with Federation weapons. We shall settle this issue in a manner that pits strength against strength. Therefore I choose hand-to-hand combat."

"Very well," said Riker. "As it happens, I have an established program that should suit you nicely." He reached for the console once more, but again Korak grabbed his hand. He stared at him suspiciously.

"What sort of program?"

"Not a very trusting type, are you?" Riker said with a taunting smile. "It's a program I use for my own training exercises. It's called Riker One. It creates no animated projections unless you want them, but provides the setting of a dojo—a training room where martial arts are practiced. It is suited for hand-to-hand combat."

"Very well, proceed," said Korak.

Riker entered the selection commands and punched up the program for Riker One. The holodeck doors slid open, and they entered the dojo the program had created.

Korak looked around cautiously. The large chamber with its imaging grids had been transformed into a martial arts dojo with a wooden deck for sparring. Various flags hung on the walls, including the Federation flag and the old traditional American, Korean, Chinese, and Japanese flags. Exercise equipment was placed around the perimeter of the chamber. Kicking and punching bags were suspended from chains, *makiwara* boards were available for striking, and various martial arts weapons hung on the walls—all actual physical props created by the matter conversion subsystem. There were *bo* staffs, nunchuks, *sai* tridents, *kamas* or sickles, Japanese swords made both of steel and of wood, spears and *shuriken,* or throwing stars.

It occurred to Riker that the weapons might offer a dangerous temptation for the Romulan, and might be interpreted as a violation of the hand-to-hand combat they'd agreed to, so he quickly said, "Computer, delete weapons."

Korak grabbed for his disruptor as he spoke, then seemed to relax when the weapons disappeared from the walls. "You will not issue spoken commands to your computer before clearing them through me," he said.

Riker gave him a small bow. "My apologies," he

said. "I often use those weapons for practice, and I did not wish you to think I was trying to violate our agreement for the match."

Korak nodded.

"Would you care to change into, uh, training clothes?" said Riker.

"We shall fight as we are," said Korak.

"As you wish." He raised his eyebrows. "Are you going to wear your disruptor?"

Korak sneered at him. "I shall keep it ready in case you try any of your human tricks."

"No human tricks," said Riker sarcastically. "But I find it interesting that a 'superior' Romulan needs the reassurance of his disruptor when fighting a 'mere human' who is unarmed."

Korak removed his disruptor. "I need no such reassurance." He stepped up onto the wooden sparring deck. Inwardly Riker smiled. So the Romulan's pride could be attacked successfully. He filed that fact away for future reference, then stepped up onto the deck and faced Korak.

"Anytime you're ready," he said, watching Korak with a level gaze. Riker relaxed into an informal fighting stance, his back straight, his body turned slightly sideways toward the Romulan, his weight on the balls of his feet, his arms hanging loose at his sides.

The Romulan snarled and charged him. Riker side-stepped quickly and used an aikido move to snare Korak's wrist and turn him in a tight circle, using his own momentum to flip him over onto his back, but the Romulan recovered quickly, breaking the hold as he fell with a jerk that would have dislocated a human wrist. He rolled quickly to his feet, his teeth bared, fury in his eyes.

Riker balanced himself on the balls of his feet, bouncing slightly, keeping his gaze locked with Korak's. "Come on, Korak," he taunted him. "Let's see what you've got."

With a cry, Korak rushed him again, seeking to seize him and bear him down to the floor, where his greater weight would give him an advantage, but using a judo technique this time, Riker dropped backwards to the floor as Korak came at him, grabbing him by his coat and planting his foot in his midsection to flip him over.

Korak rolled as he landed and came up again, more cautious this time. His eyes were narrowed to mere slits. Aware that the Romulans in Engineering were monitoring them, Riker continued to taunt him.

"That's twice I've put you down, Korak," he said. "What happened to all that Romulan superiority you were boasting about?"

Korak growled deep in his throat. He's got a temper, too, thought Riker, filing that away as well. Not only could he be pushed, but he could be pushed fairly easily. All right, he thought, let's see just how much it takes to make him lose his composure completely.

"Perhaps you're not so superior as you thought," he said. "You've been on your back twice, and I'm still on my feet. Not bad for a 'mere human,' wouldn't you say?"

Korak came at him again, only this time, he did not come in a rush. He came in a crouched fighting stance, his movements catlike, more purposeful and precise. Okay, thought Riker, we're getting serious now. He wondered if he had pushed the Romulan too far.

Korak swung at him and Riker blocked the blow with his forearm, but the jarring force of it traveled all the way up into his shoulder. Another blow came, and he was slow to block it. It felt as if a pile driver had hit him in the chest. Riker staggered, and Korak hooked an arm underneath his elbow, bracing him, and delivered two more rapid blows to his midsection.

Riker felt the breath whistle out of him as he went limp and Korak hurled him across the room. Riker flew about ten feet and landed hard, fighting for breath. He'd been hit before, but never with such force. He hoped he hadn't bitten off more than he could chew.

"Where are your taunts now, human?" Korak said contemptuously. "Come! On your feet! That is, if you can still stand!"

Riker coughed as he struggled back to his feet. He was in excellent physical condition, and he kept his muscles hard and toned, but he knew he could not absorb many more of Korak's blows without taking some really serious damage. His chest hurt like hell, and his stomach felt as if it had been struck with a sledgehammer. He wondered if any of his ribs had been fractured.

Can't let him hit me like that again, he thought. All Romulans were strong, but Korak wasn't just any Romulan; he was a trained warrior. Once his initial attack had proved that Riker would not fall prey quite so easily as he had thought, Korak had done what any trained warrior, human or not, would have done: he had resorted to his training. And that, coupled with his superior strength, made him a very dangerous opponent.

Riker stood and waited for Korak to come to him. "I can still stand, Korak," he said, partly for the benefit of the Romulans who were monitoring the scene. "What's more, I can still fight."

Korak came at him again. This time Riker did not

try to defend himself with karate-style blocks. He resorted to aikido and jiujitsu, using Korak's own strength against him. He slipped the first blow, got underneath it, delivered an elbow to Korak's midsection, and then threw him. Korak got back up and came at him again, a bit more cautiously this time. Riker launched a combination kick, feinting at Korak's groin with a front kick, then quickly snapping a kick at his temple when Korak moved to block the first kick. The second kick connected, and Korak grunted and went down on his knees. Riker immediately moved in to press his advantage, but Korak recovered quickly and fell back, twisting to sweep Riker's legs out from under him. He tried to leap on Riker, but Riker rolled and came up fast.

They both got back to their feet, this time circling each other cautiously, Korak having realized that Riker was not as weak an opponent as he had believed. Can't have him being cautious, Riker thought. That gives him the advantage. Taunt him. Make him angry. Make him lose control.

"What's the matter, Korak?" he said. "Romulan superiority is difficult to prove, is that it? Maybe Romulans aren't so superior. Maybe they aren't superior at all. Just arrogant and loud."

Korak roared and charged him once again. Riker met his rush, then sidestepped at the last moment and threw him once again. Keep it up, he thought. Make him so angry he can't think straight. And then what? His only chance was either to tire Korak out or to knock him out. Neither would be easy. But if he could win, it would certainly shake the Romulans up.

"It looks like the 'inferior human' has put you flat on your back again," he said. "And I'm not even the best fighter on this ship. The captain can take me easily, and he's older than I am. He'd make very short work of you."

Korak screamed with rage and came at Riker again. That's it, Riker thought, keep getting angrier. He caught Korak's wrist and turned it, forcing Korak to continue his forward momentum, using it to flip him over on his back once more. This time, however, he retained his grip on Korak and turned him as he fell, using his arm as leverage against him and applying pressure. Enough pressure, he thought, to break a human arm, but Korak still resisted.

"Come on, Korak," he said. "Get up, if you can."

Roaring with rage, Korak struggled against the pressure being relentlessly applied to his arm, and Riker threw his leg over it, bending the Romulan's arm back against it. Korak bellowed with pain, but still would not submit.

"Give up," said Riker, "or I'll snap your arm."

Suddenly the doors to the holodeck slid open and the projection canceled out. Three Romulan warriors came rushing in, their sidearms drawn.

"Release him!" one of them demanded.

Riker let go and Korak came up, bellowing with rage, only it was not directed at Riker. "Who told you to interfere?" he shouted at the warriors. *"Get out!"*

"But . . . Subcommander Korak, we thought . . ."

Korak moved toward them, absolutely livid with fury, not only at their interference but at their having seen him in such an embarrassing position. "Get out, I said! I have not finished with this human! How *dare* you interfere."

But at that moment, his communicator came on. "Bridge to Subcommander Korak."

"Yes, what *is* it?"

"We are approaching our destination and preparing

to come out of warp speed. Commander Valak wishes to communicate with you on the bridge."

Korak took a deep breath, trying to calm himself. "I shall be there directly," he said. He turned toward Riker. "We are not yet finished with this," he said, through clenched teeth. Then he turned toward his warriors with such cold fury that they backed off several steps. "Bring him!"

He stormed past them, out of the holodeck chamber and back down the corridor, heading toward the turbolift. The other warriors gestured at Riker with their disruptors. *"Move!"* one of them said.

Riker smiled. "That was a timely rescue," he said. *"I said, move!"* the warrior repeated.

Riker bowed to them slightly and followed after Korak, trying not to show how much his ribs and stomach were hurting him. He had made Korak lose face before his own warriors. A minor victory, but a victory nonetheless. And he now knew that Korak had a hair-trigger temper that led him to make mistakes. It was very useful information. Too bad he couldn't have gained it less painfully. But then, as the old saying went, "No pain, no gain." And he had definitely gained something. The question now was how best to use it.

Chapter Five

As THE TWO SHIPS came out of warp speed and approached Hermeticus 2 on impulse power, the Romulan warbird cloaked itself, so that long-range scanners on the planet would pick up only the *Enterprise*. Valak wasn't taking any chances, thought Picard. Despite all his best efforts to convince the Romulan commander otherwise, Valak still believed the Federation was hiding something on the quarantined world. Picard was almost certain he was wrong . . . but a nagging doubt kept tugging at the corner of his mind.

What if, indeed, someone at Starfleet had authorized a secret base deep in the Neutral Zone? Picard could not believe that anyone at Starfleet would be that criminally stupid, considering the risks involved, but he could not dismiss the possibility. Just as there were Romulans who were paranoid about the Federation, accusing it of trying to encroach upon their empire—partly to justify their own hegemony—so there were Federation officials who were just as paranoid about the Romulans. In the case of the Federation, that feeling would not be unjustified. The Romulans had more or less respected the truce, at least in the main, although they occasionally pushed the edge of the envelope. However, their intentions were certainly clear. They had long lusted to expand their empire into Federation territory, but now that there was a treaty between the Klingons and the Federation, they were a lot more cautious.

For the Romulans, respecting the truce was primarily a matter of biding their time. Still, despite the ever-present threat presented by the Romulan Empire, establishing a secret Federation base in the Neutral Zone would have been a flagrant violation of the treaty; in effect, it would have meant doing exactly the same sort of thing the Federation had long accused the Romulans of doing. Surely, thought Picard, nobody in Starfleet would risk an all-out war over the establishment of what, at best, could only be a remote intelligence outpost. It simply wasn't worth it. But still, he thought, *what if* . . .

No. He banished the thought from his mind. Hermeticus 2 had been quarantined for some reason, but it couldn't be to hide a secret Federation base. If that had been the intent, then why keep records of it in the central Starfleet data banks? Someone who was that paranoid, that obsessed with illegal covert operations, would have left no data trail at all. Valak would find no evidence of Federation presence here. The question was, what *would* he find? He was under orders to investigate Hermeticus 2, and that would clearly take some time. And time, at this point, worked in Picard's favor. Precious little else did.

Picard blamed himself for what had happened, but he was forced to admit that Valak's plan had been brilliant. How could anyone possibly have known that the Romulans had found a new drug that would simulate the appearance of death well enough to fool scanners and tricorders? There had been no way to anticipate that. The drug had given the initial advantage to the Romulans, and Valak had used that advantage for all it was worth.

He hadn't slipped once, anywhere. He had kept Picard away from the *Enterprise* crew, for the most part, denying them his leadership, and he had kept the crew divided—some of them aboard the *Enterprise,* others aboard the *Syrinx*. Since they had departed Federation space, Picard had not been able to communicate with Riker at all. Any independent action the remaining crew members aboard the *Enterprise* could have taken was stymied by the presence of Romulans in key positions everywhere, and by the fact that their officers were kept apart from them. It seemed that Valak had left them no options whatsoever. But there *had* to be options; there always were.

On the journey from Federation space to this sector of the Neutral Zone, Picard had racked his brain in search of a way out of this predicament. He kept coming up empty. What he found most galling was that Valak, thanks to the recent coup by Romulan intelligence, had been able to study him in detail. He had read his dossier; he had obviously examined carefully the records of all past encounters between Federation starships and the Romulans, and he had formulated his plan on the basis of a thorough study of his enemy. Like a fighter who studied holos of his opponents, thought Picard, Valak has studied us; the villain seems to know me like a book. He has anticipated my actions at every turn. He has planned this campaign out in his mind and he is fine-tuning it as he goes along, putting himself in my shoes, thinking of every move I could possibly make against him and systematically closing off those options.

He is a warrior with the mind of a chess master, thought Picard, and what is worse, the bastard knows how I think. That means it's time I started thinking differently. Two can play at this game, Picard told himself. He has had a chance to observe me closely, but now I have also had a chance to observe him. And he is not infallible. His weakness is his vanity, his ego. It is not enough for him merely to defeat his enemy; he needs to have the enemy acknowledge that defeat in no uncertain terms.

He needs me to acknowledge his superiority, thought Picard. And that is the contradiction in Valak's personality. Like all Romulans, he believes in the superiority of his race. Why, then, do the opinions of his "inferiors" matter to him? If he truly feels superior to me, Picard thought, then of what value is my respect? Yet he *does* seem to want my respect. And why? Because despite his capabilities, Valak is young and insecure.

When someone is insecure, Picard thought, and in a position of leadership, the one thing he most desperately wants to avoid is allowing anyone under his command to suspect that he is insecure. That holds true for anyone, human or Romulan, Picard thought. Therefore, the thing to do was play on that vulnerability. Valak may have studied us, but until now, all his knowledge has been theoretical. Now he has come face-to-face with us, and he knows his knowledge of us is going to be put to the test. Perhaps I should attempt to undermine his self-confidence, thought Picard. Convince him that he doesn't know us—that he doesn't know *me*—nearly as well as thinks he does.

His thoughts were interrupted as the doors to the first officer's quarters slid open and three Romulan warriors entered without bothering to announce their presence. "The commander wants you on the bridge," said one of them.

Picard gave them a frosty look. "How kind of him to provide me with an escort," he said. "Lead on."

They went down the corridor and entered the warbird's turbolift, which took them to the bridge. The Romulans escorting him said nothing, and Picard did not bother trying to make conversation with them. There was nothing to be gained from that. Valak was the one he'd have to work on. He needed to present to the rest of them the appearance of a man completely in control. That, in itself, would serve to undermine their confidence.

When he came onto the bridge with his escort, Valak was not seated on his command throne but was pacing nervously back and forth. He stopped immediately when he saw Picard. However, Picard let him know that he had seen him pacing by giving him a slight smile. It seemed to irritate the Romulan.

"So," said Valak, "do you still claim that there is no Federation presence in this sector?"

"I do not claim it," Picard replied confidently. "I merely state it as a fact. A fact you choose not to accept. However, I am not responsible for your flights of fancy."

"Indeed?" said Valak, his eyes meeting Picard's

with a steely gaze. "Then I suppose my long-range scanners are also having flights of fancy, for they have just detected a Federation starship in orbit above Hermeticus Two."

"That's impossible!" Picard said.

"On screen, maximum magnification," Valak said.

The viewscreen of the warbird filled with the image of Hermeticus 2, and there, still small at this distance, but nevertheless clearly visible and recognizable by its configuration, was a Federation starship.

Picard stepped forward and stared at the screen with disbelief. "What is this, Valak?" he snapped. "Some sort of Romulan trick?"

"You know better than that, I think." Valak turned back to the screen and stared at it intently. "Sound battle stations."

As the sonorous throbbing Romulan battle call sounded throughout the *Syrinx,* Picard continued to stare at the screen with astonishment. At this distance, even with the warbird's long-range scanners on maximum magnification, it was impossible to identify the ship, but they were coming in on maximum impulse power. The warbird was still cloaked, invisible to the Federation ship's scanners, or to any scanners on the planet surface, so there had been no reaction from the starship. However, as they approached rapidly, Picard could see that something wasn't quite right.

It was the lines of the ship. He frowned as he watched the screen intently. The scanners were still on maximum magnification, and the warbird was still a considerable distance from the ship, but as they approached, the screen became filled with the planet, creating the illusion that they were much closer than they actually were. The resolution continued to improve as they approached, and Picard could now make out more details of the Federation ship's configuration.

It was different from the *Enterprise,* which was a new generation Galaxy-class starship. This ship was considerably smaller, about half the size of his own ship, and as Picard stared at the screen, he realized it was one of the old Constitution-class vessels, similar to the original USS *Enterprise,* dating back some thirty years or so.

"Where are all your protestations now, Picard?" asked Valak, with a hard edge to his voice. "Now you see for yourself the duplicity of your Federation. Can you deny the evidence of your own senses?"

"Valak, listen to me," Picard said. "There is something very wrong here."

"Yes," snapped Valak, *"you* were wrong, Picard. The Federation is *wrong,* and I am about to teach all of you the error of your ways. Make ready the disruptors!"

"Valak, wait!" Picard said. *"Look* at that ship! It is thirty years out of date! You know Starfleet vessels. What does your own knowledge tell you? Your orders, as you expressed them to me, were to discover the truth about Hermeticus Two. If you destroy that ship, you may never learn anything about what happened here. *Look* at it! It does not even appear to be powered up. Don't simply take my word for it. Use your scanners!"

Valak frowned, then held up his hand to his weapons officer. "Stand by, disruptors," he said. He glanced at Picard warily, then turned to his science officer. "Scanner readings, Talar."

The science officer bent over his console. After a moment he straightened and turned to Valak with a puzzled look. "Commander, according to our scanner readings, there are no life-forms aboard the Federation vessel. And I show no power readings."

"It could be a trick," said Valak.

"You mean like the one you pulled on us?" Picard said. "Rest assured, Commander, we possess no drug that can simulate death convincingly enough to fool scanners. If we did, we might have been prepared for your deception. Besides, that is a Constitution-class starship. It could not possibly power up in time to evade your disruptors, even if it *was* capable of detecting the presence of a cloaked Romulan warbird, which it most certainly is not."

Valak furrowed his brow. "That is true."

"Readings remain unchanged," said the science officer.

"Slow to half power," Valak said. "Maintain stand-by on weapons. What is the current position of the *Enterprise?*"

"Coming up behind us on normal impulse power, bearing two point eight, mark nine," the navigator said.

Valak folded his arms and thought a moment. "Match speed with the *Enterprise* and open hailing frequency."

"Commander," said the science officer, "if we communicate with the *Enterprise,* our transmission may be picked up on the planet surface and give away our presence."

"Perhaps, but a scanner probe of the planet surface itself would almost certainly give us away if there is a Federation base there. I think we shall let the *Enterprise* make the first approach, while we remain cloaked."

"Hailing frequency open, Commander."

"Valak to *Enterprise*. Come in, Korak."

Korak replied and Valak had him put on the main viewscreen. Korak confirmed that the *Enterprise* scanners had given him the same information as the warbird's scanners had given Valak. "Commander Riker claims the Federation ship in orbit above Hermeticus is a Constitution-class vessel many years out of date," Korak added. "He insists that he is not able to identify it."

"You should be within range to read the markings on that ship by long-range scanner," Valak said. "Have Commander Riker consult the *Enterprise* computer for information about that vessel."

"I have already demanded that he do so, Commander," Korak replied, "but Riker has refused. What are your orders?"

Valak turned to Picard. "If you are telling the truth, I suspect you are as curious about that ship as I am. And if there truly is no one aboard it, then the information cannot harm anyone, can it? Or would you prefer that I compel Commander Riker to cooperate?"

"Put Commander Riker on the screen," Picard said.

A moment later Riker appeared, standing beside Korak. Picard noted that his face was bruised.

"Are you all right, Number One?"

"Fine, Captain," said Riker, without elaborating further.

Picard did not pursue the subject. "Please do as Commander Valak *requests,*" he said, stressing the last word sarcastically.

"Understood, sir."

"It may take a few moments," Picard said to Valak.

The Romulan commander nodded. "You still maintain that you know nothing whatsoever about this ship?"

"Its presence here is as much of a surprise to me as it is to you," Picard replied.

Valak said nothing.

A moment later Riker came back on. "Captain, according to the markings on that ship, it's the USS *Independence.*"

"The *Independence!*" said Picard. "Are you *certain*, Number One?"

"Yes, sir," Riker replied. "It would seem that we are looking at a ghost ship."

"Ghost ship?" said Valak. "What nonsense is this?"

"It's a figure of speech, Commander," said Riker. "Your research into Starfleet is incomplete, apparently. The *Independence* is something of a legend."

"It was reported destroyed some thirty years ago," Picard said. "A few members of the crew are believed to have escaped in one of the ship's shuttles, but by the time the shuttlecraft was found drifting in space, everyone aboard it was dead. No trace of the ship was ever found."

"If there were survivors, then there must have been a report," said Valak.

"There should have been," Riker agreed, "but the report seems to have disappeared, as well. As a result, there's not even a record of the identity of the crew members on that shuttle, and after all these years, no one seems to remember who they were. No one knows exactly what happened to the *Independence*. Its fate has remained a mystery . . . until now."

"You expect me to believe this ridiculous story?" Valak asked scornfully. "Do you take me for a complete fool? If that ship had been powered down for so long a time, its orbit would have long since decayed."

"True," said Picard, "and that means there were life-forms aboard that ship until recently."

"Then they are on the planet surface," Valak said.

"That would seem impossible, Commander," Korak said. "According to our scanner readings, there is no atmosphere on the planet capable of supporting human life. Nor have we detected any life-forms or artificial shelters on the planet surface."

"None at all?" said Valak, frowning. "But . . . they must have gone *somewhere!*"

"Perhaps there was another ship, Commander," said Korak. "That seems to be the only logical explanation."

"There has been no Federation vessel in this sector," said Picard.

"That is what you said before we found the *Independence,*" Valak replied. "You become less credible with each assertion, Picard."

Picard shrugged. "Say what you will, Valak, but I am even more anxious to solve this mystery than you are, because these were our people. I have no idea what that ship is doing here, but the concerns of the Romulan High Council certainly appear to have been justified in this instance."

"With the presence of a Federation vessel this deep inside the Neutral Zone, that is a point you can hardly avoid conceding," Valak replied wryly.

"I concede nothing," said Picard. "I merely said that Romulan concerns *appear* to have been justified. Were the situation reversed, I might well have thought as you did. However, there simply must be a rational explanation of this phenomenon. If we can determine that this situation has never represented a Federation threat to the Romulan Empire, then perhaps we can still resolve our differences in a way that will satisfy both parties and threaten neither."

"I remain skeptical of that, but much will depend upon your cooperation," Valak said.

"Then you admit the possibility of a negotiated resolution to this matter?" Picard said hopefully.

"An astute commander would do well to admit all and any possibilities," Valak replied evasively. "But my primary mission must remain my first priority."

"Understood," Picard said. "I would very much like to have a look aboard that ship."

"You shall have it," Valak replied. "I intend to board the *Independence* myself. You shall accompany me."

"If I might make a suggestion . . ." Picard began.

Valak's head snapped around. "Go on," he said, in that smug and condescending way Picard had begun to find so irritating.

"Have Lieutenant Commander Data accompany us," Picard said. "He has instantaneous access to all Federation historical records—and that information could prove invaluable."

Valak nodded.

"Acceptable, . . . Korak, have the android beamed aboard after us. And now, Captain," he said to Picard, bowing in the direction of the turbolift, "after you. I feel much more secure having you in sight."

"And here I thought you enjoyed my company," Picard said dryly.

The Romulan space suit was not a perfect fit, but it was close enough not to cause Picard much inconvenience. As he took his place on the transporter platform with the Romulan away team, Valak's voice came to him over the helmet speaker.

"Remember, Korak will be monitoring our transmissions from aboard the *Enterprise,* and my science officer, Talar, will be doing likewise from the bridge of the *Syrinx.*"

"If you think that, unarmed, I can present a threat your entire away team," said Picard, "then I fear you may be overestimating my capabilities."

"That would be better than underestimating them," Valak replied, in a tone that was almost jocular. "However, you are not the only threat I am concerned with. Should we encounter any sort of trap aboard the *Independence,* my crew, aboard both your ship and mine, will be alerted instantly." He gave the command to energize, and a moment later they materialized on the bridge of the *Independence.*

The bridge was deserted, and the ship was completely powered down. There was no sign of the crew. It was impossible to estimate by external evidence how long things had remained undisturbed; in space there were no obvious signs such as dust, cobwebs, or mice scurrying about. The crew might have departed a relatively short time ago, but Picard was acutely aware of a feeling of emptiness about the ship, an emptiness that had reigned for a long time.

The lights on their helmets were their only source of illumination as their special boots clung to the deck, holding them down in the absence of gravity. Otherwise the ship was dark. Valak's assistant science officer took readings, while the security team maintained watch, their weapons held ready, just in case. The Romulans were taking no chances.

"No residual atmospheric traces," the assistant

science officer announced. "The life-support systems have been down for quite some time. I am not picking up any power readings at all."

"What about the matter-antimatter reactors?" Valak asked.

The assistant science officer went to the science station and attempted to bring up the console. He hit several switches, without result. "No response on any of the controls, Commander," he said. He consulted his Romulan tricorder once again. "Readings indicate decay in the reactor core." He tried several other switches. "No response. No power in the warp propulsion conduits or the electroplasma system. Warp and main impulse engines are not functional. No response on readouts from auxiliary fusion generators. The warp field generator coils are inactive. This ship is dead, Commander."

"Commander Valak, if I may . . ." Picard said, indicating one of the consoles.

Valak nodded.

Picard went over to the bridge engineering console while Valak watched him carefully. He glanced at the positions of the switches. He frowned. "As I suspected," he said. "The antimatter storage pods have all been jettisoned. This ship cannot be powered up again without a major refueling operation at a starbase. It would require replacement of all the antimatter storage pods, the installation of new warp generator coils, refurbishment of the EPS system . . . in short, a major overhaul. We could easily confirm that by examining the main engineering section. However, this ship did not die of neglect, Commander. It was killed. Or put to sleep, to be more precise."

"Check the rest of the ship," Valak told his security detail.

"Commander, without power, the turbolift will not respond," one of them said.

"Use the Jefferies tubes," said Valak. Picard glanced at the Romulan, once again impressed with his knowledge of Federation ships. The Jefferies tubes were tunnels that ran throughout the ship, providing access to the utilities conduits and circuitry for testing and maintenance. "There will most likely be an access point either in the floor by the main navigational computer console or in the bulkhead by the turbolift."

The Romulan security detail found the access hatch in the bulkhead by the turbolift and proceeded to undog it and go through. At almost the same instant the shimmering form of Lieutenant Commander Data materialized on the bridge. "Captain," the android said.

"Mr. Data, it is good to see you—even under these circumstances."

"How touching," Valak said dryly. "Tell me—Captain, Mr. Data—how is it that this dead ship somehow manages to maintain a consistent orbit?" Valak shook his head. "It is impossible."

"You are correct," Data said. "Nevertheless, *something* is obviously holding it up here."

"The spirits of your ghost ship?" Valak said laconically. "That is not an acceptable explanation, Captain."

"I quite agree," Picard replied. "Since no logical explanation is to be found here, I would look to the planet surface."

"Of course," said Valak. "Some sort of tractor beam. But to reach out to this distance and maintain this ship in orbit, it would have to be immensely powerful. Our scanners should have detected the energy fluctuations."

Picard nodded. "Indeed, they should have. Assuming that it *is* a tractor beam. However, we may be dealing with some sort of force that neither of us understands."

"I told you, Picard, supernatural explanations are not acceptable to me."

"Nor to me," Picard replied. "However, any science that is sufficiently advanced would certainly seem supernatural to anyone who could not understand it."

"I believe the precise quotation is, 'Any technology that is sufficiently advanced would seem like magic to those who did not understand it,'" Valak corrected him. "Your Earth philosopher and scientist, Arthur C. Clarke."

"Have you no pithy Romulan sayings to quote?" Picard replied irritably.

Valak smiled. "Careful, Picard. Your frustration is showing."

The bastard's right, Picard thought. He was becomingly increasingly frustrated at his seeming helplessness in this situation. It was bad enough that the Romulan had the upper hand, but now there was this mystery of the Federation ghost ship. And he saw no hope of solving either problem, at least, not for the present.

"Security detail, report," Valak said, speaking into his helmet communicator.

"Readings continue to show no life aboard this ship, Commander." Picard heard the reply over his helmet circuit. "We have gained access to the crew deck corridors. Part of the team has continued on to engineering, but we are examing the crew's quarters. There is no sign of anyone aboard."

"Have you found any bodies?" Valak asked.

"None, Commander."

"Are there any personal possessions in the crew's quarters?" asked Picard.

"You are not here to ask questions, human," came the angry response.

"Answer him," said Valak.

There was a brief, surprised hesitation. Then the Romulan replied irately, "What do I know of such things? We Romulans do not clutter up our ships with frivolities. How would I distinguish human personal possessions from ship's stores?"

"Look for non-uniform garments in the closets," said Picard, ignoring the warrior's condescending attitude. "Likenesses of family members, personal mementos, items of personal hygiene in the medicine cabinets—"

"I have no time for such—"

"Do as he says," Valak said curtly.

After some time had passed, the Romulan came back on. "Personal items appear to have been removed from the quarters," he said.

"All of them?" asked Picard. "Or does it appear as if the crew departed in a hurry after packing only a few things?"

"Almost completely, although some items have been left behind," the Romulan replied grudgingly.

"So they had time to prepare to leave the ship," Picard said.

"Which means there *was* another Federation vessel here," Valak said accusingly.

"Or perhaps an alien ship," Picard said. "You said yourself a good commander considers all and any possibilities, Valak. And there is yet one other. The crew might have gone down to the planet surface."

"But the planet surface will not support human life," said Valak, "and our sensors have detected no constructed shelters."

"Something is holding this ship in orbit," insisted Picard, "and your sensors have not detected that, either."

"Nor have yours," Valak replied, a touch defensively.

"Precisely," said Data. "I would suggest that if there is nothing on the planet surface, then there must be something *beneath* the surface."

"Of course!" said Valak. He spoke into his communicator. "Valak to *Syrinx.*"

"Talar here, Commander."

"Launch a deep scanner probe to the planet surface," Valak ordered, "and report on what it finds."

"Acknowledged," Talar replied.

"Kylor to Commander Valak." It was the voice of a member of the away team elsewhere on the ship.

"Report, Kylor."

"Commander, we have reached the main engineering section," Kylor said. "Everything here has been shut down. There is no power to any of the systems, and the shutdown appears to have been a purposeful act. There is no one anywhere on board this ship. There are no bodies and no signs of violence. The ship could have been evacuated due to some sort of malfunction, but that cannot be determined at this point. Some supplies were removed from ship's stores and from the sickbay. The crew unquestionably evacuated this ship in an organized and orderly manner."

"But how long ago?" Picard wondered aloud. "None of this makes any sense, Valak. Human or Romulan, no one simply powers down a ship and jettisons all the antimatter storage pods so that the ship cannot be powered up again. Unless perhaps . . ."

"Unless what?" asked Valak.

"Unless it was done precisely to prevent the crew from ever going home again."

"Why would they have done that?" Valak asked.

"Perhaps there is something down there on the surface of Hermeticus, or beneath it, that would be too threatening if it were ever to be brought back," Picard said. "I remind you that this world was quarantined."

"And yet, according to your own story, if it is to be believed, some of the crew *did* try to go back," Valak pointed out. "Or at least they tried to escape."

"They must have known that they would not survive," Picard said. "A ship's shuttle has a very limited range, as you well know, and this far out, the odds against encountering another ship would have been astronomical."

"So what was the point of leaving?" asked Valak.

"In their desperation, they might have made a suicidal attempt to escape," Picard said. "Perhaps they felt that certain death aboard the shuttlecraft was preferable to what would happen to them if they remained behind."

"Then why did not the others do likewise?"

"I can only guess," said Picard. "Perhaps they had no choice. If they were exposed to some sort of a disease, some kind of organism that infected them or took them over, then the ones who attempted to flee in the shuttlecraft might have been the only ones who had escaped infection. Or perhaps it was not an attempt to escape but a desperate attempt to warn others to stay away."

"As you said, all this is merely conjecture," Valak replied. "In the absence of any evidence, it is all meaningless theorizing."

"Hermeticus Two was placed under quarantine some thirty years ago," Picard said. "That is *not* meaningless. And that quarantine has remained in effect for all this time, despite advances that have rendered quarantines unnecessary except in extraordinary circumstances. That, too, is not meaningless. And the location of this planet was classified top secret and has remained so for close to a century. That is the most meaningful thing of all."

"To me, the most meaningful thing of all is that you seem to be very anxious to keep us from discovering whatever is down there," Valak said.

"If you insist on believing that I am attempting to deceive you," said Picard, "there is nothing I can do to convince you otherwise."

"Talar to Commander Valak."

"Valak here. Report, Talar."

"Commander, we have launched a deep scanner probe to the planet surface, and we are receiving its transmissions, but the readings are confusing."

"What do you mean, confusing? How?"

"They are intermittent. We are not picking up any life-form readings, but we are picking up traces of enormous power emanating from beneath the planet surface. Commander . . . Hermeticus Two is hollow."

"Hollow?" Valak said. "You mean caverns? Excavations?"

"Neither, Commander," the Romulan science officer replied. "Given our readings, there is only one possible conclusion. Hermeticus Two is not a planet. . . . It is a ship."

Chapter Six

"A SHIP!" said Valak with disbelief.

"Undoubtedly, Commander," the Romulan science officer replied. "The surface of the planet is but a shielded outer crust constituting the hull of the ship. What passes for the atmosphere is merely an agglomeration of gases held by a gravity field generated from beneath the planet surface. Our analysis indicates that these gases serve two purposes: they help to disguise the ship as a planet, and they absorb waste matter expelled from the interior along with ionized particles that interfere with accurate sensor readings."

"An interstellar ark," Data said.

"What?" said Valak.

"The idea was first proposed by Earth scientists in the late twentieth century," Data replied. "It was originally called an island or an O'Neill colony, after the physicist, Gerard O'Neill, who first proposed it. It was an artificial world constructed in space, with the habitat itself built on the interior, on the curving inner surface."

"The idea that led to your starbases," said Valak.

"Precisely," said Data. "But O'Neill's model was cylindrical. Later Dandridge Cole proposed carving out an asteroid for the purposes of interstellar travel. Cole proposed utilizing giant solar mirrors constructed in space out of lightweight silvered plastics. These mirrors would then bore holes down to the center of an asteroid with a high iron content, and these cavities would then be filled with tanks of water. Spin would be imparted to the asteroid by means of hydrogen-fueled propulsion devices, and as it spun in the light bath of the solar mirrors, the asteroid would heat up and start to soften. Gravitational and cohesive forces would gradually pull it into a spherical shape, and if the whole operation was timed correctly, the water tanks at the core would explode just as the central axis of the asteroid reached its melting point. The result would be a balloonlike expansion of the asteroid, with an outer crust, or hull, and a hollow interior, ready for construction once the interior was properly sealed. The idea was further refined—"

"Yes, thank you, Mr. Data," said Picard, knowing that, given half a chance, the android would discourse upon the entire history of the concept, from O'Neill's initial formulation to the present. "I am familiar with the concept. However, Cole's idea was for a relatively small asteroid, no more than ten miles in diameter, and it was eventually discarded as more practical methods of construction in space were developed. This . . . this is on a *planetary* scale!"

"Then that is where the crew of this ship went," said Valak.

"That would seem to be the logical explanation,"

Picard replied. "But with your knowledge of Starfleet and human technology, surely you must realize that this is not a Federation construct."

Valak frowned. "Thus far, we have no evidence to prove that it is not. However, there is only one way that we shall ever know for certain, and that is to assemble an away team to beam down to the interior of Hermeticus Two."

"Valak, this discovery puts an entirely different slant on the situation," said Picard. "We know that this ark has been here for at least three decades. That in itself suggests two possibilities: either it is vacant, its crew long dead or departed, and it was merely captured by the gravitational fields in this system, or else the race that built and crewed it has reached its destination and is still present."

"There is a third possibility," said Valak. "The crew of the *Independence* discovered this ark and found it vacant, and the Federation took advantage of the opportunity to establish a ready-made base here."

"A moment's thought will tell you that is not possible," Picard said. "The establishment of a base would have required a steady stream of supplies, and traffic in this sector would have increased the odds of the base being discovered."

"Your argument, as you humans say, does not hold water," said Valak, "An interstellar ark, equipped for long-duration multigenerational voyages, would have been designed to be entirely self-sufficient and would require no periodic resupply."

"Perhaps," Picard was forced to admit, "but why advertise the presence of a secret base by leaving the *Independence* in orbit above it? That would defeat the whole purpose, would it not?"

Valak nodded. "Your point is well taken. However,

there are many unanswered questions here, and I intend to have them answered. All members of the away team report back to the bridge immediately. Talar, prepare to beam back the away team. We are going to find out what lies beneath the surface of Hermeticus Two."

"Enter," said Lord Kazanak.

The doors slid open and Valak came in. "You asked to see me, my lord?"

"Yes. I was monitoring your transmissions from the Federation ship. Do you really believe there may be Federation presence on—or perhaps I should say *in*—Hermeticus Two?"

"At this point, I am not certain what to believe," Valak replied. "However, I am inclined to think that Picard is telling me the truth."

"You trust a *human?*" Lord Kazanak said with surprise.

"It is not a matter of trust," Valak replied. "Picard's reasoning is sound. To our knowledge, the Federation has never had a craft such as this ark. And if they had a hidden base here, they would have been foolish to give away their presence by leaving the *Independence* in orbit above it, as Picard pointed out."

Lord Kazanak nodded. "Then there must be some other explanation for all this. The deep scanner probe has detected no life-form readings within this ark?"

"The readings are inconclusive," Valak said. "The power emanations from within Hermeticus Two and the charged particles in its atmosphere are causing interference. There may also be some sort of shield down there preventing accurate readings."

"If Picard is to be believed," Kazanak said, "then the *Independence* has been here for a very long time. If its crew went down to the interior of the ark, there still could be survivors?"

"Survivors or perhaps descendants," Valak said. "Yes, I suppose it is possible."

"What do you think of Picard's claim about the Federation quarantine?"

"Whether or not that is true remains to be determined," Valak said. "However, I have no doubt Picard believes it to be true."

"Indeed? You seem to have unusual faith in Captain Picard," Lord Kazanak said.

"Faith?" said Valak, raising his eyebrows. "I have faith that he will seize the slightest opportunity to act against me. That is why I do not intend to give him one."

"And yet, you seem almost to . . . like him," said Lord Kazanak, with a look of distaste.

"I understand him," Valak said, "and I respect him."

"Respect?" said Lord Kazanak. "For a *human?"*

"For an enemy," said Valak. "A highly capable enemy."

"If he is so capable, why was he defeated so easily?" Lord Kazanak said contemptuously. "Why did so capable an enemy surrender?"

"Jean-Luc Picard would never surrender," Valak replied.

Lord Kazanak frowned. "What do you mean?"

"I mean that I never asked him to surrender formally. It is, perhaps, a fine distinction, but had I demanded it, he would have fought us, to the last man," said Valak. "With all due respect, my lord, there is much about the humans that you do not understand. Particularly humans like Picard. So long as he continues to believe that he may have a chance to turn the situation to his favor, or negotiate his way clear of it without violence, he will refrain from desperate action. Had I forced his hand, I would have had to kill him, and he is of more value to me—and to the high council—alive."

"Perhaps," Lord Kazanak replied. "Still, you seem to have a fascination for these humans that escapes me. I look forward to the war that will subjugate them and put them in their proper place once and for all. It is to that end that I have designed and built this ship. Once it has proved itself, it will be but the first in a mighty invasion fleet. However, the expense of constructing this one ship was so great that the council has insisted upon its being proved. There are those members of the council who doubt the worthiness of my design, and suspect its approval to be solely the result of my father's influence. I intend to prove them wrong, Valak, wrong beyond any shadow of a doubt. This mission *must* be a success! And if there is anything to be discovered in that ark that will give us any added advantage, then so much the better. If we can bring back such a discovery, and report the destruction of the *Enterprise,* then none shall doubt me."

"Indeed, my lord," said Valak. "If there is any such discovery to be made, I shall do my utmost to bring it to you."

"Do that, Valak, and your future is assured," Lord Kazanak said. "But if there is any truth to Picard's claims about the quarantine . . ."

"I have already thought of a way to test that," Valak said.

"Absolutely not!" Picard said. "I will never agree to such a thing!"

"I did not ask you to agree or disagree," said Valak. "You have no choice in the matter."

"My people are your prisoners," Picard said. "You cannot use prisoners as guinea pigs!"

"In point of fact, Captain, I can do anything I wish," said Valak. "No formal treaties or articles of war exist between our people. We have merely agreed upon a truce, with the Neutral Zone as a buffer between Romulan and Federation space. I have found a Federation starship here, in clear violation of that truce, so if I wish, I can declare the truce null and void."

"The truce that created the Neutral Zone has been in effect for over a century!" Picard said. "I seriously doubt that your superiors have given you the authority to declare it null and void at your discretion, especially when you have not ascertained the facts of the situation."

"The fact of the situation is that the Federation ship is here," said Valak. "In any event, this debate is pointless. To minimize the risks to my crew, the first away team will be composed of crew members of the *Enterprise*. My chief of security, Kalad, will accompany them, dressed in a Starfleet uniform so that he may pass as Vulcan, in case the team encounters Federation personnel on the ark."

"And you expect me to choose which of my crew members you will place at risk?" Picard asked angrily.

"To free you of that burden, I have already chosen those who will beam down. They will be Counselor Troi, Ensign Ro, Lieutenant Commander Data, and Dr. Crusher. If there is some risk of an infection, then your own ship's doctor will be in the best position to determine that. And if any dangerous life-forms are present, Kalad is my most capable warrior, and his presence on the away team will also ensure that the Federation officers do not attempt to escape or misrepresent whatever they may find."

"If they are exposed to any sort of dangerous infection," said Picard, "it may not show up right away. You run the risk of bringing it back to your own ship."

"Captain, you know as well as I that no mission is entirely without risk. Both your people and mine accept such perils as a matter of course. I have my duty, and I intend to carry it out."

"If that is your final word on the matter, then I insist on being allowed to beam down with them," said Picard.

"You are in no position to insist on anything, Picard. I am growing weary of reminding you of that. You will remain here, where I can keep my eye on you. And that is my final word on the matter."

Despite Picard's objections, the away team was assembled in the transporter room. Valak gave them all deactivated Starfleet phasers, for the sake of appearance, but Kalad carried one that was fully charged.

Picard attempted to protest this. "You cannot send them down there without any means of protecting themselves!" he insisted.

"Neither do I intend to arm them so that they can present a danger to my chief of security," said Valak. "Your constant protests are becoming tiresome, Picard. You have no one but yourself to blame for this. If you had not erased the file on Hermeticus Two, we would have a much better idea of what is to be found down there. Since your interference caused the erasure of the data, it is only fitting that your people take the initial risk to compensate for its loss."

"May I at least speak with them?"

Valak gestured toward them, and Picard approached them.

"I tried my utmost to prevent this," he said, "but—"

"Don't worry about us, Captain," Ro interrupted. "Worry about the Romulans."

"Beverly," Picard said, "if there is any risk of an infection down there—"

"I've got my tricorder programmed to scan for all known infectious organisms," she replied, "and I will constantly monitor the condition of the away team while we're down there."

"That is still no guarantee—"

"There are never any guarantees," she said. "Don't worry, Jean-Luc. We'll find a way out of this somehow." She smiled bravely, but it was a strained smile just the same.

Picard nodded. "Mr. Data, your first priority will be the safety of the away team. Do not give Kalad any excuse to use deadly force against you. He will not hesitate to employ it."

"Understood, sir."

There was nothing else to say except "Good luck." Picard stepped back, and Valak gave the command to energize. The away team faded out of view as they were transported to the interior of Hermeticus 2.

The transporter coordinates had been carefully computed, but there was still considerable risk involved in the process. Because of the uncertain scanner readings, they had no exact idea where they were being transported to. The transporter circuitry had built-in compensators designed to reduce the risk of transporting an away team to coordinates in space that were already occupied by something else, whether a living creature or an inanimate object, but in this case, it was still a gamble.

They materialized in an open area, in a square surrounded by buildings. Kalad, the Romulan chief of security, immediately drew his disruptor and glanced around alertly, on the watch for any signs of trouble. The others, except Data, who was incapable of being amazed, all had their breath taken away.

In the artificial light flooding the interior of the ark, they could see that they were standing on the curving inner surface of a hollow inside-out world, a world that was a multigenerational starship. It was an engineering marvel. The "horizon" encircled them, and as they looked up, they saw not sky but buildings in the distance, roughly twenty miles overhead. The vista spreading out before them was a wide upcurving panorama of structures interspersed with large open parklike areas consisting of meadows, small hills, and dense forests. It was like looking at a huge city through some sort of crazy fish-eye lens that offered a 360-degree view. An equatorial "sea" encircled the ship, with a huge clifflike retaining wall designed to keep the water from flooding the city while the ark was under acceleration or deceleration. The illusion was that of a huge horizontal bay spanned by several large bridges. Perspective was completely skewed. Initially, except for Data, they experienced a breathless sense of wonder and at the same time a profound and immediate attack of vertigo.

Troi grabbed Ro's arm for support. They were in no danger of falling, but with buildings hanging upside down above them, the Federation officers—again excepting Data—experienced a sudden dizzying, spinning sensation. The Romulan, curiously, seemed uneffected, though he was obviously puzzled by his surroundings.

"I think I am going to be ill," said Troi.

"Hang on, Deanna," Dr. Crusher said. "The effect is mainly psychological. You should get used to it in a little while. Just don't look up for now."

Troi smiled, weakly. "Which way *is* up?"

"How can anyone live like this?" said Ro. "Up is down, down is sideways . . . I feel as if I'm going to fall 'up' any second."

"It's a matter of orientation," Dr. Crusher said. "It will take some getting used to, but you won't fall. Try not to think about it. Concentrate on your tricorder readings."

"It will take enough concentration merely to stop hyperventilating," said Deanna.

"The atmosphere is very close to Earth standard," Ro said, checking her instrument. "We should be able to breathe and move about comfortably without these suits."

"Keep them on for now," said Dr. Crusher, "at least until I can determine if there are any harmful bacteria present."

"Most interesting," said Data, who alone among them was not wearing a suit, as he did not require life support. "There seems to be constant control of humidity, air pressure, and atmospheric mixture as well as the artificial day and night cycles. I am not detecting any life-form readings in our vicinity, but this environment is functioning consistently. All the mechanical functions of this ark would appear to be completely automated, and whatever their power source may be, it has apparently been maintaining this closed-system environment without interruption all this time."

A communication came through from the ship: "Valak to away team. Are you receiving me?"

"Affirmative, Commander," replied Kalad. "However, there is some interference in the form of static on the comm circuit."

"We are picking it up on this end as well," Valak replied, as the others listened over their helmet comm circuits. "Give me your report."

As Kalad described their surroundings to the Romulan commander the others continued to take tricorder readings. When Kalad had finished, Valak asked Dr. Crusher for a report.

"My readings do not indicate the presence of any harmful bacteria," she replied. "The ark has a closed environmental system. The air is breathable, and it appears to be filtered somehow, with all impurities drawn out. There is no pollution of any sort, and the temperature is a constant seventy degrees. We have not detected the presence of any life-forms, but the range of our tricorders is limited and our readings are still being thrown off somewhat. However, there is nothing in the atmosphere down here that should cause any harm."

Aboard the *Syrinx,* Valak turned to Picard and said, "Thus far there seems to be no reason for a quarantine."

"It is still too early to draw such a conclusion," Picard replied.

"We shall see," said Valak. "But the more we learn, the more it seems as if the Federation has taken great care to conceal something. Rest assured, Captain, that I shall find out what that is."

Night watch. Riker sat alone in his quarters aboard the *Enterprise,* confined there by order of Korak, who seemed to want him out of his sight unless Valak needed to speak with him. I got him where it hurts, thought Riker, in his pride. Bad enough I managed to put him down in hand-to-hand combat, but I did it in sight of his subordinates. That's something he's not going to forget . . . or forgive. But the important thing, he thought, is that it threw Korak off-balance. It shook him up, and badly.

Obviously, it was the first time the Romulan had ever fought a human who had been trained in martial arts. It was probably the first time he had ever fought a human, period. Korak had been well trained himself, and his fighting style prepared him to handle karate more or less, but he had been completely thrown off by aikido. It made sense, thought Riker. The Romulans were a combative, conquering race, and their modes of fighting would be powerful and aggressive ones. A fighting style designed to be primarily defensive would be a new concept for them. They respected strength, but there was a difference between strength and force. The idea of using an opponent's strength as a force against him had taken Korak by surprise.

Riker was grateful now for the time he'd spent honing his skills in the ancient martial art. It had been a long time since he'd trained formally, but while Tasha Yar was with them, he'd spent many hours working out with her. She had been a master in the art, and she had taught him a great deal and helped him set up his own holodeck training program. For a long time he had used it partly as recreation, partly to keep in shape, and partly to keep his reflexes sharp. Now it had paid off. Without it he would have been no match for the Romulan. Korak could easily have crippled him. There was a lesson to be learned here, and Korak was not the only one who had received an education.

There was little contact between Romulans and humans. What Korak knew of humans was probably just what he'd been told, and he'd been told that they were weak, decadent, and inferior. Valak apparently had considerably greater knowledge, but even his knowledge was primarily theoretical. For a commander of a warbird, especially one as advanced as the *Syrinx,* Valak was quite young. He couldn't have had much, if any, direct experience of humans. But he was much less overconfident than Korak, and he seemed much more even-tempered, if there could be such a thing as an even-tempered Romulan.

Riker knew that as he was studying Korak for weak points, the captain would be doing the same with Valak. The Romulan commander was smart to keep them apart as much as possible, so that they could not compare notes and put their heads together to come up with a plan of action, but at the same time, Valak had separated himself from his own first officer. Korak was more impulsive, much brasher than Valak. The two of them together would have been formidable antagonists indeed. But without Valak, Korak was the weaker link in the Romulan chain.

The trouble was, Korak was now more wary. He was keeping Riker separated not only from Picard, but from the rest of his crew as well. He had been left alone in his quarters only after they had been carefully searched and the computer terminal disconnected.

And there were guards just outside the door. Somehow, thought Riker, I've got to figure out a way to communicate with the others, so we can try to come up with a plan.

Suddenly, the lights in his room went out. Then just as suddenly they came back on again. He glanced up. They went off, then on again, then off for a bit longer this time, then back on. It took a moment for the meaning of the occurrence to sink in, and then he grinned. Geordi! It couldn't be anyone else. He was using the lights in Riker's quarters to signal him in Morse code.

Riker quickly grabbed a pen and started writing down the dots and dashes on a notepad. God, he thought, my Morse code is so damn rusty, I may have to look this up to make sure I get the message right. He scribbled furiously. Not so fast, Geordi, dammit! After a few moments, the lights stopped flashing on and off and Riker softly read aloud the message he had written down: "Vent shaft your quarters 0300 hours. Acknowledge. Disconnect light circuit service panel."

He smiled. Of course. All Geordi had to do was use a tester to see that the circuit for the lights in Riker's quarters had been interrupted and he would receive his acknowledgment that his message had gotten through. He quickly complied with La Forge's instructions and plunged his quarters into darkness. Now all he had to do was wait until 3:00 A.M. But the ventilation shaft? Geordi wasn't a big man, and he was very trim, but it would still be one hell of a tight fit for him to squeeze through the air ducts. Riker would have to wait about three and a half hours. It would probably take La Forge all that time just to crawl through the ductwork to his quarters, assuming he did not get caught . . . or stuck. Riker settled down to wait.

It was the longest three and a half hours of his life. It grew even longer as the time stretched agonizingly to three and three-quarters hours, and then to four hours, and then—*finally*—he heard the soft sounds of Geordi squirming his way through the shaft. Riker got up to remove the screen and helped pull him through.

"Damn!" La Forge swore in a whisper. "Now I remember what it feels like to be born."

"I was starting to get worried," Riker said. They kept their voices very low, to avoid alerting the Romulan guards outside.

"For a while there, I didn't think I was going to make it," La Forge said. "It's a hell of a tight squeeze there in some spots."

"Here, have a drink," said Riker, handing him a glass.

"Thanks, I could use it." He downed it in one gulp. "Boy, some mess, huh?" He handed Riker a small communicator. "Here, I managed to squirrel a couple of these away when nobody was looking. I altered the frequency, so that it broadcasts on a different band and with a lower power level. It won't go outside the ship, but if we're real careful we should be able to communicate with each other without them picking it up."

"Well done. How are you holding up?" asked Riker.

"Okay, I guess, except that I've got a damned Romulan engineer crawling all over me and watching every single thing I do. Atalan knows his stuff, but he's not familiar with our systems and he doesn't trust me as far as I can throw him."

Riker grinned. "At least you've still got your sense of humor."

"That's about all I've got," said La Forge, still rubbing his cramped muscles. "I've about flat run out of patience with these people. Commander, we've *got* to do something!"

"Tell me about it," Riker replied. "The trouble is, they're holding the captain and half the crew hostage on the warbird, and I've had no contact with them at all. They've beamed Dr. Crusher, Troi, Ro, and Data down to Hermeticus Two to look around. Sort of a test case, I guess, before Valak sends down his own people."

"What's the deal with this place, anyway?" asked La Forge.

"That's right—you've been out of the loop, for the most part," Riker said. He quickly brought him up to date.

"Damn," said La Forge. "It looks like they've really got us by the short hairs. We need to come up with a plan—fast."

"I've been working on that," Riker said. "Valak hasn't left us a whole lot of options. But if some of us could find a way to get aboard the *Independence* . . ."

"What good would that do?" La Forge said sourly. "Without new antimatter pods and generator coils, that ship can't be powered up. We couldn't do a thing with it."

"Maybe not with the ship itself," said Riker, "but if we can get at the arms storage lockers, we could get our hands on some phasers."

"Maybe," La Forge said, "if they're still there . . . if the Romulans didn't confiscate them."

"I listened to the reports of the away team that beamed aboard the *Independence*," Riker said, "and they said nothing about finding any weapons. Even if they had, after all this time, the phasers would be outdated and the sarium krellide cells would have long since expired. The Romulans would have figured they'd be useless."

"But sarium krellide cells can be recharged by tapping the ship's electroplasma system," La Forge said. "If the emitter crystals and the recharging coils are still in decent shape—"

"If the weapons have been stored all this time, there's no reason why they shouldn't be," said Riker. "And we'd need just enough phasers to seize back our own arms storage locker, and we could make up the deficit out of that."

"Whoa, wait a minute," La Forge said. "We're putting the cart before the horse here. I might be able to figure out some way to tap the EPS for a recharge of the power cells without getting caught, but we'd first have to seize the transporter room to get aboard the *Independence*. Even if we could overpower the guards there without alerting the others, they'd still pick it up on the bridge the moment the transporter was activated. We might be able to get over to the *Independence,* but the Romulans would be on us before we could do anything."

"Not if we don't use the transporter," Riker said.

"A shuttlecraft would be a sitting duck," said La Forge. "Besides, I thought you said they used all the shuttles to transfer the hostages to the warbird."

"That's right, they did," said Riker, "but I wasn't thinking of using a shuttle."

La Forge whistled softly. "You mean *EVA?*"

Riker nodded.

"Jeez, that might work, but we'd be taking one hell of a chance. We wouldn't be as easy to spot that way, but if they *did* spot us . . . and how would we get aboard the *Independence?* There wouldn't be any power to the emergency hatches and . . ." His voice trailed off. "Wait a minute, you mean blow the emergency bolts from *outside?*"

"Exactly," Riker said. "I know it would be risky, but it's the only thing I can think of."

La Forge shook his head. "It could work," he said, "but to blow the bolts from the outside, we'd need to remove the outer access panels and tap into the circuits with a portable power source, which means we'd be practically *next* to the damn things when they blew."

"I didn't say it was going to be easy," Riker said.

"No, you sure didn't. How are we going to get at the EVA suits?"

"The same way you got in here," said Riker.

"No way," said La Forge. "It would never work. I was just barely able to squeeze through where the ducts narrow. You'd never make it."

"I wouldn't have to go very far," said Riker. "We'd only have to crawl far enough to reach an opening into the first Jefferies tube, and then we could crawl through and take the tubes the rest of the way. It would have to be during night watch, when the Romulans would think we were asleep. We'd need as much time as possible."

La Forge took a deep breath and exhaled heavily. "All right," he said. "Let's say it all works and we manage to get our hands on some antiquated phasers from the *Independence*. And let's assume we can get back safely and I can get them charged up. *Then* what?"

"Then the next step will be up to you," said Riker. "Korak's been keeping a close watch on me, and when he's not with me, he's keeping me confined to quarters. You'll have to pass the word somehow to your crew down in engineering. They're the ideal people for what I have in mind anyway."

"And what's that?"

"We're going to fight them the one way they won't expect us to," said Riker. "And our weapon is going to be the *Enterprise* itself."

Chapter Seven

"KALAD TO *Syrinx.* Come in, Commander." The Romulan frowned as, for the third time, there was no response. "Kalad to *Syrinx.* Please acknowledge."

There was no reply from the warbird.

The Romulan frowned. "My communicator seems to be malfunctioning," he said.

"Let me try mine," said Dr. Crusher. "Crusher to *Enterprise.* Come in, please." She waited a moment and then tried again, this time calling the *Syrinx,* but still with no result. "Strange, mine doesn't seem to be working, either," she said with a frown.

Data lowered his tricorder. "There may be nothing wrong with our communicators," he said. "My readings indicate that there is considerable interference."

"What sort of interference, Data?" Troi asked.

"I cannot pinpoint the source," the android replied. "However, I am picking up highly irregular readings on my tricorder."

"I am, too," said Ro, looking down at the readout screen of her own instrument. She tapped it
slightly on the side. "Something is affecting our instruments."

"There was no interference with the signal earlier,"
Kalad said suspiciously. "Why now?"

"I cannot say," Data replied. "But numerous power
fluctuations are taking place all the time aboard this
vessel. Most of its automated systems still appear to
be functioning, coming on line at different times, and
it is possible that one or more of them is generating a
field that is causing the interference."

"What will Commander Valak do when he does not
hear from us?" asked Dr. Crusher.

"He will either locate us and beam us back aboard
the *Syrinx* or beam down another away team to
investigate," said Kalad.

"Perhaps we should return to our arrival point,"
said Troi.

"No," said Kalad. "We were sent down here to
investigate and to report our findings. I see no immediate danger. I shall attempt to communicate with the
Syrinx later. We shall carry on, for the present." He
gestured with his disruptor. "Continue. I mean to
have a look inside some of these structures."

They approached an arched entryway that led inside one of the buildings. There were no doors. They
entered a sort of lobby with a corridors leading off it
in three directions—to either side and straight ahead.
The ceilings were high, and the corridors wide, like
boulevards. Daylight came in through large windows
in the outer walls, though from the outside, no windows were visible. Here and there, placed in islands in
the corridors, were clusters of abstract sculptures.

Data raised his tricorder and frowned. "The interference is increasing," he said. "It is greater here. I am not picking up any clear readings at all now."

"This architecture is fascinating," Dr. Crusher said as she looked around her. "But it doesn't tell us much about the people who built it. They might have been large and very tall, or they might simply have wanted to achieve a sense of space in this closed environment. But they obviously appreciated art." She approached a cluster of sculptures. "These are beautiful."

She reached out to touch one, but Troi caught her hand. "Wait," she said.

"What is it?" Dr. Crusher asked.

"I . . . don't know," said Troi, frowning as she gazed at the strangely shaped forms. They were dark and their surface textures were varied. Some shapes appeared sleek and glossy; others were rough and irregular. Some were as tall as humans, others taller, still others shorter, but they were all clustered in groups. No one individual sculpture stood alone.

"Are you getting something?" Crusher asked.

Troi shook her head. "I'm not sure," she said in a puzzled tone. She reached out tentatively toward one of the graceful forms. Her hand hesitated, inches away; then she touched it, barely grazing it with the tips of her fingers. It felt hard and cool to the touch. She shook her head as she drew her arm back. "I feel nothing now," she said. "Perhaps it was some sort of residual aura from whoever created this."

Data stepped forward and reached out to touch the sculpture. "Curious," he said. "I have never seen material like this. It is neither stone nor metal. It appears to be synthetic, and it seems to have been molded into this shape."

"The shapes are all different," Ro said. "Some are

smooth and flowing; others are angular and blocky. But they all seem to fit together."

"They appear to serve no practical purpose," Kalad said.

"They serve an aesthetic purpose," Dr. Crusher replied.

Kalad scowled. "We are wasting time. I see nothing of value to be learned here."

They proceeded down the corridor, past other strangely shaped clusters of sculptures, but they saw no doors anywhere. It was as if they were walking through some sort of gigantic endless maze. There were places where other corridors branched off, and they passed several other graceful archways leading into interior plazas with gardens planted in them and more sculptures placed around them. They entered one of these small plazas and saw that it was an atrium with an open shaft extending all the way up through the building. From the upper levels balconies looked down over the plaza. The plants in the well-tended garden were unlike any they had ever seen before.

"Someone has been taking care of these gardens," Troi said, examining one of the strange willowy trees growing in the center of the plaza. It was surrounded by fragrant, well-trimmed shrubbery and smaller succulents that echoed the shape of the sculptures.

"So there *is* someone aboard this ship," said Kalad.

"I am still not getting any clear readings off my tricorder," Data said. "However, it is possible that some automated function is maintaining these gardens. That would appear to be the case with the rest of this vessel."

"You mean some sort of robotic droids?" asked Dr. Crusher. "We haven't seen anything like that."

"As yet, Doctor, we have seen very little of this vessel," Data pointed out.

"True," she replied, "but it certainly doesn't *feel* deserted, although I can't really say why."

"No, it does not," Troi said, looking around her. "I have the distinct sensation that we are being watched."

Kalad glanced around quickly, his disruptor held ready. "I see no one."

"Nor do I," said Troi. "But I still feel as if someone or something is watching us."

"Why are there no doors?" asked Ro, in a puzzled tone. "Nothing but endless corridors and plazas, and no doors anywhere. What's behind these walls, and how does one get inside them?"

"Perhaps there are doors, but we just don't know how to recognize them," Dr. Crusher said.

"Well, so far we have not seen anything that looks like a door," said Troi. "Merely archways connecting open areas and corridors. The walls all appear to be quite smooth. Perhaps the doorways are concealed."

"We haven't seen anything that looks like a lift or a stairway, either," Ro said, "yet these buildings have upper levels. There must be *some* way to get to them."

Kalad tried using his communicator once more, but it didn't work. "Perhaps the interference is being caused by something behind these walls," he said. "We shall retrace our steps and go back outside to where we did not encounter this difficulty."

He herded the others ahead of them, and they went back the way they came, but after they had walked for a while, Ro, who was leading the way, stopped and looked around. "We must have made a wrong turn somewhere," she said.

"No, I'm sure we came this way," said Dr. Crusher, looking around uncertainly.

"Then where's the archway leading to the outside, where we came in?" asked Ro.

"We have to go back," said Troi. "Obviously we took a wrong turn somewhere."

"Negative, Counselor," Data said. "I have kept careful track of our progress, and we have retraced our steps exactly."

"Then where is the archway leading out?" asked Kalad.

Data cocked his head in that curious, almost bird-like manner. "It *should* be here," he said.

"Clearly it is not," Kalad said irritably. "You are mistaken."

"I am most definitely *not* mistaken," Data insisted. "This is where we came in." He turned toward a corridor that branched off from the one they stood in. "That corridor was ahead of us when we entered, and we turned right. The archway was there." He pointed at a blank wall.

"That is absurd," said the Romulan. "There is nothing there but a wall."

"I assure you that I am not mistaken," Data said. "This is where we came in."

"Impossible," said the Romulan.

Dr. Crusher walked slightly away from the others, toward a group of sculptures. "No, he's right," she said. "This is the same sculpture we were looking at earlier."

"Perhaps it only looks similar," said Ro.

"No, it is the same one," Troi agreed. "I am certain of it."

"Then why is there no way out here?" asked Kalad.

"The way out *was* here," said Data. He approached the wall and felt it. "However, it is here no longer."

"What do you mean?" demanded Kalad.

"I mean that this is the precise spot where we came in," Data replied. "but the opening through which we entered has now been sealed in some manner I cannot detect."

"You mean we're trapped in here?" said Ro.

"Unless we can locate another exit or find a way to open this one, it would seem so," Data replied.

"Something has gone wrong." Valak, aboard *Syrinx,* had repeatedly tried to raise the away team, with no result. He turned to Picard. "If your crew members have anything to do with this, Picard, both you and they will regret it, I assure you."

"Do you think they would try to overpower your chief of security and escape, thereby endangering the hostages?" Picard asked. "Where would they escape to? With your people in control of the *Enterprise,* you control the only means of bringing them back up."

"One would certainly think so," Valak said. "However, there remains the fact that they are not responding."

"Perhaps they cannot respond," Picard said. "They might be injured . . . or perhaps worse. Send me down there, Valak. Beam me down with one of your away teams and let me see what's happened to them."

"I shall do better than that," said Valak. "I shall go down myself with an attack group, and you shall accompany me." He addressed the guards. "Conduct the captain to the transporter room and wait for me there." Valak faced Picard. "If you have lied to me and there are Federation personnel waiting for us down there, I shall wipe them out to the last man."

After Picard left with his guards, Valak quickly gave orders to assemble an attack group, then left the bridge and made his way to Lord Kazanak's private chambers.

"Enter," Lord Kazanak said from within.

The doors opened and Valak went inside. Lord Kazanak was seated at his table. He looked up as Valak entered. "Ah, Valak. I have been preparing my report on this mission. I am including your log entries as well as my own observations. Have you anything new to add?"

"We are receiving no response from the away team, my lord," Valak said. "I am preparing to beam down with an attack group to ascertain what has become of them."

Lord Kazanak frowned. "You suspect treachery?"

"Until I know for certain what has occurred, I suspect everything," Valak replied. "I am leaving Korak in command of the *Enterprise*. Until I return, my science officer, Talar, will be in command of the *Syrinx*. He will see to your comfort and keep you informed of any new developments."

Kazanak nodded. "Very well. I shall monitor your communications with the bridge from here. And I shall consult your first officer aboard the *Enterprise* for periodic reports."

"If we fail to return, my lord," said Valak, "this mission must be abandoned and the ark destroyed. I leave the fate of the Federation prisoners to you."

"Our warriors will be more than sufficient to deal with any threat you may encounter," Lord Kazanak replied.

"My lord, Picard's warning about a quarantine may have some substance," Valak said. "If there is danger of infection, the ark must be destroyed."

"Yes, well, we can make that decision when and if the time comes," Lord Kazanak replied. "Until then I shall eagerly await your reports."

Valak bowed and left. He took the turbolift to the transporter room, where Picard was waiting with his guards. The attack group was also waiting, thirty Romulan warriors armed with disruptors and dressed in battle armor. They made an imposing sight. Valak armed himself and turned to them, quickly dividing them into three squads of ten, each with an officer in command.

"Antor, your squad will beam down first and secure the area," he said crisply. "Torak, your squad will follow, and then Captain Picard and I will beam down with Sirok's squad. If you encounter any resistance, crush it immediately. Proceed."

The attack groups snapped to, and the first group of warriors took their places on the pad. Valak gave the order, and the transporter was activated on wide beam. The warriors dematerialized, and the second squad quickly stepped up to take their place. Finally it was the last group's turn. Picard stood with Valak on his left and Sirok on his right. He alone was unarmed. Valak had allowed him to carry only a tricorder. It did not make for a great feeling of security, he thought wryly, but for the moment, his greatest concern was for the members of his crew on the away team.

"Energize," said Valak.

Moments later they were standing in an open area, on the same coordinates to which the first away team had been transported. The Romulan warriors were deployed all around them, their weapons held ready, alert for any sign of movement. But Picard only just barely noticed their presence. His entire attention was occupied by his surroundings.

"Good Lord!" he said as he looked around him.

It was absolutely breathtaking. In their initial reports, the away team had understated the case considerably. Intellectually, Picard had been prepared for what the away team had described, but actually experiencing it for himself was overwhelming.

He had been in similar habitats before—some of the older starbases had been constructed on the O'Neill model—but he had never seen anything built on this scale. Artificial light flooded the interior of Hermeticus 2, illuminating the breathtaking panorama that surrounded him. Cities hung above him where one would expect to see the sky. It was almost like seeing a world photographed through some sort of bizarre fish-eye lens.

The buildings surrounding them were Cubist, vaguely reminiscent of the twentieth-century architecture of Paolo Soleri. Rather than individual buildings that stood side by side, these were irregularly clustered atop one another like crystalline formations. It was as if some impossibly large child with a skewed sense of perspective had been let loose with building blocks. Aside from the sheer spectacle of it, the inside-out world possessed a surreal beauty that was awesome to behold.

"On the outside, it's camouflaged to resemble a planet. On the inside . . . *this,*" Picard said. "You still believe the Federation could have constructed such a ship, Valak?"

The Romulan commander was equally impressed. He shook his head. "No," he said, staring around him with amazement. "Clearly, this was not built by humans. But that does not mean there are no humans here." He held up his communicator. "Valak to away team. Report."

There was no answer. He tried again.

"Valak to away team. Report, Kalad!"

He waited a moment, but there was still no response. As he tried calling the ship, Picard glanced at his tricorder.

"Valak to *Syrinx.*"

Nothing.

"Valak to *Syrinx.* Talar, respond!"

"I think I know why there has been no word from the away team," Picard said, still looking at his tricorder.

"Valak to *Syrinx!* Talar, are you receiving me?"

"He can't hear you, Valak," said Picard. "Some sort of interference is affecting the instruments. My tricorder readings are completely jumbled."

"This interference did not affect our earlier communications with the away team," Valak said suspiciously.

"Well, it is affecting them now," Picard said. "This tricorder is useless. And so, I suspect, are your communicators."

Valak drew his disruptor and fired it at a spidery tree. The tree disintegrated. "This interference does not seem to affect our weapons," he said.

"It may be only a localized phenomenon," Picard said. "Or perhaps a temporary one. Your probe registered unusual power fluctuations down here. It is possible that these fluctuations are affecting communication signals. And since tricorders operate on a similar frequency, that may explain the malfunction."

"That seems logical." Valak holstered his weapon and turned to his warriors. "We shall split up to search by squads," he said. "Torak, search that section." He gestured to his left. "Antor, take your squad the other way. I shall take the others and search the immediate area. Meet back here in one hour."

"In one hour it will be dark," Picard said.

"How can it be dark?" said Valak. "There is no sun to set in here."

"Perhaps not," Picard said, "but whoever constructed this ark apparently succeeded in simulating day and night. You will observe that the light is slowly fading."

Valak looked up and frowned. "The light *is* fading," he agreed, "but I see no source for it."

"Nor do I," Picard said. "Perhaps it is being diffused throughout the interior of the ark with automated solar mirrors. Or there may be an artificial power source. However, night is most assuredly about to fall inside this vessel."

"Then let us waste no time," said Valak. "Split up and look for the away team. Meet back here when it grows dark."

"We've been wandering these damned corridors for hours!" Kalad said, with exasperation. "There *must* be a way out somewhere!"

"We've been going around in circles," Ro said. "We passed these sculptures before."

"And that's the garden atrium we went into earlier." Dr. Crusher pointed, then sighed. "I'm getting tired."

"It's getting dark," Troi said as she walked out into the garden atrium and looked up.

"Dark?" said Kalad. "But I thought the light in this vessel was artificial."

"Then someone is turning down the lights," Troi replied. "See for yourself."

The rest of them walked out into the garden atrium. It was indeed getting dark. Dr. Crusher sat down on one of the benches. "It looks as if we're going to have to spend the night here."

Kalad tried his communicator again. "Kalad to *Syrinx*. Kalad to *Syrinx*. Please acknowledge."

There was no response. *"Aarrgh!"* The Romulan snarled in frustration.

"They're bound to send someone down to look for us," Troi said somewhat uncertainly.

"Perhaps they already have," said Ro. "But how would they ever find us in here?"

"It is possible that we inadvertently tripped some type of security device when we first entered this complex," Data said, "thereby activating a mechanism that sealed the entrance."

"Either that or someone sealed us up in here on purpose," Dr. Crusher said.

"That was the second possibility I was about to mention," Data said.

"Do you really think there is a chance of that, Data?" Ro asked.

"There is always a chance," the android replied. "How remote that chance may be is a matter for conjecture. Without accurate tricorder readings, it is impossible to ascertain whether or not there are any life-forms aboard this vessel. However, the automated functions of this ark appear to be operating smoothly, and these gardens are being maintained. Those two facts do suggest the presence of sentient beings."

"Then why don't they show themselves?" demanded Kalad angrily.

"Without more specific information, that is impossible to determine at this time," Data replied.

"I am growing tired of your flat, unemotional

responses," snapped Kalad. "We are trapped in here, and you prattle on as if nothing were the matter! Does nothing arouse any feelings in you?"

"No," said Data. "I am an android. I have no feelings. And I do not prattle. I was merely replying to your question to the very best of my ability."

"Bah!" The Romulan turned away from him angrily. "I am tired of seeking a way out of this place! I am going to blast my way out!"

"That may not be wise," said Data. "We know nothing of the composition of this structure, and the energy beam of your disruptor may cause—"

"Silence! I have had enough of this! If you are afraid, then you can all wait here. I shall come back for you after I have blasted open an exit. And if you value the lives of your comrades aboard the *Syrinx,* you had all best be here when I return!"

"Where would we go?" Dr. Crusher asked wryly.

"Humans!" Kalad said contemptuously. Unholstering his disruptor, he left the atrium and strode back out into the corridor.

They sat for a while in silence. "It's getting darker," Troi said, looking up through the shaft of the atrium. "It seems so strange to see buildings suspended overhead in the evening sky. But I suppose one would grow accustomed to it eventually."

"I hope we won't have to," Ro said. "You think we're ever going to get out of this?"

"We've been in tight situations before," said Dr. Crusher, "and the captain's always found a way to pull us out of them."

Ro took a deep breath and exhaled heavily. "I wish I had your confidence."

"They will send a team down to search for us," said Troi. "I am certain of it."

"And if they do not find us?" Ro said. "Remember that, to Valak, we're expendable."

"There's Kalad," Dr. Crusher reminded her.

"One warrior?" Ro said. "I doubt that the Romulans consider Kalad irreplaceable. If they did, Valak never would have sent him down here with us. We're the guinea pigs, remember?"

"The captain would never allow Valak to simply leave us down here," Dr. Crusher said.

"With the Romulans in control of the *Enterprise,* the captain may not have any choice," said Ro. She sat down on the bench beside Crusher. "It looks as if we're really in a tight spot this time."

"Well, unless Kalad can blast a way out of this maze, it appears that we will be spending the night in here," Troi said.

Data frowned. "It occurs to me that we should have heard Kalad firing his disruptor by now."

Dr. Crusher looked up. "That's right," she said. "He's certainly been gone long enough."

They all exchanged apprehensive glances.

"You don't suppose he would simply leave us here?" said Troi.

"He could not have blasted his way out without us hearing his disruptor firing," said Data.

"Unless he managed to *find* a way out," said Ro. "Perhaps the entryway where we came in has opened up again. We'd better go check, Data. I don't trust that Romulan."

"I'll go with you," Troi said. "Perhaps you had better come with us, Beverly."

Crusher smiled and got up. "All right, we'll all go. If he's managed to find a way out, I'm all for getting out of here. I'm utterly exhausted."

"With all the stress we've been under and all the

walking we've done, I'm about worn out myself," said Ro. "How are you holding up, Deanna?"

"As well as could be expected, I suppose." Troi smiled. "I wish I had Data's stamina."

"Actually, Counselor, it is not really a matter of stamina," said Data. "Stamina relates to physical endurance, and as such—"

"I know, Data, I know," Troi said with a weary smile. "It was merely an idle comment."

They went back into the corridor and looked both ways, but there was no sign of Kalad. "Where could he have gone?" asked Dr. Crusher, with a frown.

"I don't know," said Ro. She tried calling him. *"Kalad!"* There was no response. Her shout echoed down the long corridors. *"Kalad!"* She waited a moment, and then tried once more. *"Kalad! Can you hear me?"*

Nothing.

"I don't like this," Troi said apprehensively.

"He couldn't have simply disappeared," said Dr. Crusher.

"Something's happened to him," Troi said.

"Perhaps we should spread out and look for him," said Data.

"Absolutely not," said Ro. "We should all stick together. Remember, we're not armed."

"That's not exactly a comforting thought." Dr. Crusher sounded worried.

"I think we should go back to the point where we came in and see if that doorway has opened up again," said Ro.

They walked back down the corridor toward the place where they had come in, but they found no opening to the outside.

"Are you sure this is the same spot?" asked Ro.

"I'm sure this is where we came in," said Troi. "I remember those sculptures."

Ro shook her head. "They all look pretty much alike to me."

"No, these are the same ones, I'm sure of it," said Dr. Crusher.

"Well, there's still no opening," said Ro, running her hand along the wall. It felt completely smooth. "It's as if there never even was one in the first place."

"We do, however, know there *was* an opening," said Data. "Therefore, that means it was sealed in such a manner as to present a perfectly smooth and seamless surface."

"Great," Ro said wryly. "So how does that help us?"

"At the moment, perhaps, it does not," replied Data. "However, it would seem to explain why we have seen no other doorways. There may be similar sealed passageways all around us, only we cannot detect them."

"That doesn't make any sense," said Ro. "Why would anyone make doorways you can't even see? And how is it possible to construct a door that seals so tightly there's not even the faintest trace of a crack or a seam?"

"I did not say I knew how it was done," said Data, "I merely pointed out that it clearly *has* been done. One logical possibility, however, is molecular engineering."

"You mean nanotechnology?" said Dr. Crusher.

"Precisely. To date, Federation scientists have only scratched the surface of what could be accomplished with nanotechnology. Properly developed, the techniques of molecular engineering could produce sophisticated nanocircuitry capable of programming the functions of this structure on an atomic level."

"You mean the molecular structure of this wall could actually alter itself to create a doorway?" asked Troi.

"Theoretically, it is possible," the android replied. "In fact, given the knowledge and the technology, this entire structure could have been designed along such lines."

"So what are you saying?" asked Ro. "This building can assume any shape it wants?"

"It would be more precise to say that the molecular components of this structure may have been designed with a certain limited flexibility dictated by the desired function," the android replied.

"In other words," said Dr. Crusher, "a solid wall could rearrange itself on the molecular level to form an open archway or a door, but not a chair or a staircase, because that's how it was designed."

Data cocked his head. "A rather curious and simplistic way of putting it, Doctor," he said, "but essentially correct."

"Great," said Ro. "So where's the doorknob?"

"Doorknob?" said Data. "Ah, you mean the mechanism that controls the function." He shook his head. "I fear I do not know."

"You're a lot of help," said Ro.

"I perceive by your tone that you are being sarcastic, Ensign," Data said. "I fail to see the reason for sarcasm, however. I am doing the very best I can, given the little information we possess."

"She didn't mean to snap at you, Data," Troi said. "It's just that we are all tired and frustrated."

"And on top of that, it's getting dark in here," Ro said.

"I would feel a lot safer if Kalad hadn't disappeared," said Dr. Crusher. "At least he had a disruptor."

"Well, whatever happened to him, the disruptor didn't seem to help him any," Ro said.

"We still do not know for a fact that anything has happened to him," Data pointed out. "He simply went off and had not returned."

"Deanna's had the feeling that we've been watched ever since we came in here," Ro replied. She shook her head. "No, something happened to Kalad all right. He never would have left us alone this long. If he lost us, he'd have to answer to Valak."

"What are we going to do?" asked Dr. Crusher.

"Well, we can't stay awake all night," said Ro. "We don't even know how long the night is in here. We'll have to find somewhere to bed down as best we can. We'll take turns standing watch."

"That will not be necessary," Data said. "Since I require no sleep, I am perfectly capable of standing watch all night long."

Ro glanced at him and sighed. "Of course. Sometimes I forget you're not really human, Data."

"Thank you," Data replied.

Ro smiled wanly. "You're welcome."

"That garden atrium would make as good a place to sleep as any," Dr. Crusher said. "We could stretch out on the benches there. Right about now, that seems almost as good as a warm bed."

"I am not sure I would go that far," said Troi, "but I suppose it will have to do under the circumstances."

"Let's just hope the circumstances are temporary," Dr. Crusher said as they headed back toward the garden. "I don't much care for the thought of being trapped in here much longer."

"I don't much care for the thought that an armed Romulan warrior simply disappeared without a trace," said Ro. "I have a feeling that we're not alone in here."

Troi moistened her lips nervously. "I have that feeling, too," she said.

Chapter Eight

As NIGHT FELL in the ark, Valak's search party returned to the arrival coordinates. They were the first ones back. There was no sign of the groups led by Torak and Antor. They had found no sign of the first away team, either, and Picard was worried. Valak, too, seemed concerned, but for other reasons.

"Kalad would not have simply wandered off exploring," he said. "As soon as he discovered his communicator was not functioning, he would have returned to the arrival coordinates. I am concerned that I cannot account for his disappearance."

"I am equally concerned about my own people," said Picard.

"Are you?" said Valak. "Perhaps they encountered friends aboard this ark."

"You *still* believe there may be Federation personnel aboard this ark?" said Picard. "We have seen no signs of life at all."

"This vessel is very large," said Valak. "And it would take a long time to search it all."

"If there were Federation personnel present here," Picard said, "don't you think they would have responded to your presence by now?"

"Perhaps they are biding their time." Valak tried to use his communicator again, but it still wasn't functioning. He swore. "If this interference is affecting communications, it may also affect the transmissions from the scanner probe on the surface. Talar will be unable to get a fix on our position."

"And a blind transporter beam sweep of our arrival coordinates may prove ineffective as well, so long as the interference persists," Picard said.

"You had best hope that it does not," said Valak.

Picard frowned. "Why?"

"I have given orders that the ark is to be destroyed if I do not return within a reasonable length of time," said Valak.

"Destroyed!" Picard said. "And what of my crew aboard the *Syrinx* and the *Enterprise?*"

"That will be Korak's decision to make, as he is next in command," Valak replied. "So for your own sake as well as that of your crew you had best hope that this *interference* with our communications does not continue."

"You suspect your signals are being purposely jammed?" Picard said.

"The possibility has occurred to me," replied Valak. "I find it curious that we were initially able to communicate with the away team without difficulty, and now all of a sudden our communications devices are inoperative. It is possible that the interference may be the result of power fluctuations aboard this vessel, as you have suggested, but there may also be another explanation."

Before Picard could reply, there was a shout, and Antor's team appeared, moving toward them quickly. "Something has happened," Valak said.

As Antor and his team came running up to them, Valak frowned, noting that some of them were missing.

"Commander," Antor said breathlessly, "we have lost several of our warriors!"

"What do you mean, you *lost* them?" demanded Valak. "What happened?"

"We were searching the streets in the area assigned to us, and Dalok saw movement in the entryway to one of the buildings. I sent him to investigate, along with Eivak, Istak, and Jalad. We saw them enter the building, and then, moments later, the doorway disappeared!"

Valak frowned. "It *disappeared?* How?"

Antor shook his head. "I cannot explain it, Commander," he said. "One moment there was an arched entryway leading into the building. The next moment it simply was not there! The wall . . . moved."

"Be more precise," Valak said irritably. "What do you mean, it moved? You mean a panel of some sort came down to seal the entrance?"

"No, Commander, I mean the wall *moved!* It seemed to *flow,* to actually alter its shape until the archway disappeared. The entrance rapidly grew smaller, the opening shrinking rapidly before our very eyes! I thought at first that I was seeing things. Before we could react, it was no longer there. Where once there was an opening, there was now a solid wall, as if there had never been an opening there to begin with. And our warriors were trapped inside."

"And you simply *left* them there?"

"We fired our disruptors at the wall, Commander, but they had no effect."

"Impossible," said Valak.

"By the gods, Commander, I swear it!" Antor insisted. "All six of us fired our weapons at it, but the structure sustained no visible damage!"

"How can a solid wall flow, and then remain impervious to disruptor fire?" said Valak.

"Perhaps the wall is composed of a structural material with molecular memory and the density to withstand such damage," said Picard.

"Molecular memory?" said Valak. "What is that?"

"Something that was first developed on Earth many years ago," explained Picard. "The earliest examples entailed metal alloys that were designed to return to a specific shape if heat was applied. However, on a much more advanced level, molecular engineering could produce materials capable of being programmed for specific functions. It is something we have only begun to develop."

"Explain," Valak demanded.

"The term for it is 'nanotechnology,'" said Picard. "In essence it involves the manufacture by molecular chemistry of tiny machines that are smaller than living cells. The applications of such technology would be almost limitless. Applied to medicine, for example, it could result in nanomachines capable of being injected into the bloodstream and traveling to specific areas of the body to repair injuries and heal diseased tissue. Applied to structural engineering, it could result in building materials that could reassemble themselves on a molecular level."

"I have never heard of such a thing," said Valak.

"Admittedly, it is supposition," said Picard, "but in

theory, it could explain what happened. None of the structures we have seen so far have any visible entryways, except the one your warriors found, and they actually saw that entrance seal itself, or so they claim. You asked how a solid wall could alter its shape. I merely offered one possible explanation. Can you think of another?"

"All I can think of at the moment is that four of my warriors have been sealed inside a building, with no way out," said Valak tensely. "And now Torak is overdue."

"Commander, look!" Antor said.

All around them, like islands in the street, were abstract sculptures surrounded by small trees and shrubs. Some of the sculptures were tall, cylindrical, and spindly, like the undulating stalks of underwater plants; others were blocky, hard-edged, and angular. They varied in height from four or five feet to eight or nine feet, and most were arranged in clusters interspersed with plants. At first they had appeared to be artworks constructed of stone or metal, but now several of the sculptures began to emit a soft glow while others remained dark, creating artful shadowy effects in the sculpture gardens.

"Streetlights," said Picard.

"So the forms are functional as well as decorative," said Valak, in a tone that dismissed the matter as being of no consequence. "I have rather more pressing concerns at the moment."

"This may touch on one of your concerns," Picard replied. "Note that the lights appear to be coming on only in our immediate vicinity."

Valak saw that he was right. Everywhere up and down the streets at the crossroads where they stood, similar sculpture gardens were spaced out at regular intervals. However, they all remained dark. The "streetlights," as Picard had called them, had come on only in the area where they were.

"There may be sensors placed to react to our proximity, controlling the lights only in areas where they are needed," Picard continued. "We can test that easily enough by moving to a darker area and seeing if the lights come on."

"And what if they do?" said Valak.

"If the lights are controlled by sensors designed to detect movement," said Picard, "then there is also movement over there."

Valak's gaze followed in the direction he was indicating. Picard was pointing almost straight up. Above them, in another section of the ark, they could see similar dots of light.

"The missing away team?" Valak said.

"That seems unlikely," said Picard. "We are standing in the area to which they were beamed down. Those lights are nearly on the opposite side of the ark. The away team has only been missing for a matter of hours, surely not enough time to travel that far on foot."

"On a ship of this size, there must be some means of transport other than walking," Valak said. "Perhaps they discovered some sort of shuttle connecting the various points of the ark."

"Perhaps," Picard agreed. "However, as you have already pointed out, one has to wonder why they would have ventured so far from their arrival point once they discovered that their communicators were not functioning."

"So then there *is* someone else aboard this vessel," Valak said.

"I never discounted that possibility," replied Picard. "I merely stated that there was no secret Federation base here. And I expect by now, even though you seem reluctant to admit it, you have concluded that I was telling you the truth."

"Commander, someone is beaming down!" said Antor.

They all turned to see the shimmering images resolve themselves into another landing party from the *Syrinx,* headed by the Romulan science officer.

"Talar!" said Valak.

"We were unable to raise you, Commander," Talar said, as he approached with his party. "There was concern that something might have gone wrong."

"Our communicators are not functioning, due to some sort of interference," Valak said. "But why have you beamed down with a landing party? I left you in command aboard the *Syrinx!"*

"Lord Kazanak has assumed command in your absence," Talar replied. "He directed me to lead this landing party."

"Lord Kazanak has assumed command?" Valak was clearly astonished.

"And who is Lord Kazanak?" Picard asked.

"The son of a member of our high council," Valak replied, "and the designer of the *Syrinx."*

"Indeed?" Picard said. "I have never met a member of the Romulan nobility. A pity you neglected to introduce us."

"It was a pleasure Lord Kazanak chose to deny himself," said Valak. "He is not fond of humans."

"I see," Picard said. "And he is now in command of your ship, with members of my crew aboard it. I take it he has the authority to assume command?"

"He is the high council representative on this

mission," Valak replied, flatly. "That gives him the authority."

"And you do not like it," said Picard.

"What I like or do not like is no concern of yours!"

Picard smiled. "You most definitely do not like it."

"Lord Kazanak acted unwisely," Valak said grimly. "Now we have three away teams down here with no way to get in contact with the ship."

"I anticipated that possibility and suggested to Lord Kazanak a way to solve that problem," Talar said. "In one hour's time the transporter will be activated once again, on a wide pattern aimed at the same coordinates. We may not be able to effect communication and have the *Syrinx* properly lock on to our signal, but if we are standing in the right place at the appropriate time, the transporter should be able to beam us up."

"One hour may not be enough time," said Valak. "Several of our warriors are missing, and we have found no trace of the first away team."

"Lord Kazanak feels the humans are expendable," Talar said.

"Does he, indeed?" Picard said tensely. "What about your own chief of security? I suppose he is expendable as well?"

"I have no intention of abandoning one of my officers unless I am left with no other choice," said Valak. "And if we find Kalad, we shall probably find your people as well. Perhaps they became trapped inside one of these buildings, as did my four warriors."

"Trapped?" said Talar.

Valak quickly told him what Antor had reported. "And Torak has not yet returned with his squad," he added. "We must find them, and seek a way to free Dalok and the others."

"I can send a party out to search for Torak," said Talar, "but if disruptor fire has no effect on the walls of these structures, how can we free the four who are trapped?"

"If there is a way to close a door, then there is a way to open it as well," said Valak. "You are the science officer, Talar, you tell me. Captain Picard thinks this 'flowing wall' may be the result of something he calls nanotechnology."

"Molecular engineering?" Talar said.

"You know of it?" Valak seemed surprised.

"It is something our own scientists have been researching. We have heard the humans are pursuing it as well," Talar replied. "We have not had much success, but neither have the humans."

"Well, whoever built this ark seems to have succeeded," Valak replied dryly. "Go with Antor and find a way to open that door. The rest of you, come with me. We shall search for Torak and the others."

"Has it occurred to you that someone may have *purposely* closed that door on your warriors?" asked Picard. "Antor said that one of them saw movement in the entryway of that building. It may have been meant to lure them inside. Something similar could have happened to Torak and his group."

"That thought has already occurred to me," said Valak. "And if that is what happened, the parties who are responsible, whether they be Federation personnel or otherwise, will have cause to regret their actions."

The door to Riker's quarters opened and Korak entered without announcing himself, as if he owned the place. "Don't Romulans believe in knocking?" Riker asked him.

"Knocking?" the first officer said, in a puzzled tone. "What is . . . knocking?"

"Apparently not," said Riker. "Never mind. It's not important. What do you want, Korak? Are you looking for a rematch?"

Korak sneered. "The next time we face each other —and you can be sure there will be a next time, I shall be ready for your tricks."

"Then I guess I'll have to think up some new ones."

"Joke all you like," said Korak. "But you will not feel like joking when next we face each other."

"I'm shaking in my boots," said Riker. "Is there a point to this visit, or did you just come down here to scare me?"

"I merely thought you would be interested to know that there has still been no word from the first away team. And since Commander Valak beamed down with your Captain Picard and another away team, there has been no word from them, either. I have just been informed that a third away team has beamed down from the *Syrinx,* and contact with them has been lost as well."

"It sounds as if you can't keep track of your people," Riker said lightly. Inwardly he felt concerned, but he'd be damned if he'd allow the Romulan to see it.

"In Commander Valak's absence, Lord Kazanak has assumed command of the *Syrinx,*" Korak continued, ignoring Riker's dig.

"Lord Kazanak?"

"He is the designer of the *Syrinx,*" Korak replied, "but what is more significant, he is the son of a member of the Romulan High Council. He has informed me that if Commander Valak fails to return, I will be in command of the *Syrinx* and of the human prisoners. In that event I will claim the *Enterprise* as a prize of war."

"I wasn't aware that we were officially at war with the Romulan Empire," Riker said dryly.

"With more warbirds like the *Syrinx,* we soon shall be," Korak said, "and your starships will not stand a chance against us. The Federation will be utterly destroyed."

"It seems to me I've heard that kind of talk before," said Riker. "Notice we're still here."

"Yes, and notice your current predicament," Korak countered. "Commander Valak wanted to return to Romulus with the crew of the *Enterprise* as his prisoners, but Lord Kazanak does not much care what happens to you, one way or the other."

"I see," said Riker. "So if anything happens to Valak, *you* get to decide what to do about us."

"Precisely." Korak smiled maliciously. "I shall leave my intentions to your imagination while you remain here to brood on the fate of your crew. But I can promise you one thing, William Riker. We shall have our rematch. I intend to let you live at least long enough for that."

Riker's gaze bored into Korak's back like a laser as the Romulan turned and left his quarters. The muscles in his jaw bunched as he gritted his teeth. The door slid shut with a soft hiss, and Riker realized that he was gripping the edge of his desk so hard that his knuckles were cracking. He let go of the desk with an effort and retrieved the altered frequency communicator he had tucked beneath him a split second before Korak entered the room.

"Geordi?"

"I'm still here," the chief engineer replied. "What happened?"

"Our buddy Korak just paid me a call," Riker said tensely. He exhaled heavily. "That was close. He almost caught me talking to you."

"What did he want?"

Quickly Riker recapped the conversation. "It looks as if we've got our work cut out for us," he said when he had finished.

"And not a lot of time to do it in," La Forge replied.

"The trouble is, there's nothing I can do locked up and under guard in here," said Riker. "I humiliated Korak in front of his men, and he's confined me to my quarters so my presence won't cause him continued embarrassment. The bastard wants me to sit here and squirm over what he plans to do to us if he gets the chance. Have you been able to make any progress?"

"I've spoken with four of my crewmen in engineering so far," La Forge said, "but it's not easy with those Romulans watching practically every move I make." The frustration was evident in his voice.

"Well, counting us, that makes six so far," said Riker. "If we could get around a dozen, we might have a shot at it. A long shot, maybe, but at least a shot."

"I'm doing the best I can under the circumstances," said La Forge. "That Atalan keeps us on pretty tight rein."

"I know you're doing your best, Geordi," Riker replied. "But we haven't got much time left. If we're going to make our move, we've got to do it soon. Korak's got himself a bad case of ambition."

"That sounds like the least of our worries," Geordi replied. "We're going to have to space walk to the *Independence* without anyone noticing, find some phasers, come back, and charge them somehow, then seize control of the *Enterprise* while the Romulans are still holding part of our crew hostage on the warbird. And then we've got to figure out how to get the captain and the others back. Talk about long shots! There's about a million ways this whole thing could go wrong."

"It went wrong when we let the Romulans take us by surprise and seize our ship," said Riker. "That's about as wrong as it gets. Now we've got to make it right, and we don't have a lot of options."

"I hear that," said La Forge with an air of resignation. "Can you give me one more day?"

"I don't know if we've *got* one more day," Riker replied.

"Then I guess I go back to crawling through the ventilation ducts and the Jefferies tubes again," said La Forge wearily. "That's the only way I'll be able to get to any of the others tonight."

"Do what you can, Geordi," Riker said.

"Yes, sir."

"And Geordi? Don't get caught. . . . Riker out."

Data stood watch in the garden atrium while the others slept. They had removed their suits, for there seemed to be no risk in breathing the ark's air, and the tanks had run out after three hours, anyway. Troi and Dr. Crusher had stretched out on the benches, and Ro slept on the ground. It was not completely dark. In the center of the atrium several of the curiously shaped sculptures were glowing softly. Others were casting long, strange shadows in the ethereal light.

There had been a moment of consternation when the sculptures began to glow, but they soon realized that they were designed for illumination as well as for aesthetic reasons, and Data had suggested that they were probably controlled by motion sensors concealed somewhere nearby, perhaps built into the sculptures themselves. They did not flood the atrium with light, but instead gave off a gentle illumination. "Night-lights," Dr. Crusher had called them.

Data occupied his time with analyzing everything that they had seen and experienced so far, searching for a way out of the building they were trapped in. They had found a way in, so it seemed logical that there should also be a way out. They had found no other doors anywhere and no means of access to any of the upper levels. There had to be doorways and lifts or stairways—some way of gaining access to the upper levels of the building—but they seemed to be concealed. Data could not see how concealment would serve any useful purpose. The ark had clearly been designed as a multigenerational starship, its primary purpose to house its crew—or rather its inhabitants —and to convey them to their destination. The builders of the ark had taken pains to create a comfortable and aesthetically pleasing environment for those who came here, so why would they have constructed doorways that were difficult to find?

The obvious answer was that for those who had inhabited this ark, the doorways were *not* difficult to find, any more than the doors aboard the *Enterprise* were difficult for the members of its crew to find.

At first Data had thought, as had the others, that the archway through which they had entered had sealed itself automatically, either as part of some periodic program, the purpose of which was not readily apparent, or because their entrance had triggered some sort of sensor. Now, however, with the inexplicable disappearance of Kalad, another answer had suggested itself: someone or something had sealed them in on purpose.

Without accurate tricorder readings, they could not disallow the possibility that they were not alone aboard the ark. And then there was the fact that Deanna Troi felt that they were being watched. Data was not capable of intuition, but he knew Counselor Troi relied on it and was usually accurate. He assessed the possibilities. Kalad had either found a way out of the building or had stumbled through another portal and been sealed in behind it. He might have triggered some sort of automated defense mechanism, but if that was so, they should have done the same thing earlier when they were all wandering around inside the building. If there was someone aboard the ark with them, then perhaps the Romulan had been captured or even killed. Without more information, it was difficult to tell which possibility was more likely.

There were other problems as well. They were unable to communicate with anyone. And they were all unarmed, because Valak had not trusted them with active phasers. Data stood guard while the others slept, but he was not sure that he could actually protect them. Kalad had carried a disruptor, and it apparently had not done him any good. At a time like this, thought Data, a human would be worried, perhaps even frightened. He was incapable of such emotions, though he understood them, more or less. The others did not seem frightened, but Data knew that humans often concealed their fear. They did, however, seem very worried. Even as tired as they were, it had been difficult for them to get to sleep. They had talked among themselves for a long time before they finally drifted off one by one. I am now responsbile for their welfare, Data thought. For their safety. How best can I ensure it?

He moved slowly around the atrium, pacing softly back and forth so as not to disturb the others. He had observed that Captain Picard often paced while he thought. He seemed to find it helpful. Knowing that the others were asleep and could not see him, Data imitated Captain Picard's pacing, walking back and forth with a purposeful, measured tread, his head down, his hands clasped behind his back. Perhaps this pacing helped Captain Picard think better, but it did not seem to be doing much for him. He continued to walk steadily back and forth, his footsteps making soft sounds on the smooth surface of the atrium. And then he heard another footstep just after his own. He stopped suddenly and turned around.

Everything was quiet. He peered intently into the shadows, but he could see nothing. All he heard was the sound of Dr. Crusher breathing evenly as she slept. He took a tentative step. And then another. And another. And then he raised his foot, but did not put it down.

But there was the unmistakable sound of a footstep.

"Is someone there?" he said.

There was no answer. But then, there was no reason to believe the occupants of the ark could understand English. Ro stirred. Data moved closer to the others. Now he heard several footsteps.

"Ro," he said.

"What?" she said, coming awake. "What is it?"

"I think we are about to have visitors."

She was on her feet in an instant, instinctively

reaching for her phaser. As she recalled that Valak had given them inactive weapons, she swore. "Deanna! Beverly! Wake up!"

The other two women came awake quickly, long accustomed by service in Starfleet to come alert immediately to deal with any emergency that might arise.

"What is it?" Dr. Crusher asked.

"Data says somebody's coming."

Even as she spoke, a hooded, black-robed figure stepped out of the shadows at the far end of the atrium. There were sounds of movement, and several more robed figures stepped out on either side of him.

"I think it would be prudent to indicate that we are not hostile," said Data.

He slowly raised his hands. The others did likewise.

The hooded figures came closer. And then one of them spoke in English. "Who are you?"

"We are from the Federation starship *Enterprise,*" said Dr. Crusher. "We mean you no harm."

Troi's eyes grew wide. "They are human!" she said, picking up on that fact with her Betazoid sensitivity.

The man who spoke pulled back his hood. "Yes, we are human. We are the crew of the Federation starship *Independence.*"

The man approached them, followed by the others, who also pulled back their hoods. Some of them looked to be in their fifties and sixties, while others seemed much older, including the man who had spoken. And some were only in their teens and twenties.

"The *Independence* was reported destroyed over thirty years ago," said Ro. "We found it here, in orbit, a dead hulk."

"Indeed," the old man said. "And we have been here ever since."

"You certainly appear old enough," said Troi, "but some of these other people are scarcely twenty years old."

"Our children—and grandchildren," the old man said. "They have grown up here. They have never known any other existence. I am Commander Morgan Llewellyn, first officer of the *Independence* and leader of this colony."

The stunned *Enterprise* crew members introduced themselves, then Llewellyn indicated the man on his right, who was also very old. "This is Lieutenant Commander Giorgi Vishinski, our ship's doctor. Lieutenant Charmayne Jamal, our weapons and chief security officer." He gestured toward an African-American woman. "Lieutenant Commander Sven Nordqvist, our chief engineer." A white-haired man smiled a greeting. "And Lieutenant Kiri Nakamura, our science officer." A slight Asian woman gave them a curt nod.

"That is all that remains of our bridge crew," said Llewellyn. "Captain Wiley and Lieutenant Commander Glener attempted to escape in a shuttle with two other crewmen, Chief Connors and Ensign Morris. We have no idea what became of them."

"Apparently the shuttlecraft was discovered drifting in space, with everyone aboard it dead," said Troi. "But that was over three decades ago and there is no official documentation of the incident. The record was either lost or classified along with all other information concerning Hermeticus Two."

"Hermeticus Two?" Llewellyn said with a puzzled frown.

"That is the official designation given to this planet," Data explained. "That is, it was assumed to be a planet, though quite obviously it is not. We have a great many questions to ask you, Commander."

Llewellyn frowned. "What *are* you, a robot?"

"The correct term is 'android,' sir," Data replied.

"Amazing," said Llewellyn. "The Federation seems to have made great strides."

"You should know that there is a Romulan warbird here in addition to our own ship," said Troi. "The situation is very complicated and dangerous. The Romulans are in control of both vessels."

"We know," Llewellyn said simply. "Is the Federation currently at war with the Romulan Empire?"

"Strictly speaking, no, sir," Data replied. "However, Romulans feel that our uneasy truce has been violated by the presence of your vessel in the Neutral Zone."

"The Romulans have seized the *Enterprise,*" said Dr. Crusher, "and they are holding members of our crew hostage aboard their warbird. Their mission was to investigate Hermeticus Two. They seem to believe there is a secret Federation base here."

Llewellyn nodded. "I understand. It sounds as if, with regard to the Romulans at least, nothing much has changed. It would seem that we have much to discuss. However, I think you may prefer to do that in more comfortable surroundings."

"Commander," Data said, "there was a Romulan officer with us who has apparently disap—"

"Yes, I know," said Llewellyn, interrupting him. "Do not trouble yourself about him. All your questions will be answered, I assure you. Now if you will come with me, please . . ."

He led them toward the back wall of the atrium. As

he approached it, the wall began to flow, as if it had turned to liquid, and in an instant an archway appeared where there had been a solid wall.

"That's amazing," said Dr. Crusher. "How did you *do* that?"

Llewellyn smiled. "I recall my own astonishment when I discovered this for the first time," he said. "That was a very long time ago. Now I take it for granted. You will find much here to astonish you, Dr. Crusher. The level of technology is far superior to our own."

"But . . . how did you open the wall?" asked Troi.

"I willed it open, Counselor," said Llewellyn.

"You mean . . . it is controlled by *thought?*"

"In a manner of speaking," Llewellyn replied as they walked through the archway and into another corridor. "I do not pretend to know exactly how it works. Most people can learn how to use computers, for example, but knowing how to use one and having the knowledge to write sophisticated programs are two rather different things. The builders of this incredible vessel achieved a level of engineering that is beyond our understanding. To follow the computer analogy, they somehow learned how to program at the molecular level."

"Nanotechnology," said Data.

"Exactly," said Llewellyn. "They developed a means of structuring matter so that it was capable of reassembling itself on the molecular level. In our time, nanotechnology was only in the realm of theory. Have we since passed beyond that point?"

"Science has made considerable progress in protein engineering and microcircuitry," Data said, "but true nanotechnology is still in the theoretical realm."

"Well, the builders of this ship have taken it far

beyond the theoretical realm," Llewellyn said, "as you have just seen. In fact, in my day *you* would have been in the theoretical realm, Mr. Data, yet now here I am, conversing with an android as calmly as you please. You see, I have learned something in the years I've spent here, or perhaps I should say I have remembered it. In childhood we all believe that anything is possible, although probability is another matter. That archway we just passed through, for example— nanotechnology controlled by thought, but a rather specific kind of thought. It is not enough merely to think that you want the door to open. You have to know *how* to think it."

"You mean as in a specific command?" asked Dr. Crusher.

"Partly," replied Llewellyn, "but it is also a matter of how you direct your mental energy. This begins to enter the realm of parapsychology. You are familiar with the concept of telekinesis?"

"Moving objects by thought energy?" said Troi.

"Just so. We have discovered that the machinery of this vessel works on roughly similar principles. I did not actually open the wall with my mind, although in a sense I did. The procedure involves what I call telepathic sensors. The trick is to train your mind to generate a particular type of mental energy—the same type of faculty, I suppose, unconsciously developed by psychics and clairvoyants and people who possess other paranormal abilities."

"How did you learn to do this?" Troi asked.

"All in good time, Counselor Troi. All in good time. I cannot condense thirty years' worth of experience and study into a simple explanation."

"You appear to be in excellent health—incredible health, considering that some of you must be over a hundred years old," Ro said. "Your colony seems to have thrived, and your offspring have developed normally. How did you survive here all these years? And why did you abandon the *Independence?*"

"Excellent questions," said Llewellyn. "And you will receive your answers, I promise you. We are as eager to ask *you* questions as you are to find out about us. However, as I have already explained, it will take time, and for the moment we need to concern ourselves with more immediate problems. This way . . ."

He turned toward another archway, through which they saw a mazelike corridor stretching out into the distance, but when he walked through it, he disappeared completely.

The crew members of the *Enterprise,* except for Data, stared open-mouthed. There had been no transporterlike shimmering image, no discharge of energy of any sort. It was like the old story of stepping through the looking glass, except that there was no glass or mirrored surface, merely an open archway much like those they had seen while wandering through the building.

"There's no cause for alarm," said Dr. Vishinski. "This is merely a form of transporter. It is considerably more sophisticated than the ones you are accustomed to, but its function is the essentially the same. Please step through."

Data was the first to step through the archway, and like Llewellyn, he disappeared from sight. Troi and Dr. Crusher exchanged glances, then they, too, stepped through. Ro hesitated.

"Please," said Vishinski. "It is safe, I assure you."

She thought to herself, How do I know I can accept your assurances? How do I even know you are who you claim to be? However, the others had already gone through, and there was nothing to do but follow. She still had her suspicions about these people, whom the others had apparently accepted at face value, but now was not the time to reveal them. She and her colleagues were unarmed and outnumbered, and they were in a completely alien environment, most of which was still a mystery to them. The answers, whatever they were, lay on the other side of that curious portal.

Ro took a deep breath and stepped through it.

Chapter Nine

"I'M GETTING SICK AND TIRED of sitting here doing nothing," Chief Miles O'Brien said in a low voice. "Are we going to just give up without a fight?"

"I feel much as you do," Worf replied, "but we have had no word from the captain. We must also think of the children. If we make an attempt to break out of here, we might endanger them."

"They are endangered already," replied Keiko O'Brien, coming to her husband's support. They all lay together on the bedding the Romulans had provided for them in the large shuttle bay, whispering softly. "What chance will they have at the mercy of the Romulans?"

"She's right, sir," whispered Ensign Tyler, the ship's environmental systems officer. "The Romulans can never let us go. They'll have to kill us all.

"Or we'll wind up in their slave markets," added Lieutenant Arthur, Worf's deputy chief of security.

"I'd rather have my child die than end up as a Romulan slave," said Keiko vehemently.

"Keep your voice down," Worf cautioned her, glancing around at the guards posted by the doors to the shuttle bay. They had turned out some of the lights in the bay to enable their prisoners to sleep, but they had left enough on so they could still keep an eye on them. "I am a Klingon warrior," Worf said. "You think I like this any better than you do? My blood boils at being held captive, but what would you have me do? The captain told us to wait. I do not have the authority to initiate any action."

"You're the senior officer present," said O'Brien. "And for all we know, the captain and Commander Riker may already be dead."

"And if they aren't, their hands are tied because of us," said Arthur.

"Our hands are tied as well," said Worf. "We have no weapons. If we attempt to rush the guards, they will shoot us down before we even reach them, or they will simply retreat and leave us locked inside here. If we attempt to break out, they can either open the outer bay doors, cancel the force field, and kill us all, or else purge the life-support system in the shuttle bay and suffocate us."

"But we can't just sit here. We've got to do *something!*" said Chief O'Brien in exasperation.

"Sir, I've been thinking," Tyler said. "If I can manage to get behind that shuttlecraft over there, I'll be blocked from the guards' view. I noticed a large access panel in the bulkhead back there. Unless I miss my guess, it's a maintenance panel for the outer bay doors. If I can get inside it, I might be able to temporarily disable the controls so the Romulans couldn't open the outer doors from the bridge."

"That would still not eliminate the threat presented by the guards," said Worf. "Besides, you would never be able to reach the panel without them seeing you."

"He might have a chance if there's a distraction," O'Brien said hopefully.

"Even so," said Worf, "it would take time to open the panel and trace the unfamiliar circuits. The slightest sound would alert them, and if any of the guards moved away from their present position, they would see what Tyler was doing."

"Not if I did it during night watch," Tyler said. "That whole area's in shadow right now. And it wouldn't take much to cover up any noise I might make. A loud argument, a fight among the hostages, anything that would distract the guards."

"Perhaps," said Worf, thinking it over. "And then?"

"If I could disable the controls for the outer bay doors, it would buy us some time," said Tyler. "I could get inside that shuttlecraft and fire it up. That would get the guards' attention, and you might have a chance to rush them. And I could use the shuttlecraft to block the entrance doors and prevent them from getting any reinforcements."

"Even if we were able to overcome the guards," said Worf, a plan he had already been considering himself, "we would not do so without casualties. For myself, I do not fear death, if I can die like a warrior, but to risk the lives of the children . . ."

He glanced over at his own son, Alexander, who was sleeping. It seemed ironic to Worf that he, of all people, should be the one to counsel caution instead of following the dictates of his Klingon warrior spirit and urging the others on to battle. However, as the senior officer among them, he had responsibilities, and above all he had a responsibility toward his own son.

He could understand now how Captain Picard must have felt during the crises they'd faced in the past. A captain of a ship was, in a very real sense, a paternal figure, not only a figure of respect and authority but also a custodian of his "children," the crew. His duty was always clear, but the manner in which he carried out that duty frequently called for agonizing decisions, decisions that often went against his nature.

Worf's nature was to fight, to prevail over the enemy or go down in battle as a warrior should rather than submit to defeat. But as Captain Picard knew, what seemed like a defeat could often be turned into victory through boldness or clever use of strategy. There was merit in Tyler's idea, but Tyler was young, and the enthusiasm and boldness of the young had to be tempered by the wisdom of their more experienced elders. Resistance was always preferable to submission, but now was not the time for what French-speaking humans referred to as a *beau geste,* a noble gesture of self-sacrifice. While it might be noble to die in battle against the Romulans, it would be pointless if it did not accomplish anything, and tragic if it resulted in the death of children.

Worf recalled how ill at ease he'd felt at first with Alexander. He hadn't been prepared for the discovery that he had a son, and he was even less prepared to assume the responsibilities of fatherhood. He had felt awkward around the child, and while Deanna Troi had offered invaluable counsel to him in his new role, he had felt uncomfortable at having to seek that counsel. It seemed to undermine his self-sufficiency. It had taken time for him to realize that no one was truly self-sufficient, and that those who thought they were merely took refuge in a form of weakness, the weakness of being unable to ask for help and guidance and thus find greater strength in reliance on close friends and comrades.

That was Picard's strength, he realized. Emotionally, the captain was the strongest human Worf had ever known. Yet Picard relied as much upon the strength and counsel of his immediate subordinates as he did upon his own. In this situation, Worf thought, I must do the same if I am to lead effectively.

These thoughts all flashed through his mind as he gazed at the sleeping form of his young son. He glanced around at the other children, the older ones all huddled together in a group, the little ones clinging to their parents, some of whom were sleeping, but most of whom were lying awake and watching him. They knew something was going on, but they could not hear the soft, whispered exchanges between him and the others. They simply watched and waited expectantly. Worf saw some of them nod at him as his gaze swept over them. It was as if they were reassuring him. They were all depending on him to make the right decisions. He could not let them down.

"Your idea may have some merit," he told Tyler cautiously. "However, let us consider it carefully. If we could overcome the guards, we could fortify our position by blocking off the entrance doors. We could then hold the Romulans off, but not for long." He glanced at Tyler. "They could still purge the life-support system in the shuttle bay and suffocate us. Our only option would be to open the outer bay doors ourselves and attempt escape in the shuttles. It is possible that we could reach the *Enterprise*, but with the Romulans still in control of our ship, we would be recaptured as soon as we brought our shuttles aboard.

And then our situation would be no different from what it is now."

"At least we'd be back aboard our own ship," said O'Brien. "And I don't intend to allow myself to get captured again without a fight."

"If we could seize some weapons from the guards, that would at least improve our chances," Arthur said.

"And it might prove enough of a distraction to allow our shipmates aboard the *Enterprise* to act," said Tyler.

"You are forgetting one thing," said Worf. "If we attempt escape aboard the shuttles, someone will first have to open the outer bay doors. With the bridge controls disabled, the doors will have to be opened from in here, at the maintenance panel."

"Yes, I could do that manually by reconnecting the outer bay door controls and leaving the bridge controls out of the circuit," Tyler said.

"Disabling the controls would also disable the forcefield that maintains atmospheric integrity in the shuttle bay with the outer bay doors open," Worf said. "It would then undoubtedly register as a malfunction both on the bridge and in the engineering section. That would give away our intentions and enable the Romulans to disconnect the forcefield generators from their main engineering section. If they were to do that—and it would be the obvious countermeasure—then any attempt to open the outer bay doors would be suicide."

Their faces fell as they realized that Worf was right. He had obviously already considered the idea.

"Not necessarily," said Tyler. "If everyone got aboard the shuttles first and we brought one of the shuttles around right next to the maintenance panel, then I could reconnect the circuits to open the outer bay doors from in here and still get inside the shuttlecraft before the vacuum sucked all the air out of the bay."

"Perhaps," said Worf, considering the plan. "It could work. But it would be dangerous. You would have only seconds to get aboard the shuttlecraft. And we would still have to reach the *Enterprise*. The Romulans in control there could simply leave the shuttle bay doors closed. We would not be able to get aboard, and our life support aboard the shuttles would eventually run out. We would all die within sight of our own ship."

"But not until our life support ran out," said O'Brien. "And once our shipmates knew we had escaped from the *Syrinx*, they would be free to rise up against the Romulans aboard the *Enterprise*."

"The warbird would not attack our ship," Arthur pointed out, "not with their own people aboard. We'd stand a fighting chance, at least."

"Sir," O'Brien said to Worf, "I understand what you're doing. You're playing devil's advocate, pointing out all the flaws in our plan so we can see the potential consequences. We all know that no one wants to take a crack at these Romulan bastards more than you do. You just want to make sure we've thought the whole thing through. Well, maybe we stand a chance and maybe we don't, but unless we do something, we don't stand any chance at all. So long as we're held hostage here, there's not much our shipmates back aboard the *Enterprise* can do. Even if we die, we'll have succeeded in giving our crewmates the freedom to act. And at least we'll go down fighting."

Worf gazed at O'Brien for a moment, then turned to the others. "Is this how you all feel?" he asked.

Tyler nodded. So did Arthur. Keiko O'Brien said, "We all knew the risks when we joined Starfleet. We knew the risks when we decided to start our families. All the people here know and respect you, Worf. They'll follow you regardless of what you decide."

Worf looked at them all for a long moment, then nodded. He felt proud of them. He glanced around at the others lying all around him, a few of the women sitting on the bedding and rocking their small children. Worf asked himself what the captain would have done in such a situation. The others all met his gaze steadily and nodded, as if to say, whatever you decide, we're with you. And he had his answer.

The sound of disruptor fire echoing through the streets galvanized Valak and his warriors and they ran toward it, several of them flanking Picard and keeping a close watch on him. The glow of the curious sculpted streetlights followed them as they moved, the lights going on as they drew close to them and then going out again as they passed. When they reached the spot where they thought the disruptor fire had come from, they saw nothing. The warriors spread out, their weapons drawn, their eyes alert for any sign of movement, but there was no sign of any of the others.

Picard came up beside Valak as the Romulan commander issued orders to his warriors. "Spread out! Secure the area, but maintain visual contact with one another." He looked all around him anxiously. "Torak!" he called out. *"Torak!"* There was no answer. "Talar? Antor, can you hear me? *Respond!"*

"You seem to be losing track of your warriors,

Valak," Picard said. "How many does that make so far—eighteen disappeared without a trace?"

Valak turned an angry gaze on him. "I remind you that your own people have disappeared as well!"

"Believe me, that thought remains foremost in my mind," Picard replied. "As does the fact that if we do not find a way to reestablish contact with your ship, this ark might be destroyed at any time, due to your ill-considered orders."

Valak's frustration was clearly evident. The muscles in his jaw worked as he struggled to control his temper. "Damn you, Picard, if I die here, then so do you."

"I am prepared for that," Picard replied in a level tone. "But as you said yourself, this game is far from over."

"Commander!" one of the warriors called out. He came running over. "I found this," he said. He held out a Romulan disruptor. "It was lying on the ground over there."

"No warrior of mine would abandon his weapon unless he was dead," said Valak.

"There was no trace of any bodies, Commander."

"Then they must have been removed," said Valak. "If they were killed by a disintegrating weapon, this disruptor would have disintegrated as well. And if our opponents lack such weapons, I cannot imagine them leaving this one behind. Call everyone back."

"What do you intend?" Picard asked.

Valak turned to face him. "We are going over there," he said, pointing to the lights on the opposite side of the ark. "I am going to bring the fight to them. And if the others aboard this cursed vessel want to stop us, they will have to show themselves and face all of us together!"

"It will take several days to reach that place," Picard said. "You may not have the time."

"Then I shall die," said Valak. "But I shall not remain here helpless while they pick us off at their leisure. If they want a war, then by the gods, I shall give them one!"

"As yet you have not even *seen* them, whoever they may be," Picard pointed out. "This may be exactly how it started with the *Independence*. First one landing party beamed down; then interference knocked out communications and another away team followed, and then that team disappeared . . ."

"You think Lord Kazanak would be foolish enough to risk sending down another team when three have already been transported down and there has been no contact with them?" Valak said.

"You did not think he would send down Talar and his team," Picard reminded him. "The captain of the *Independence* was no fool, and yet his entire crew disappeared without a trace. There were only four survivors, all of whom committed suicide by attempting escape in a shuttlecraft. The *Independence* has been here for thirty years, Valak. Thirty years! Why hasn't its orbit decayed? What is holding it up there? If something can reach out from here and affect the *Independence*, what makes you think your own ship will be invulnerable?"

"Commander, someone else is beaming down," said one of the warriors.

"What?" Valak turned around and saw another Romulan away team materialize a short distance away.

"You were saying, Valak?" said Picard dryly.

Valak hurried toward the new away team, followed by the others. The new arrivals came to meet him.

"Zorak!" the Romulan commander said. "What are you doing here?"

Zorak looked at his commander with a puzzled expression. "But, Commander . . . you yourself gave the order for us to beam down!"

"I?" said Valak. "Are you mad? I did no such thing! We have been unable to contact the *Syrinx* ever since we arrived here!"

Zorak looked utterly confused. "But . . . I do not understand, Commander. Lord Kazanak received a message from you that there was no more interference with the communications signals and that you required more personnel to—"

"Impossible! I sent no message!"

"So it begins," Picard said softly.

Valak turned on him furiously. "I have heard about enough from you, Picard!"

"You may have heard," Picard said, "but you have not *listened.* I warned you that there was danger here, but you chose not to believe me. If Lord Kazanak received a message from here, then we can draw only one possible conclusion: the interference is no accident; the signal frequency of your communicators is purposely being jammed, just as you suspected. However, *someone* obviously managed to get through, someone who was able to convince Lord Kazanak and your bridge crew that the message came from you. Whoever is aboard this ark is not afraid of you, Valak. They *want* more of your people to beam down. And once they are here, they will never be allowed to leave."

"We shall see about that," Valak replied, though he no longer seemed quite so sure of himself. "Remember that whatever happens to us, Picard, will happen to you as well."

"Obviously," Picard said wryly, "since I am your prisoner. Only now it would seem that *you* are prisoners too."

Valak raised his hand as if to strike him, but at that moment one of the warriors shouted and fired his disruptor. Instantly the others also began firing. Valak turned quickly and drew his own weapon, then shouted at them to stop when he saw that there was no return fire being directed toward them.

"Cease firing! Cease firing! What are you all shooting at?" he shouted.

"Over there, Commander," one of the warriors said, pointing across the street toward a shadowed area between two buildings. "I saw someone running."

"Who?"

"I do not know, Commander. A figure . . . all in black. Wearing a hooded robe."

"So they are showing themselves at last," said Valak. "Zorak, take your team over there and investigate. The rest of you, come with me."

The group split up, with Zorak's team moving toward the area where the shadowy figure had been seen, and Valak leading the rest of the warriors to the opposite side of the street, to set up a field of covering fire in case it was a trap. Once they had taken up position, Valak tried using his communicator once again.

"Valak to *Syrinx*. Respond!" The only answer was a crackle of static. He tapped the communicator and tried again, with no better result. He swore vehemently.

Valak's self-control was starting to slip, Picard noticed. Up to now the young Romulan commander had been confident of his superiority, secure in the knowledge that he had planned everything out to the last detail. Now, separated from his ship and unable to communicate with his crew, Valak was suddenly faced with the unknown. Without the might of the Romulan war machine behind him, he was caught in a situation where he could make no plans, map out no strategy. He would have to improvise and depend entirely on his own resources. In this, his youth and temperament worked against him.

Picard, on the other hand, had often found himself in circumstances where he was forced to improvise. This current situation certainly looked bad, he thought, but as long as a man could think clearly, there were always options. He had been in some pretty tight spots before, but for Valak, this was a new experience, and he was starting to fray at the edges.

Suddenly a voice came over the communicator. "Zorak to Commander Valak. Are you receiving me?" The transmission crackled with static, but it was still audible, though barely.

"Zorak!" Valak turned up the gain on his communicator. "Zorak, can you hear me?"

"Barely, Commander," came the static-filled reply. "There is still interference, but I can hear you. Apparently the communicators will function only within very close distances."

"At least that is something," Valak said. "Report."

A burst of static came back over his communicator, with only a few words audible.

"*Again*, Zorak," Valak said. "I did not receive you clearly."

Another burst of static, then, ". . . sign of . . . here, Commander. Whoever . . . has disappeared. Wait! There is something moving farther . . . We see them!" The transmission ended in a burst of static.

Valak tapped his communicator in frustration. *"Zorak!* Respond! *Zorak!"*

"He must have moved just out of range," Picard said. "Or been decoyed out of range."

"I did not *tell* him to move, blast his soul!" said Valak angrily. He beckoned to the others. *"Come on!"*

They ran across the street in the direction Zorak had taken with his team. They reached the point where the others had gone around a corner of the building and down an alleyway. There was no illumination in there, and they could see only a few yards ahead of them.

Valak tried his communicator again. "Zorak! Respond!" There was no answer. *"Zorak!"*

The communicator crackled with static.

Valak cursed and led the way into the alley. Picard felt someone shove him from behind, and then he was running with the rest of them. The dark alley extended for several hundred yards, then opened out onto another street that ran parallel to the one they had come from. There was no sign of Zorak and his party.

"Zorak!" Valak shouted, his voice echoing off the buildings all around them. *"Zorak!"*

There was no reply. The soft glow of the sculpted streetlights illuminated the immediate area, but there was no light farther down the street to indicate where Zorak and the others might have gone. They had simply disappeared, just like the others.

"That brings the total missing to what, about thirty?" said Picard.

Valak spun around and grabbed him by the front of his tunic, pushing him back and slamming him against a wall. "Damn you, Picard—"

Picard quickly brought up his hands and broke the

Romulan's grip, then shoved him away hard. "Take your hands off me!"

Valak stumbled and fell, and the others immediately trained their weapons on Picard. He tensed, waiting for them to fire.

"No!" said Valak. He got to his feet, his eyes narrowed with fury. "If anyone kills him, it will be *me!"*

"And here I thought you wanted to take me back to Romulus with you and show me off," Picard said sarcastically, though inwardly he sighed with relief.

"Do not overestimate your value to me, Picard," said Valak, a hard edge to his voice. "I could easily do without you. You have sorely tested my patience, and you are beginning to grate on my nerves."

"Only because you are allowing your emotions to cloud your judgment," said Picard. "You are not thinking, Valak; you are merely reacting. I thought you were a better officer than that."

"I do not need you to point out my responsibilities!"

"For better or for worse, Valak, we are in this together," said Picard. "My people are missing too. And unless we can put aside our differences, we shall *all* fall victim to whatever fate befell them."

Valak stared at him for a long moment, then took a deep breath and exhaled heavily. He nodded. "Very well, then. I shall listen. Speak."

"Brute force will not get us out of here," said Picard. "Your warriors were all armed with disruptors, and yet they vanished. Whatever they saw was obviously a lure intended to draw them into some sort of trap. The same thing occurred with all the others."

"Divide and conquer," Valak said.

"Precisely," said Picard. "We have been watched all

along, and those who are watching us could have chosen to attack us at any time."

"But they have not, which means they must lack the strength to do so," Valak said.

"Perhaps," Picard said. "This ark was obviously designed to accommodate a crew numbering in the tens of thousands. Yet it appears to be almost deserted. If we are dealing with the original occupants of this vessel, then it would seem their original number has been significantly reduced somehow."

"If we are faced with the original occupants of this vessel," Valak said. "For all we know, we could be dealing with the survivors of the *Independence."*

"Thirty years have passed since the *Independence* was reported missing," said Picard. "Even if there were survivors, which seems doubtful, they would all be in their sixties and seventies."

"Humans reproduce, do they not?" Valak said wryly.

"If they found a way to survive here, then that is indeed a possibility," Picard said, "though I consider it remote. If they're human, I undoubtedly have less to fear from them than from you. Still, why would the crew of the *Independence* have chosen to disable their own vessel and remain here? Surely you realize by now that there cannot be a secret Federation base here. If there were, why would they leave the *Independence* in orbit to advertise its presence? Perhaps it was left there as a warning."

"A warning against what?"

"Against whatever prompted the Federation to impose a quarantine on Hermeticus Two," said Picard. "The logical assumption in this case is the presence of a life-form too dangerous for us to have contact with, or the existence of a disease for which there was no cure. Either possibility could explain what happened to the original crew of this ark."

"But *someone* is still alive here," Valak said.

"True," Picard said. "If the crew members were struck with a deadly disease, perhaps some of them survived and developed an immunity. But if so, they are probably carriers of that disease. And if, on its journey to this sector, the ark encountered some life-form that destroyed all of its occupants, then that life-form could still be here."

"This is nothing but idle speculation," Valak said. "It still fails to address the problem."

"Before a problem can be solved, it is first necessary to know precisely what it is," Picard said. "We still know very little about what we are faced with here. What we *do* know is that whoever or whatever is aboard this ark possesses enough intelligence to utilize the technology that holds the *Independence* in orbit and interferes with our communications. They also possess enough intelligence to communicate with your ship and make your crew believe the message came from you. Zorak and his away team were beamed down on what they thought were your orders. What is to prevent another message being sent and more of your people ordered down in your name?"

Valak's face looked grim. He was starting to listen at last. "Lord Kazanak is eager to discover something here that will give the Romulan Empire an edge in competing with the Federation. If he believes I have made significant discoveries here, he will be only too glad to beam down more away teams to investigate. Yet I fail to see how that would work against us. It would only serve to reinforce our strength. Besides, it is not the Romulan way to avoid our enemies rather than confront them."

"Be that as it may," Picard replied, "your people will still have no idea what they are getting into unless someone warns them as soon as they arrive."

"Then I shall station warriors at the arrival coordinates to brief any more teams that may arrive," said Valak.

"But what guarantee do you have that they will not disappear as well, or that anyone else who beams down will arrive at the same coordinates?" said Picard. "Whoever sent that message in your name could easily have given them new coordinates. They could have away teams transported down anywhere inside this ark, effectively splitting up your forces even as they arrive."

Valak exhaled heavily and nodded. "I must admit there is sense in what you say," he replied. "So what are we to do?"

The other Romulans looked on with amazement as their commander asked advice from a Starfleet officer. It was absolutely unprecedented. They had no idea what to make of it. But at the same time, they were profoundly unsettled. Since they had arrived, some thirty of their fellow warriors had disappeared without a trace. And Valak had been unable to do anything about it. They all knew they could be next, and the man they had looked to for leadership no longer seemed sure of himself whereas Picard remained calm and in control. And that, coupled with his frequent subtle use of the word "we" in referring to them all together, was having its effect. They *were* all in this together, and even though Picard was human, the things he was saying made sense.

"We must assess the situation calmly and logically," Picard said. "Some of your warriors have disappeared. However, up to this point, we have not actually been attacked or fired upon. What does that suggest to you?"

"Either they possess weapons that function silently or else no energy weapons are being used against us," Valak replied.

Picard nodded. "If they possessed such weapons, they could easily have used them on us by now. So either their weapons are of a different order or they are not using any weapons as we understand them. We have also seen no bodies. If your warriors were killed, then their bodies have all been taken away. But why? On the other hand, perhaps they may still be alive."

"No Romulan warrior would ever allow himself to be captured and taken prisoner," Valak said.

"Spare me the bombastic rhetoric," Picard said. "Given the proper circumstances, anyone can be captured and taken prisoner, as you yourself have demonstrated by seizing my ship."

"Very well, for the sake of argument, I shall concede the point," Valak said. "But why would they want to take us alive?"

"Perhaps they are a nonaggressive species," said Picard. "That is something you seem not to have considered. Remember, it is *we* who are presenting a threat to *them*. We have invaded their home, and we have come with weapons of war. They may only be seeking to defend themselves."

"And I suppose if we all lay down our weapons and surrender, they will come out and welcome us with open arms?" Valak said scornfully. "Is that your advice, Picard? I expected more from you."

"I did not say we should surrender," said Picard, "but there is always the possibility of negotiation."

"I did not come here to negotiate with anyone, Picard," said Valak. "Whoever we are facing—the survivors of the *Independence* or the original occupants of this vessel—I intend to find them. And when I do, this matter will be settled once and for all."

"You may not have long to wait," Picard said. "Observe."

He indicated the lights on the opposite side of the ark. They were spreading out. And they were moving closer.

Chapter Ten

WHEN RO STEPPED through the archway, she felt a very brief tingling sensation, then found herself in another part of the ark. Troi, Data, and Crusher stood in front of her with Llewellyn, and seconds later Vishinski, Jamal, Nordqvist and Nakamura followed, materializing as they came through the archway behind her.

"You see?" said Vishinski with a smile. "There was nothing to worry about."

Ro noticed that only the elders, the members of the *Independence* bridge crew, had come through. The others, the younger ones, had apparently remained behind. She glanced at her surroundings. They stood in a wide, brightly illuminated corridor, similar to the one they had just left, only a short distance away from them there was an arched opening to the outside.

"Please come this way," Llewellyn said, walking toward the opening.

They followed him, and as they approached the opening, they could see that they were on one of the upper levels of the building. It was not a balcony. They were simply looking out through an opening in the building wall. Visibility was limited by the darkness outside, but in the distance, they could see the glow of lights on the far side of the ark.

"We are now on the opposite side of the ark," Llewellyn explained. He pointed toward the lights in the distance. They seemed to be moving. "Those are your Romulan friends," Llewellyn said.

Data cocked his head to one side. "I beg your pardon, Commander, but the Romulans are *not* our friends."

Llewellyn smiled. "I was speaking ironically, Mr. Data."

"Ah," the android said. "I see. The use of words to convey the opposite of their literal meaning for humorous or rhetorical effect."

"Quite so," Llewellyn said.

"What are those lights over there?" asked Troi, pointing to where trails of lights below them seemed to be moving slowly to either side of where they stood, spreading out and heading away from them. Due to the illusion created by the curved inner surface of the ark, they seemed to be moving across the sky, like fireflies.

"Merely a sort of diversion, nothing more," Llewellyn replied, enigmatically. "It will be dawn soon—at least we like to think of it as dawn, even though one does not literally see the sunrise. This way . . ."

He turned and led the way back down the corridor. Ro glanced over her shoulder as they went back the way they had come. "Look," she said, quickly nudging Troi. Behind them the wall seemed to ripple and flow, and a moment later the arched opening disappeared and was replaced by a solid wall. "That's how we got sealed in," she said.

"We have prepared quarters for you," Llewellyn said, stopping before a completely blank section of the wall. "I hope you will find them adequate." An instant later, the wall flowed and rippled and formed an arched opening wide enough to admit one person at a time. He gestured them inside, and when they hesitated, he smiled again and said, "Very well. I shall precede you." He went in first and they followed him. The other elders came in after them.

It was a large room, easily four or five times the size of their private quarters aboard the *Enterprise* and as luxurious as that of a five-star hotel. The floor was sleek and smooth, and the room contained a large horseshoe-shaped sofa upholstered in black leather, with a heavy carved-mahogany coffee table set inside the curve, matching recliner chairs and end tables with ceramic-based lamps on them, an elegant dining set, and even a small bar. The large arched window in the far wall was similar to the one they had just seen in the corridor. Troi and Crusher stepped close to it and looked out.

"The window has no glass," Vishinski said from behind them, "but you will find there is no need for it. The temperature in the ark is kept uniform at around seventy degrees; there is no wind or precipitation, nor are there any annoying insects."

"You will find a food replicator in the wall behind the bar," Llewellyn added. "It functions like the ones aboard Federation starships—at least, the ones found on the ships of thirty years ago. I believe you will find the cuisine uniformly excellent. There are separate bedrooms down that small corridor, with doors that function in the normal fashion, as I am sure you will be relieved to know."

"Speaking of the doors, Commander," Data said, "I have noticed that the walls in all the buildings we have seen are uniformly smooth and blank. There are no outward indications of where any doors should be. Given the assumption that with nanotechnology, you are capable of creating a doorway or an opening in any of the walls, how do you locate the precise area?"

"That was a bit confusing for us as well, at least in the beginning," said Llewellyn. "To put it in simple terms, how does a blind man find his way around his own home? At first, it would be a matter of rote memorization, learning to take so many steps in one direction, turn to the left or right, take so many steps in that direction, and so forth. After a while, it becomes automatic and he does it without thinking."

"That would suggest that the builders of this ark possessed an absolutely unerring sense of direction," Data said.

"I suppose one could use the analogy of a homing pigeon," said Nordqvist. "No matter where it is released, the bird always finds its way back to its own roost. Needless to say, we did not possess that advantage in the beginning, but we discovered that once we learned how to interact with the thought sensors that control the walls, we could mark the doorways by them. We also played with creating individual patterns on the walls where the doors should be."

"We amused ourselves with making different patterns," said Nakamura with a smile. "We were unable to make the walls change color, but we could create patterns in relief, spelling out our names and creating pleasing visual designs, and to that extent we were limited only by our imaginations. Our own quarters in this building still have those identifying designs, though we no longer really need them. My quarters on the level below this one, for example, are marked by a dragon in relief."

"If you wish to rest," said Llewellyn, "we can leave and come back later, after you have had some sleep."

"Sleep?" said Crusher. "I don't think I could sleep a wink! I have about a thousand questions to ask you, and I hardly know where to begin!"

Llewellyn smiled. "Perfectly understandable," he said. "Please, sit down. "Ski, why don't you get some refreshments for our guests?"

"Be happy to," said Vishinski, heading for the replicator behind the bar. "What would you folks like?"

"I'm too keyed up to eat right now," said Dr. Crusher, "but I'd love a cup of coffee."

"Plain? With cream? Or would you prefer cappuccino? We also have espresso, Irish, Viennese . . ."

"Just plain black coffee, thanks."

"Coming right up. . . . Counselor?"

"I would love a cup of tea," said Troi.

"Ceylon, Chinese, jasmine, orange pekoe, herbal . . . sky's the limit."

"Some jasmine tea would be very nice, thank you."

"Mr. Data?"

"I do not require solid or liquid nourishment, thank you," said the android.

"Of course. What about you, Ensign?"

"I could use a stiff drink," said Ro, feeling a bit overwhelmed.

"How about Bajoran brandy?"

She glanced at him with surprise. "That would be wonderful."

"Coming right up."

They all took their seats on the sofa. Llewellyn and Nordqvist sat in two of the large chairs. Vishinski brought their drinks, and they were all excellent. Ro took a tentative sip of her brandy and found it to be of a vintage superior to any she had ever had before.

"Why don't we begin at the beginning?" Llewellyn said. "About thirty years ago, we were on routine patrol when our long-range scanners picked up some unusual power signals emanating from this sector. We discovered that they were coming from the Neutral Zone. We decided to investigate. It was a calculated risk, but we thought the Romulans might be up to something. In any case, there wasn't supposed to be anything out here. We entered the zone on yellow alert and discovered what we first thought was a small planet that didn't appear on any of our charts. Long-range scanners showed no ships in the vicinity, so we came in closer and established orbit. At that point we began to experience some interference with our scanners. We were unable to get consistent accurate readings, so we dispatched several probes to the surface and discovered, much to our surprise, that the planet was hollow.

"The power readings we picked up clearly suggested that this was an artifical world—not a planet at all, but an interstellar ark created for multigenerational voyages. Needless to say, this was a tremendously exciting discovery. We attempted to make hailing contact with anyone who might be aboard, but after repeated attempts, we received no answer. Our probes indicated that there was a breathable atmosphere aboard the ark, but we were unable to pick up any life-form readings, and so the next step was to send down an away team."

"Excuse me, Commander," Ro said, "I do not

mean to be rude, but much of this we have already surmised. You seem to have very little concern about the current Romulan threat. If there are already Romulan landing parties aboard this ark, then—"

"There is no need for concern, Ensign, I assure you," said Llewellyn. "The situation is well in hand."

"Commander," Ro insisted, "I am not sure you understand the gravity of the situation. The Romulans have an advanced warbird in orbit above the ark, larger and much more powerful than any you may ever have encountered. They have also seized the *Enterprise,* a Federation starship much advanced over the *Independence.* That makes for enough firepower to reduce this entire ark to slag."

"I appreciate your concern, Ensign," said Llewellyn, "but once again let me assure you that the Romulans do not pose any real threat. In fact, a number of them have already been captured and are safely in detention at this moment. Their warbird and your own starship will be seen to presently."

"What do you mean?" Troi asked with a frown.

"In due time, Counselor, I will explain," Llewellyn replied. "However, before we can get to that, there are some things that you will have to understand first. Now, if you will allow me to continue . . ."

They nodded, though both Ro and Troi looked vaguely dissatisfied with his reply. Dr. Crusher merely sat there listening to Llewellyn and watching him carefully.

Llewellyn went on with his story. "I led the first away team. With me were our science officer, Lieutenant Nakamura; our chief weapons and security officer, Lieutenant Jamal; Dr. Vishinski; and two other crewmen who, regrettably, are no longer alive. We beamed down not far from where we sit right now, and we were confronted by essentially the same things you saw. We did not find any sign of life. The ark appeared to be deserted, but all the systems that maintained it were apparently still functioning. Our instruments, like yours, would not work properly, and we could not get any accurate readings, although at first we *were* able to communicate with our ship. We began to explore the ark.

"It was daytime aboard the ark when we arrived, so we spent most of that first day simply looking around, wandering through the streets. We did not attempt to enter any of the buildings because we could not find an entrance. So far as we could tell, the buildings were solid cubes, stacked in patterns resembling crystalline formations. We thought they might be residential structures with concealed entrances, or perhaps sealed power plants that ran the ark. All we could do at that point was theorize."

"It was obvious that this ark was constructed by an advanced civilization," added Nakamura, "at least as advanced as we were, possibly more. As we soon discovered, they were advanced far beyond our own technological capabilities."

"When we were satisfied that we seemed to be alone aboard the ark, we brought down more personnel," continued Llewellyn. "We had decided to make a complete survey of this huge vessel and learn as much about it as possible. The captain, figuring it would be a long-term project, prepared a dispatch for Starfleet Command, reporting our discovery. To the best of our knowledge, that message never reached its destination. It was only after a good number of our people had beamed down that we began to encounter problems."

"Some of our people began to disappear," said

Lieutenant Jamal. "They simply vanished without a trace. And at about the same time we lost the ability to communicate with our ship."

"The same thing happened to us," said Dr. Crusher.

"I know," said Llewellyn. "Initially we believed that power fluctuations aboard the ark were responsible for some sort of interference, but we soon realized that our signals were being purposely jammed. We suspected it might be the result of some sort of automated defense program, but we were unable to discover anything that looked like a central control station for this ark. We figured it had to be inside one of the buildings, but they all looked more or less alike, and we had no idea which one it might be, much less how to gain entry."

"We'd had several reports of our people finding arched entryways to buildings and going inside to investigate," said Nakamura. "Then we simply lost contact with them. Nor could we find those entryways. It was not until we actually witnessed one of the walls sealing itself that we understood what had happened to them."

"We attempted to use our phasers to blast our way inside the buildings," said Jamal, "but our weapons had absolutely no effect. That seemed impossible, until we realized that the structural material was actually repairing itself as it was being damaged by our phasers. It was happening so quickly we couldn't even see it."

"You stated that you believed the interference with your communications might have been the result of some sort of automated defense system designed to jam your signals," Data said, "and yet you had not experienced any initial difficulty in communicating with your ship. Our experience was the same, at first. It is possible that an automated system might have required time to detect your presence aboard this vessel and then lock on to your communications frequency so that it could be jammed, but your tone of voice suggests that you do not believe that to have been the case."

"Very good, Mr. Data," said Llewellyn. "You are exactly right. That was not the case."

"Then what was responsible for jamming your communications?" Data asked.

"Very simple, Mr. Data," said Llewellyn. "We were not alone aboard the ark. The original crew, or at least the descendants of the original crew, were—and are—still present."

Dr. Crusher leaned forward. "You mean they are still here?"

"That's correct," Llewellyn replied.

"But . . . where?" asked Troi.

"Where?" said Llewellyn. "Why, all around us. I'm not sure exactly how many of them there are, but excluding ourselves I would estimate the present population of the ark at roughly thirty thousand."

"Thirty thousand?" Ro said.

"More or less," Llewellyn replied, as Troi and Crusher stared at him with astonishment. "If it hadn't been for them, we never would have survived. They've been taking care of us all these years, and our colony, such as it is, has thrived. That is very fortunate, for you see, we can never leave."

Riker grunted as he painfully squeezed his way through the duct, following La Forge. Neither of them, fortunately, possessed a husky build, but Geordi was smaller, and it had been a tight squeeze for him in places. For Riker, inching his way through the ductwork like a worm was an ordeal.

"Just a little bit farther, Commander," La Forge said, from just ahead of him.

"I'm . . . going . . . on a diet," said Riker, wincing as he dragged himself about another foot. He had to inhale, then exhale heavily, emptying his lungs and inching forward as he did so. He had been repeating the whole process over and over, with painful slowness, wondering if he was ever going to reach the point where the duct vented into one of the Jefferies tubes.

"Come on, Commander, you're almost there," said La Forge.

"I . . . don't know . . . if I'm going . . . to make it," Riker said, gasping for breath. He was starting to develop claustrophobia. The narrow passageway had not been meant to accommodate a human body, and he could barely move. He raised his head very slightly, just enough to see about a foot or two in front of him, then stretched his arms out almost completely straight and pulled himself along by pressing down with his elbows and pushing a little with his knees, making slow, tortuous progress. What worried him most of all was not discovery by the Romulans, but the thought that he might become stuck.

"Just a few more feet," said La Forge, urging him on.

Riker grunted and dragged himself forward once again, scraping his shoulders painfully and ripping his tunic. *"Damn!"* he said, gritting his teeth as he felt his skin being scraped away along with the cloth. They were trying to move along quietly, but inside the duct, it sounded to him as if they were making enough noise to wake up the whole ship. It seemed like an eternity before Geordi finally helped him through the vent opening and out into one of the ship's maintenance tubes.

Riker took a deep breath, filling his lungs gratefully, and closed his eyes as he exhaled heavily. *"Whew! After that, the rest of this mission will be all downhill."*

"I'm not sure I'd go that far," said La Forge. "You know how long it's been since either of us walked in space?"

"Not as long as it took to crawl through that damned duct," said Riker. He glanced around at the Jefferies tube they stood in, part of a vast, interconnecting network of maintenance tubes that ran throughout the ship. It was close in there, and there wasn't enough room for him to straighten up completely, but he wasn't anywhere near as uncomfortable as he had been inside the ductwork. "I used to hate coming into these damn things," said Riker. "Can't stand up straight, got to crawl through on your hands and knees in places—it made me feel closed in. Brother, not anymore. After what I just went through, this feels as roomy as an open field."

La Forge grinned. "Welcome to how the other half lives," he said. "At least we won't have to crawl through any more ducts. We can follow the tubes down to Deck Thirteen and suit up, then exit through the emergency hatch in Shuttle Bay Two."

"How's the rest of your team going to get to the shuttle bay?" Riker asked.

"Same way," said La Forge. "Through the ducts to the nearest vent into the tubes, then on to the shuttle bay from there."

"Well, I sure hope you picked a bunch of skinny guys," said Riker, with a grimace.

"Not much chance for us to get fat down in the

engineering section," La Forge replied. "We spend most of our time working, unlike you goldbricks up on the bridge."

"Sure, we just sit around playing computer games on the main viewer," Riker said, grinning back at him. "Okay, let's get this show on the road."

"Right," said La Forge, leading the way as they moved off down the tube. "You know, Commander, I was wondering. . . . Assuming we get that far, what happens if we *don't* find any phasers aboard the *Independence?*"

"You'd better hope we do," said Riker, "otherwise we'll have to cannibalize whatever we can find to rig up for weapons, and you'll get to show me what a hot engineer you are."

"Yeah, I was afraid you'd say that."

They wound their way through the maze of the maintenance tubes, then climbed through a narrow hatchway and down a steel ladder that led to the lower decks. "You know, it's been so long since I've been down in the guts of this ship that I'm not sure I can find my way around in here," said Riker.

"Well, if you see a large rabbit with a pocket watch, you'll know we took a wrong turn somewhere," said La Forge, with a grin.

"Hold on," Riker said, freezing on the ladder as they descended. "I hear something."

La Forge stopped. They listened for a moment, then heard a muffled clanking sound.

"What's making that noise?" Riker asked softly. "Mice?"

"You don't suppose the Romulans heard us moving through the ducts?"

"I don't think so," La Forge said. "But it's possible."

"Valak knows about the Jefferies tubes," said Riker. "If he's sent a search party in here after us, we've had it."

The sounds were getting closer.

"It's coming from just below us," said La Forge.

"Not much room in here to maneuver," Riker said. "And we don't have any weapons."

"Yeah, this could get interesting."

A moment later a head poked into the tube from an accessway just below them. "Commander Riker?"

Both La Forge and Riker exhaled heavily. It was one of Geordi's engineers. "Lewis!" La Forge said, shaking his head. "You scared the hell out of us."

"Sorry about that, sir," said the bearded crewman. "I heard noise over this way and figured it had to be you."

"You have any trouble getting here?" asked Riker.

"Bit of a tight squeeze through the duct, sir, but except for leaving some skin back there, it was no trouble at all. I'm pretty sure none of the guards heard me. They won't be checking on us till the next watch."

"We'd better get moving, just the same," said Riker.

They continued climbing down the ladder down to Deck 13. By the time they got there, several members of La Forge's engineering crew had joined them. They continued on until they reached the access hatch that led out into the shuttle bay. La Forge put his ear up against it and listened intently for a few moments, then slowly and carefully opened the hatch. "It's all right," he said. "Come on."

They climbed out into the shuttle bay and La Forge took a quick head count. Not counting himself and Riker, there were six of them. "We're missing two," he said. "Rogers and Chan."

"They'll probably be along any minute," Lewis

said. "It's not exactly easy making it through those ducts."

"We can't afford to wait," said Riker. "Let's get suited up. If Rogers and Chan don't arrive in the next few minutes, we'll have to go without them."

They crossed the darkened shuttle bay to the opposite side, where the suit lockers were. As they were getting into the suits, the other two arrived, first Rogers, and then Chan, about two minutes later.

"Sorry I'm late," Chan said, as she came running up to the group. "I had trouble getting the vent grill off in my quarters. Somebody stripped one of the damn screws."

La Forge handed her a suit. "Never mind," he said. "You made it, that's what counts. Let's move it."

She quickly slipped into the suit. Then they all helped one another strap on the EVA packs. La Forge, Rogers, and Lewis also strapped on some tool kits.

"Okay," said Riker, just before he put on his helmet. "Now listen up. I don't want any chatter out there. We maintain strict radio silence. The last thing we need is for the bridge to pick up our suit communicators. So it's hand signals only, got that?"

They all nodded.

"Good. Keep each other in sight. Use the buddy system. Does anyone have any questions?"

"Sir?"

"What is it, Chan?"

"Is there any way we can get out of this lousy detail?"

The others chuckled and Riker grinned. He was glad to see they still had their sense of humor. It helped dissipate the nervousness they were all feeling. Riker knew, because he was feeling it himself. "Okay," he said. "Let's move it. Geordi, don't forget to disable the warning light. We don't want them to see it on the bridge."

"Got it," La Forge said.

They donned their helmets and checked one another's seals, then quickly checked their life support backpacks, giving thumbs-up signs as the systems checked out. Then they trooped over to the emergency hatch. La Forge disabled the circuit that would indicate an open emergency hatch up on the bridge; then he and Lewis opened it and they all crowded into the small chamber on the other side. La Forge closed the hatch behind them, then opened the outer hatch. Riker took a deep breath. Well, he thought, here goes, and he stepped out into space.

As he started to drift away from the ship, he used the small jets on his EVA pack to direct his flight. La Forge floated close beside him. He gave him a thumbs-up signal to indicate that everything was okay. The others followed them in pairs, heading across the gulf of space that separated the *Enterprise* from the *Independence*. They had achieved orbit fairly close to it when they first went on board to investigate, but while the ships were near enough to each other to be within easy transporter range, for EVA, thought Riker, it wasn't exactly close.

He couldn't even remember the last time he had taken a space walk. Damn, he thought, how long had it been? Probably back when he was still a young ensign. There wasn't any call for extravehicular activity in the normal routine of a ship's crew. Hardly anybody did it anymore except shipwrights at construction docks and refitting teams at starbases. We really ought to do more drills on this, Riker thought to himself. In a way, it was like riding a bicycle—once you learned how, you never forgot—but that didn't mean you wouldn't feel a bit shaky at first if enough time had gone by since your last walk. Come to think of it, he hadn't ridden a bicycle in years, either. There were a lot of things he hadn't done in a long time. Things that never seemed important until there was a very real chance of never being able to do them again, ever.

Fortunately the *Enterprise* was between them and the warbird, so they probably would not be seen from the *Syrinx*. And the *Enterprise* was positioned so that the bridge was facing away from them, as they floated in the opposite direction toward the *Independence*. However, there was still a possibility they could be spotted, and at this stage that was the greatest risk. About all they could do was keep their fingers crossed and hope that none of the Romulans felt like gazing out of any of the starboard viewports. However, most of the Romulans aboard the *Enterprise* would probably be sleeping or standing watch in the areas of the ship where they had sequestered the crew.

With any luck, thought Riker, we might get through this. He could hope that the arms lockers of the *Independence* had not been stripped completely bare. Even so, he had never known an ordnance officer who didn't squirrel away a few spare cases of weapons somewhere among the supplies, just as he had never known a chief engineer who didn't always make certain he had at least twice as many spares as he would need. He glanced toward La Forge, then back over his shoulder. The others were all strung out behind them, still keeping roughly abreast of their partners, so they could stay in visual contact with each other. Riker wished he could talk to them, but he didn't dare break radio silence. That would have been a sure way to give themselves away to the Romulans.

They were about halfway to the *Independence* by now. So far, so good, thought Riker. Now if only they could gain access to the ship without trouble. Even if everything went smoothly at this stage, they could still run into a snag while getting back to the *Enterprise*. A little more than half a dozen crewmen with phasers would not stand much chance against a full ship's complement of Romulans. Fortunately, some of the Romulans were aboard the *Syrinx* and others had beamed down to the ark, so the odds had been reduced somewhat, but they were still pretty stiff. There were still enough of them on board the *Enterprise* to quash the rebellion if the Starfleet team didn't move very quickly and take advantage of the element of surprise.

No matter what, thought Riker, they had to get back to the *Enterprise* before the watch changed. If the Romulans discovered any of them missing, there would be a full alert and that would be the end of it. They stood a chance of freeing and arming their fellow crew members only if they could get back and overpower the guards before the Romulans realized what had happened. The whole project was a monstrous long shot. And then there would still be the problem of the *Syrinx* and the hostages aboard it, and the people who were still down inside the ark—the captain, Deanna, Ro, Beverly, and Data.

He pushed the thought from his mind. He could not afford to think about them right now. He had to fix his concentration on one thing at a time. There were so many ways this could go wrong, they could not afford the slightest slipup. They did, however, have one thing in their favor. With Valak down inside the ark, Korak was in command, apparently under the authority of this Romulan lord, Kazanak or whatever his name was. He seemed to be a government bureaucrat of some sort; Riker was reasonably certain he wasn't in the Romulan military. Romulan lords did not command starships; they became colonial governors or served on the Romulan High Council. That meant Korak was the senior military officer in charge. And Korak wasn't half the officer that Valak was. Riker had found that out the hard way.

His body was still sore from the pummeling Korak had given it, and the scrapes and bruises he'd received worming his way through the ductwork hadn't improved things any. That Romulan bastard could hit like a jackhammer. Riker still had a score to settle with Korak, and the Romulan felt exactly the same way. There would be a rematch, no doubt about it. The question was, would it occur on Riker's terms or Korak's?

Riker gave the jets another squirt and brought himself up alongside the *Independence*. La Forge joined him a moment later, and then the others came floating up. They were directly underneath the engine nacelles and were now effectively hidden from view. If the Romulans had seen them on the way over, they would probably find out very soon—one or two well-placed photon torpedoes would solve all their problems permanently.

Slowly they worked their way along the outer hull toward the shuttle bay doors. The emergency hatchways could be opened from the outside during extravehicular work on the hull, while a routine refitting was in progress, but not if they were locked from the inside. Standard operating procedure called for the hatches to remain locked at all other times, so they had come prepared to blow them open.

Using hand signals, he directed La Forge to begin

the operation. Lewis and Rogers moved in to help him begin the work. They used small portable power drivers to open up the access panel, then La Forge rigged a small power pack and switch to the wiring that would blow the explosive bolts. He turned toward Riker and nodded, giving him a thumbs up to indicate that he was ready. Riker took a deep breath, then nodded back and signaled the others to get clear. La Forge had to remain where he was to throw the switch. It would have been far better to use a timer switch for the job, but La Forge had been limited to what he could scrounge together unobtrusively without alerting the Romulans. Under the circumstances, it was the best he could do, but it also meant that he would be at risk when the bolts blew—assuming they *would* blow. Riker backed off with the others, then waved to La Forge. He couldn't see the chief engineer tense up in his suit, but he could easily imagine how he felt. A moment later Geordi threw the switch.

There was, of course, no sound when the bolts blew, but Riker saw them come flying out at great speed. In the blink of an eye it was over, and the outer hatch drifted loose. As the others moved in, Riker reached La Forge first and saw him raise his right hand, holding his thumb and forefinger about two inches apart to show how close one of the bolts had come to hitting him. Riker exhaled heavily. If the bolt had struck Geordi, it would have penetrated the suit, and even if it hadn't hit a vital organ, he would have died when the integrity of his suit was violated.

Moments later, they went through the inner hatchway and safely entered the ship. They still had to wear their suits and maintain radio silence, for the life-support systems on the *Independence* were not functioning and there had been no opportunity for La

Forge to alter the frequencies of their helmet communicators. Time was of the essence.

Now all they had to do was search through the ship's ordnance and hope there were some spare phasers stashed away somewhere, then return to the *Enterprise* with the weapons, get back aboard without being spotted, and free some of their fellow crew members so they could take back control of their own ship without giving the Romulans time to alert their friends aboard the *Syrinx*.

Right, thought Riker grimly. Piece of cake.

Chapter Eleven

THE ROMULANS WAITED TENSELY, uneasily holding their weapons as they took shelter beside the buildings and behind the low walls of the illuminated sculpture gardens in the street. Valak had dispatched them in groups, so they were all in visual contact with one another and capable of laying down fields of fire covering all approaches to their position. Picard waited beside him, along with several other warriors, as they watched the lights spreading out toward them.

What had initially appeared to be several trails of lights moving away from the illuminated area on the opposite side of the ark had now branched out into dozens of light trails coming toward them from all directions. It was like watching dozens of huge torchlight processions from a distance. A distance that was steadily closing.

"There must be literally *hundreds* of them coming toward us," said Picard.

"They will find us waiting for them," Valak replied grimly, although he sounded tense.

"Don't be a fool," Picard said. "You are hopelessly outnumbered."

"A Romulan warrior does not fear great odds," said Valak. "Are you afraid, Picard?"

"I have been afraid for my crew and for my ship ever since this whole thing started," said Picard. "Your arrogance and your inflexibility and your damned Romulan aggression will get all of us killed."

"I am not afraid to die."

"Nor am I, if it is for a good cause," Picard said. "But what cause is being served here? The occupants of this vessel are merely defending themselves against an invader, and that invader is you, Valak. I cannot say I do not sympathize with them."

Valak watched the lights drawing ever closer, moving in from all directions. Although he tried, he could not quite hide his anxiety. He's young, Picard thought, and undeniably a brilliant officer, but he has never truly been put to the test before. The might of the Romulan war machine and his skillful use of it had made his early victories easy. But now, perhaps for the first time in his life, Valak was truly under pressure, caught in a crisis that seemed completely beyond his ability to control.

Over half of the Romulans who had beamed down to the ark had disappeared, and those who remained had lost confidence in Valak. They kept glancing toward him nervously, looking for leadership, but Valak did not know what to do. Faced with what clearly appeared to be overwhelming odds, he had dug in like a cornered animal and prepared to make a stand. He either could not or would not consider any other options.

"Whatever we accomplish or fail to accomplish here no longer makes any difference," Valak said in a fatalistic tone. "When none of the away teams return to the *Syrinx,* Lord Kazanak will realize my mission here has failed and he will obliterate the ark. So either way, we shall probably all die here."

"Then why not attempt to negotiate?" Picard said. "What have you got to lose?"

Valak stared at him curiously. "You know, Picard, I have always sought to understand humans, in particular, the top field commanders of Starfleet, because I believed the best among the humans had the most to teach. I see now I was wrong. There is nothing I can learn from you, and I do not think I shall ever truly understand you. I expected you to resist me to your dying breath, to fight me with every last measure of energy you possessed. I expected you to be a difficult and challenging opponent. On all those counts, you have been a disappointment. I did not think your spirit could be broken so easily."

"You are correct in at least one thing," Picard replied. "For all your scholarship, you have failed to understand us. When pressed to the last extremity, humans will fight, and you will find them formidable opponents. But we have learned that violence and aggression are the least desirable options, and we employ them only when no other choice is left. When you seized my ship, you closed off as many options for resistance as possible, but you never pushed us to the point where we had no choice except to fight or die."

"I was merely determined to take you alive, if possible," said Valak.

"And as long as there is a possibility, however slight, that we can resolve our differences through negotiation without destroying one another, I am determined to pursue it," said Picard.

"Negotiation is the way of cowards," Valak said contemptuously.

"No," said Picard. "It is the way of an enlightened species, Valak. For all your advancement, you Romulans still seek to subjugate and conquer rather than to cooperate and coexist in peace with others. The Federation does not want war with the Romulan Empire; we have not yet exhausted all the options for peace. And you Romulans hesitate to begin an all-out war with the Federation because for all your contempt of us and our so-called weakness, you are wary of our strength. We may never leave this place alive, but as long as we *are* alive, there is a chance that we can resolve this situation without violence. Even if it is only a slight chance, it is worth taking. Violence is easy, Valak. You say you seek the stimulation of a challenge. Then choose the more challenging alternative."

"Unfortunately I do not believe there are any alternatives in this situation," Valak said.

"Then let me try to find one," said Picard. "Let me go out there and see if I can communicate with them."

"Let you try to run away, you mean?" said Valak, misinterpreting the request. "No, Picard, you are my prisoner, and my prisoner you shall remain. If I accomplish nothing else, I shall at least have the satisfaction of having beaten you."

One of Valak's men shouted and fired his disruptor. Immediately the others started firing as well. There was movement out there, but they could not really see what they were shooting at. The Romulans were all keyed up and they poured their fire out into the darkness. It was impossible to tell if they were hitting anything, but Picard heard shouts, in Romulan, and realized they were coming from the figures out there in the darkness. And then it hit him. *In the darkness*.

"Cease firing! Cease firing!" Valak shouted. "You fools, you are shooting at our own people!"

The firing died down as Valak's confused warriors stared out into the slowly dissipating darkness. Picard glanced up and saw that the ark was entering its day cycle.

"Commander Valak?" a voice shouted at them.

"Talar?" As Valak lowered his weapon, Picard suddenly lunged toward him. He seized Valak's disruptor just below its emitting cone and quickly wrenched it out of his grasp. He had moved so quickly that before the startled Romulan even had a chance to react, Picard was behind him, twisting his arm up behind his back.

Valak cried out with surprise and pain, and the other warriors turned toward him, their eyes widening with shock when they saw Picard with their commander at his mercy.

"Tell them to drop their weapons," said Picard, twisting his arm up behind him and reaching around his neck with his other hand to press the emitting cone of the disruptor up beneath Valak's chin.

"Never!" Valak said. *"Shoot!"* he called out to his warriors.

"If you shoot, then your commander will die with me!" Picard called out.

They hesitated.

"Shoot!" Valak shouted at them, as Picard started to back away with him. "Shoot, I command it! Shoot us both!"

Valak struggled against Picard's grasp, but Picard

twisted his arm up even higher, causing what had to be excruciating pain.

"Hold your fire!" Talar called out.

Valak continued to struggle, forcing Picard to apply more pressure. There was a loud crack and the Romulan gasped with pain as his arm snapped. He ceased to struggle momentarily, allowing Picard to quickly shift his grip, encircling Valak's throat with his arm while keeping the other warriors covered with the disruptor.

"I have no time to deal with your heroics," Picard said as he applied pressure with his forearm against Valak's throat, choking him. "Stay where you are!" he shouted as the warriors started to move toward him.

Picard continued to back away slowly as Valak's struggles diminished. Then the Romulan's body sagged as he lost consciousness. Picard waited a moment, continuing to apply pressure to make sure Valak wasn't faking. Then he quickly bent down and swung the Romulan up onto his shoulder fireman-style. He continued to back away slowly, covering the others with Valak's weapon.

The Romulans slowly moved forward and spread out, knowing he couldn't cover all of them. Then, one by one, they collapsed to their knees, dropping their weapons and grabbing their heads before they fell to the ground and remained motionless. Only Talar remained standing, gazing at Picard steadily as all of the missing Romulans came up behind him.

Picard felt Valak's deadweight across his shoulders and realized that he could not run while carrying the heavy Romulan. He would never be able to outdistance them. He felt absolutely helpless. There was nothing he could do.

And suddenly he realized that he was living out his dream.

The heavy weight on his shoulders, being separated from his crew and powerless to help them, fighting the instinctive urge to run . . . this was the dream. He felt his stomach muscles knotting up and decided that whatever happened next, he would face it *his* way, the way in which he had been trained, the way he had always believed in. He put the disruptor down, then eased Valak off his shoulders and stood up straight.

"I come in peace," he said, holding his arms out from his sides to show that his hands were empty.

And as he watched, Talar and the others began to change.

"I am sick and tired of your ceaseless whining and complaining!" Worf shouted, angrily.

"And I'm sick and tired of *you!*" Arthur shouted back. "Ever since they brought us here, you've done nothing but give orders! You're not the captain! Who the hell do you think you are, anyway?"

"I am the senior officer!" Worf shouted. "It is my duty to take charge in the absence of Captain Picard and Commander Riker!"

"Well, I don't remember anyone putting you in charge!" Arthur replied angrily.

"You are being insubordinate, crewman!"

"And your stupid plan to escape is going to get us all killed!"

"Be silent, fool!"

By now they had the attention of the guards, who had started moving in toward them, their weapons held before them. At the back of the crowd that had gathered around Worf and Arthur, Tyler waited, watching the Romulan guards intently. The people around him moved in toward the argument, extending themselves diagonally in a way that effectively screened Tyler from the guards' view. He started inching toward the back of the shuttle bay.

"I will *not* be silent!" Arthur shouted. "I have no wish to die simply because you want to be a damned hero! If you want a pointless warrior's death in battle merely to satisfy your stupid Klingon pride, then that's your business, but there are children here, and I will not allow you to endanger their lives!"

"*You* will not allow it?"

"That's right! I've had it up to here with your damned Klingon arrogance!"

"Shut your mouth, crewman, or I will shut it for you!"

"Take your best shot, you Klingon freak! I've had about all I'm going to take from you!"

Worf snarled and swung at Arthur, connecting with his jaw. Arthur went down, but he was up in an instant, charging the Klingon in a headlong rush. He ran at him full tilt and hit him in a football tackle, carrying him backwards to the deck. The others surged around them, shouting and calling out encouragement.

"Get him, Worf!"

"Take him, Arthur! Hit him!"

"Kill the bastard!"

"Give it to him!"

The guards ran toward the prisoners, clubbing them with their weapons and trying to push their way through the crowd to reach the two antagonists. Tyler sprinted to the bulkhead and ran toward the shuttles at full speed, not even daring to glance back and see if any of the guards had spotted him. He expected them to fire some warning shots or, worse yet, fire into the crowd—a risk they all knowingly faced—but instead, the overconfident guards actually waded into the crowd of prisoners—an unexpected bonus that changed everything. The maintenance panel for the outer bay doors would have to wait for now. Two of the guards had remained behind, by the entrance to the shuttle bay, but their attention, at least for the moment, was on the conflict. If even one of them happened to glance in his direction, Tyler knew he'd be spotted in an instant and it would all be over. Right now, speed was everything.

He had taken off his boots and socks, and he ran barefoot so as not to make any noise, although his footsteps would have been drowned out by all the shouting anyway. He sprinted like a track star, pumping with his elbows, and managed to reach the shuttles parked at the far end of the bay without being seen. He plunged through the open hatchway of the nearest shuttlecraft and jumped into the pilot's seat. Whatever you do, he thought, don't give me a hard time starting, *please.* He hit the button for the engines and as they whined to life, he risked a glance out the front viewport.

The two Romulan guards who had remained near the doors looked toward him with astonishment and he saw them shout out to the others, but a full-scale melee had broken out at the far end of the shuttle bay. The other guards suddenly found themselves being attacked by the prisoners and borne down by the sheer weight of their numbers.

"Come on! Come on!" said Tyler, gritting his teeth.

The shuttlecraft rose off the deck as the two guards raised their weapons, and Tyler slammed the stick forward. The Romulans fired. One of them rushed his shot and it missed, but the second guard's shot struck the shuttlecraft. Tyler felt it rock as it moved forward, picking up speed as it accelerated toward the two guards. They started backpedaling toward the doors, but before they could fire again, Tyler banked the shuttlecraft sharply, trapping them between its hull and the wall of the shuttle bay. He felt the impact as he struck the wall, crushing the two guards against the bulkhead. Then he shoved the stick forward once again and the shuttle flew ahead, just above the floor, until he brought it even with the entrance to the shuttle bay and landed it, wedging it firmly against the doors.

He then jumped out and raced over to where the two guards had fallen, knocked out by the impact of the shuttle. He grabbed their disruptors and ran back toward the others. With the crowd surging all around them, the Romulans had no opportunity to fire their weapons. All they could do was lash out, using them as clubs. A number of the hostages had fallen, bleeding from their wounds, but a number of the guards had fallen as well.

Three guards managed to break free of the crowd and raised their weapons to fire. Tyler fired the two disruptors, one in either hand, and dropped the Romulans.

Worf had already killed three guards with his bare hands, and as he tore another one off Arthur, he felt a jarring impact on his neck and shoulder and sank to his knees. As the Romulan behind him raised his disruptor to finish him off, a fierce, high-pitched scream cut through the other noise as Alexander landed on the Romulan's back. The guard struggled to throw him off. Worf got to his feet and smashed a hard right into the guard's chest, crushing his rib cage. The Romulan went down. Worf looked at his son and nodded proudly, then swept up the guard's weapon and waded back into the fray.

It was over quickly, and all of the guards were dead. They had grown overconfident from watching over prisoners who had been docile up to this point. They had never expected all of them, even the women and children, to turn on them. As Picard had told Valak, when pushed to the last extremity, humans would fight, and when they did, they were formidable foes.

Worf quickly took charge, ordering some of the crewmen to see to the wounded while Tyler and Arthur disabled the bridge controls for the outer bay doors. Then Worf started herding all the others toward the shuttles and assigning some of the men to help carry the wounded. Tyler had said the guards by the door did not have time to raise an alarm, but he knew that the Romulans could discover their escape attempt at any moment. They would discover it for certain the moment the computer registered the malfunction as the bridge controls for the outer bay doors were disabled.

"Quickly, quickly!" he urged the others. "Get aboard the shuttles! There is no time to waste!"

"Sir," one of the medical corpsmen said, "we've got at least three dead and six critically injured."

"We must take them all with us," Worf said. "Hurry! Get them aboard the shuttles."

"There's too many of us, sir," said one of the other crewmen. "With that other shuttle blocking the entrance doors, we've only got three shuttles left. They'll be dangerously overcrowded."

"We have no other choice," said Worf. "We cannot leave the wounded and the dead behind. Their sacrifice was not made in vain. They *will* get off this ship!"

"Understood, sir."

As the hostages boarded the shuttles, Tyler and Arthur worked feverishly at the maintenance panel. "Come on, Tyler, for God's sake!" said Arthur. "Can't you hurry it up? If they open the outer doors before we're ready, we've all had it."

"I'm doing the best I can," said Tyler. "This isn't the *Enterprise,* you know. I've got to figure out how these damn circuits are wired and I can't exactly run a diagnostic. Now shut the hell up and let me think!"

Worf came up to check on their progress. "The shuttlecraft are almost filled," he said. "We do not have much time. Perhaps you should simply concentrate on opening the outer doors."

"No," said Tyler, "the bridge controls have to be disabled before we can open up the outer doors ourselves, otherwise they're liable to override us from the bridge before the shuttles can get out."

Worf nodded. "Very well. Do the best you can."

"There! I think that does it," Tyler said. "I hope."

"We'll find out soon enough," Arthur said tensely.

"Okay, is everyone aboard?" asked Tyler.

"Go on, sir," Arthur said to Worf.

"Good luck," said Worf, running back toward the shuttle.

"You go with him," Tyler said to Arthur.

"But what if—"

"Go! Just get that shuttle over here fast, so that when I open up the outer doors, I can get inside in one hell of a hurry."

"All right," said Arthur. "I hope you know what you're doing."

"So do I. Now *get!"*

Tyler waited until everyone was aboard and the shuttlecraft had started their engines. Two of the shuttles had their hatches closed, ready to move out.

The other one still had its hatch open, with Worf standing in the opening, watching. As all three shuttlecraft lifted off, it was obvious that they were overloaded. They rocked slightly as they rose unsteadily several feet above the deck. The shuttle with the open hatch moved closer to Tyler. *"Now,* Tyler!" shouted Worf.

"Well . . . here goes nothing," Tyler said, as he made the connection. There was the heavy sound of machinery engaging, and the outer bay doors began to open.

At almost the same time, two things happened. The alarm siren went off throughout the ship as the bridge controls registered the malfunction, and the air in the shuttle bay started to rush out into the vacuum of space. Tyler leapt for the shuttle as soon as he heard the machinery gears engage, but the suction of the air rushing out the shuttle bay caught him almost at once. For an instant he actually hovered in midair, the forward momentum of his leap halted by the suction, and Worf reached out and grabbed his wrist just before he was sucked out. Holding on to the shuttle for all he was worth with one hand, while clutching Tyler with the other, Worf strained against the pull as the air inside the shuttle bay whooshed out into space.

"You've got to close the hatch!" Tyler shouted. *"Let me go!"*

Worf grimaced as he struggled to pull Tyler in. *"We all . . . go . . . together!"* he shouted over the noise of the air rushing out. Then Arthur was behind Worf, being held by a chain of his fellow crew members as he leaned out and grabbed Tyler's arm just above where Worf was holding on to his wrist. Together they managed to haul him in.

"The hatch!" Worf said. "Quickly!"

It was already closing, and the other shuttles began moving out through the doors, as soon as the gap grew wide enough. Moments later all three shuttlecraft had left the ship and were moving toward the *Enterprise*. Tyler and Worf both lay breathless on the floor of the shuttle, surrounded by their crewmates as the life-support system in the small vessel pumped in air to breathe. Tyler looked up at Worf and sighed with relief. "Thanks," he said. "I owe you one."

"You may buy me a drink when we get back aboard the *Enterprise*," said Worf.

Tyler smiled. "Deal," he said.

Riker and Geordi had to break into the arms lockers in the ordnance section of the *Independence*, but their efforts yielded them an unexpected bonus. They found two unopened crates of early Type I phasers and a crate of carefully packed and sealed sarium krellide power cells. It was all Geordi La Forge could do not to whoop with joy when he opened up that crate and found all the seals still intact. Properly sealed and stored, sarium krellide power cells held their charge indefinitely, and even after thirty years, the intact seals meant that the cells had not decayed.

We're in business, Riker thought, as he gave La Forge a thumbs-up. Now we've got at least a fighting chance. As the others broke open the seals and started to load the cells into the phasers, Riker said a silent prayer of thanks to the supply officer of the *Independence*. And he resolved never again to give his own supply officer a hard time about redundant requisitions. This one had probably saved their lives.

Riker helped them unpack the phasers, break the seals on the power cells, which came a half dozen to the pack, load them into the phasers, and then place the charged phasers back in the crates. They each took one phaser for themselves and placed them safely in the outer pockets of their suits. Then, carrying the crates of phasers, they started to make their way back to the *Enterprise*.

Riker knew they were still a long way from being home free. They still had to get back aboard the *Enterprise* without being discovered, distribute the weapons to their fellow crew members, then seize control of their ship before Korak could alert the *Syrinx* and thus endanger the hostages. And as if that wasn't enough to worry about, Riker still didn't know what had happened to the captain, Deanna, Ro, Beverly, and Data. He had no idea whether they were alive or dead.

As they left the *Independence* and began the space walk back to the *Enterprise* with their precious cargo of weapons, Riker wondered if the others felt as tense as he did. Just let us get back aboard the ship, he thought. How much time had elapsed since they had left? It seemed like hours. Could it possibly have been that long? What if their absence had been discovered? What would the Romulans do? They'd probably search the ship first, he thought. They'd realize how they got out and they'd go through the Jefferies tubes, looking for them. That would buy some time . . . unless Korak figured out that they'd left the ship.

As they drifted back across the space separating the two ships, Riker tried to assess the odds. So far, luck had been with them, but the hardest part still lay ahead of them. He was worried about the captain and the missing away team, but he was also concerned about the hostages. If Valak was in charge, he would keep them alive to use as his hole card, but with Korak commanding in Valak's absence, there was no telling what might happen. Korak had it in for Riker. He might even execute the hostages just to hit Riker where it would hurt the most. In fact, thought Riker, that was exactly what Korak would do. The question was, how could he prevent it?

The captain always spoke about options. Well, in this case, there just didn't seem to be any. Riker tried to steel himself for the possibility of the hostages being killed. My friends, he thought, and all those children. His stomach was tied up in knots. But they were committed to their plan to seize the starship. No matter what happened, they had to carry it through.

As they approached the *Enterprise,* Riker felt the tension mounting. Only another hundred yards to go. They came in low, under the belly of the ship, to minimize the chances of being spotted. Riker could now see the huge bulk of the *Syrinx* just beyond the *Enterprise,* and—he caught his breath—shuttles! Three of them coming over from the *Syrinx!* La Forge saw them at the same time, looked toward him, and pointed.

We've had it, Riker thought, with a sinking feeling. Somehow they must have been spotted from the *Syrinx,* but he didn't see how they could possibly have seen them from that angle . . . and then he realized that the shuttles were from their own ship. And even as they approached, he could see the *Syrinx* slowly turning toward them to bring its weapons to bear.

The hostages! It couldn't possibly be anybody else! Somehow they had managed to escape. But the shuttles had to be badly overloaded. They'd be crammed in there like sardines. Riker realized that his team would reach the *Enterprise* before the shuttles did. They had to get the outer bay doors open for them. Had the shuttles seen them? It was pointless to maintain radio silence now. As he reached the emergency hatch together with La Forge, he turned and beckoned the others over to the side of the ship.

"Riker to shuttlecraft, Riker to shuttlecraft!" he said, over his suit communicator. "Come in!"

"We have seen you, Commander," Worf's voice replied, and Riker's heart gave a leap.

"Come around to Shuttle Bay Two," said Riker. "We'll open the doors for you. Move it! The *Syrinx* is coming around."

"Acknowledged," said Worf.

"Geordi, the rest of you, move back away from the hatch. I'm going to open the inner emergency hatch."

"But with the outer hatch still open, that will depressurize the bay!" said La Forge.

"Exactly," Riker said.

"Right!" said La Forge, comprehending instantly.

During normal shuttle bay operations, the annular forcefield maintained atmospheric integrity in the bay, allowing shuttlecraft to pass in and out of the open outer doors without depressurizing the bay. As they moved through the forcefield, as if through a membrane, some of the air inside would escape, but not enough to make any significant difference. However, there was no forcefield in the emergency hatchway, for which reason there was an outer and an inner door, with a decompression chamber between them. If Riker opened up the inner door without first closing the outer hatch, the air inside the shuttle bay would come rushing out into the vacuum. That meant the Romulans would be unable to enter the shuttle bay until it had been repressurized. And that would give the shuttles time to enter safely.

Riker grabbed the wheel and unlocked the inner door. Then, hooking his arm through the wheel, he yanked back on the lever that controlled the latch. The hatch slammed open and Riker barely got his feet up in time to keep from getting smashed against the wall as the atmosphere inside came rushing out with explosive force. He held on with all his might to keep from getting sucked out. The others were all safely out of the way. Moments later the pressure let up and Riker and the others were able to enter the shuttle bay, though they had to keep their suits on.

The *Syrinx* wouldn't dare fire now, with the shuttles so close to the ship, thought Riker. They wouldn't sacrifice their own people aboard the *Enterprise.* Or would they? No, thought Riker, as he rushed to the controls for the outer doors of the shuttle bay, they'll assume that we'll be recaptured the moment we get back on board. But we may have a few surprises for them.

While the others were entering through the emergency hatchway and closing it up behind them, he threw the switch to open the outer bay doors. The machinery engaged, and the outer doors began to open. Then they stopped, and slowly started to close again. Riker swore.

"The bridge controls! Geordi—"

"I'm way ahead of you, Commander," La Forge replied, as he threw open the maintenance panel. The doors continued to close as the bridge overrode Riker's controls, but as La Forge disabled the system, they stopped. Through the gap, Riker could see the shuttles approaching.

"Riker to Worf: we've disabled the bridge controls, and we'll be opening the outer bay doors from in here. But the shuttle bay is depressurized. Repeat: the shuttle bay is depressurized. Remain inside the shuttlecraft until I give the signal."

"Understood, Commander," Worf replied.

It didn't matter if the Romulans heard them now. In fact, it would keep them out of the shuttle bay. They would not be able to enter without suits until it was repressurized, and by then, with any luck, thought Riker, we'll be ready for them.

The outer bay doors started to open once again and Worf brought the first shuttlecraft in before they were open all the way. Riker stood at the flight deck officer's station, controlling the short-range tractor beams designed to help bring the shuttles in and out smoothly. With the shuttlecraft as overloaded as they were, Worf and the other pilot were going to need all the help they could get.

Worf's shuttle touched down inside the bay, and then the other two came in close behind it. Riker locked on to them and helped the pilots bring them in. The others, meanwhile, were busy unpacking the phasers and preparing to hand them out the moment it was safe for the passengers to leave the shuttles. As the third shuttlecraft touched down, the outer bay doors began to close and Riker watched the indicators on the console, waiting tensely for atmospheric integrity to be fully restored inside the shuttle bay. The seconds seemed like minutes as he waited, and the minutes seemed like hours. And then Korak's voice came booming over the loudspeaker.

"An admirable attempt, Riker," he said, "but you have only succeeded in trapping yourself anew. None of you will leave the shuttle bay alive."

Chapter Twelve

As VALAK CAME AROUND, his eyelids flickered open and he saw Picard standing over him. The disruptor Picard held was aimed squarely at his chest. Valak started to sit up and winced. "Curse you, Picard," he said. "My arm is broken."

"You gave me little choice," Picard replied.

Valak glanced around at their surroundings. Morning had come to the ark, and he saw that they were in a different area. They were in a park, on a wooded rise overlooking a garden with a fountain in the center and curving, paved paths radiating out from it, cutting through a blue-green carpet of low-growing, mossy vegetation interspersed with clumps of shrubbery and spidery trees. More of the sculptures they had seen— the streetlights, as Picard had called them—were placed throughout the park, and the only thing lacking to complete the bucolic scene was the sound of birds twittering in the tree branches. Except for the two of them, there was no sign of life anywhere.

"So you managed to get away somehow," Valak said with a grimace. "It will gain you nothing. You may have the advantage over me for the moment, but my warriors will hunt you down."

"I think not," Picard replied. "Encumbered as I was with your weight across my shoulders, they should have had no difficulty giving pursuit. Yet they did not follow. Perhaps they were unable to give chase."

Valak grunted as he propped himself up against the tree behind him. "What do you mean?"

Picard countered with another question. "Did it not strike you as a coincidence that Talar and the others should suddenly reappear precisely at that moment?"

Valak frowned. "What are you getting at, Picard?"

"Once darkness fell, everywhere we have gone inside this ark, the lights have followed us, illuminating the areas we passed through. However, Talar and his warriors came *out of the darkness*. Their approach failed to activate the lights. Why? The obvious explanation is that the streetlights are not controlled by sensors, after all. We have been under close surveillance ever since our arrival. Our way was merely lighted for us."

"Then all those lights we saw . . ." said Valak. "Of course. They were a ruse meant to play upon our nerves and make us anticipate an attack so that we would fire on Talar and the others when they approached out of the darkness. It was all a trick."

"That is one possible explanation," said Picard, "but it does not explain how your people have been disappearing, nor does it explain why Talar and the others should suddenly reappear the way they did. Nor does it explain how a message was transmitted to your ship, mimicking your voice well enough to fool your bridge crew and have an additional away team beamed down, perhaps more than one. If they were able to do that, they could just as easily have sent *another* message, in your voice, requesting that a team be beamed *back up*."

"Then my men would have taken them the moment they materialized in the transporter room," said Valak.

"Would they? What if the occupants of this ark are able to mimic more than just a voice communication? Consider the *Independence*, Valak. What happened to its crew? The ark's residents might have induced a few landing parties to beam down through some similar subterfuge, but surely not the entire crew. At some point, they would have realized something was wrong."

"What if the crew had been thoroughly infiltrated before they realized what was happening?" said a *second* Picard, stepping out from behind a tree. Valak's eyes grew wide and his jaw dropped as his gaze went from one Picard to the other. They were absolutely identical.

"Fascinating, is it not?" the first Picard said. "Which of us is the real Jean-Luc Picard?"

"Perhaps neither of us is the real Picard," the second one said.

There were the sounds of running footsteps, and Talar and the others came racing up the hill, weapons drawn. They stopped when they saw the two Picards.

"Shoot, Talar!" yelled Valak. "Shoot both of them!"

Talar lowered his weapon. "I fear you have mistaken me for someone else, Commander," he said.

Valak stared at him wildly, his mouth open with disbelief. The science officer spoke into his communicator, only the voice he used was not Talar's but Valak's own. "Valak to *Syrinx,*" he said.

"Go ahead, Commander," came the response.

Valak tried to shout out a warning, but a sudden white-hot pain lanced through his brain and he collapsed, gasping for breath. Sparks danced before his eyes and he tried to scream, but could not utter a sound.

"We are ready to beam up."

Riker watched the gauges on the console, and the moment atmospheric integrity was restored to the shuttle bay, he removed his helmet and gave the signal for Worf and the other hostages to leave the shuttlecraft. As they came out, Geordi and the others started passing out phasers.

"I don't know how you managed to escape," said Riker, "but I sure am glad to see you. Your timing couldn't have been more perfect."

"Happy to oblige, Commander," Worf replied.

Riker grinned. "We're not going to have much time. As soon as they realize the shuttle bay's repressurized, they'll come in here after us."

"Then we shall give them a warm reception," said Worf.

"We'll use the shuttles for cover," Riker said, "and try to get them as they're coming in. Keiko!"

"Yes, sir?"

"Take some of the others and get the children into the Jefferies tubes. Stay in there until you hear from me."

"Understood," said Keiko. She and the other mothers started herding the children into the narrow maintenance tube hatchway.

"Geordi," Riker said, "take your crew and work your way up through the tubes to Ten-Forward. Take some extra phasers with you. And good luck. Now move it!"

"I'm on my way," La Forge said.

Riker made sure that all the children were safe inside the maintenance tubes, then joined Worf over by the shuttles, where the others had taken up position with their phasers. "They already know we've disabled the bridge controls for the outer doors," he said. "Their next step will probably be to try cutting off the life support in here, but Geordi's already bypassed the individual cutoff switches. They won't be able to close down the system in here without shutting it down throughout the entire ship. As soon as they figure that out, they'll come in here after us."

"Unless they attempt to come in through the tubes," said Worf.

Riker shook his head. "They'd have to come through one at a time, and we could simply pick them off as they came out. No, that isn't Korak's style. He'll come in with a strong frontal assault. He's got a score to settle with me, and he's not about to let anyone else settle it for him."

Worf glanced at Riker questioningly. "A score?"

"We started something we didn't get a chance to finish," Riker said. "He'll want a crack at me himself, and I'm just dying to give it to him."

The doors leading into the shuttle bay slid open.

"Here they come," said Tyler, holding his phaser ready.

A squad of Romulans rushed into the shuttle bay,

firing their disruptors. A score of phaser beams lanced out to meet them. A number of them were struck, and the rest fell back, but one of the shuttles was struck in the hull right over its tanks and the fuel exploded. There were screams as a number of *Enterprise* crewmen were blown backwards while others scrambled for cover. The Romulans retreated as the fire triggered the automatic control system in the shuttle bay and jets of mist shot down from the ceiling, filling the shuttle bay with chemical fog.

"Korak!" shouted Riker. "Can you hear me, Korak? You wanted a rematch? Come on! Let's finish it! Just you and me!"

"Do you take me for a fool, Riker?" Korak shouted over the roar of the fire-control system. "Do you expect me to come in there alone so you can shoot me down?"

"I'll put down my phaser and meet you in the center of the bay!" shouted Riker. "That way my people can't fire without the risk of hitting me, and your people can't fire without the risk of hitting you! We'll finish our business first. Or are you afraid to have your warriors see you lose?"

"Come out where I can see you!" Korak shouted back. "You have my word of honor as a Romulan warrior that you will not be fired upon!"

Riker started to move forward, but Worf grabbed his arm. "You would trust the word of a Romulan?" he said.

"I never thought I'd hear myself saying this," said Riker, "but in this case, yes."

Worf shook his head. "This is not wise."

"It will give Geordi and the others time to reach our people in Ten-Forward," Riker said. "Besides, this is personal."

Worf scowled, then nodded and let go of Riker's arm. Riker stepped out from behind the shuttle and moved toward the center of the bay. Through the fog from the fire-control jets, he saw a figure coming toward him—Korak.

They stopped about fifteen feet apart. Keeping his eyes on Korak, Riker slowly held up his phaser, then laid it down on the deck and stepped away from it. Korak did the same with his disruptor.

"I have waited for this moment," Korak said. "This time, Riker, you die."

"This time there won't be any interruptions to save you," said Riker.

With a snarl Korak moved in to attack.

The transporter chief aboard the *Syrinx* was unprepared for the sight of two Jean-Luc Picards appearing on the pads, supporting Valak between them and surrounded by the rest of the Romulan away team. In his moment of shock and hesitation, he lost any chance he might have had to act. As he reached for his sidearm a searing pain exploded in his brain. He grabbed his head and dropped to his knees in agony, gasping for breath. An instant later he was stretched out on the deck, unconscious.

"Quickly," said Picard, "we have no time to lose."

"I have already communicated our arrival to the others," his doppelgänger replied, in a voice indistinguishable from his. "I perceive your concern for the safety of your ship. Rest assured, the *Syrinx* will present no threat to the *Enterprise.*"

Valak was conscious but helpless. The Romulan commander was pale and he trembled slightly. His mouth worked, but no sound came forth. He struggled against the control being imposed upon him, but could not resist it.

Picard's double approached the transporter controls. Two of the Romulan doppelgängers stepped down off the pads, while the others, with Valak, remained where they were. Picard glanced at his double questioningly as he started entering commands into the controls.

A voice spoke in his mind, replying to his question before he could even speak it: *"I have obtained the necessary knowledge from the transporter operator's mind to beam the others to the* Enterprise *from here. We will join them as soon as this vessel is secured."*

Picard merely nodded, watching as his double activated the transporter. The thought had been communicated with such confidence that he had no doubt in his mind that they could do it. It was more than a little frightening.

"There is no cause to be frightened," said the voice in his mind. *"We mean you no harm."*

"I believe that," said Picard. He took a deep breath and exhaled heavily. "However, the thought that you feel you can secure my ship so easily is rather unnerving."

"I understand. The humans from the Independence *felt much the same at first. But they have come to accept us, as we have come to accept them."*

"Then they are still alive?" Picard said with astonishment.

"Regrettably, they did not all survive."

"I see. After thirty years I suppose that is to be expected," said Picard.

"I regret that those who died did not expire of natural causes."

"What happened to them?" asked Picard.

"We killed them."

As his double stepped away from the transporter controls, his features seemed to melt, and an instant later Picard was looking at a facsimile of Commander Valak, right down to his uniform. It was the second time he had witnessed such a transformation, the first being when he saw one of them turn into an exact double of himself, but it still took him aback.

"Come."

They went out into the corridor and headed for the turbolift. Along their way, they passed the prostrate forms of several dozen crew members of the *Syrinx,* simply lying on the deck where they had fallen.

"Are they dead?" Picard asked uneasily.

"No. Merely inactive."

The turbolift took them to the bridge of the warbird. As the doors opened and they stepped out, Lord Kazanak turned toward them, panic in his eyes. "Valak! Thank the gods you have returned! The human hostages have escaped, and there is something wrong aboard this ship! None of the sections are responding, and I am unable to raise our people on the *Enterprise!*" He saw Picard, and his features contorted. *"You!* You are responsible for this!"

"Much as I would like to claim that honor," said Picard, "I fear that I cannot. I assume I have the honor of addressing Lord Kazanak, the designer of this ship?" Picard stood before the Romulan, smiling, then sat down in the command throne. "Allow me to compliment you. This vessel is a truly brilliant piece of design."

Kazanak stared at Picard with astonishment, then turned back toward Valak's double. "What is the meaning of this, Valak? I demand an explanation!"

"Commander Valak is, at this very moment, our

prisoner aboard the *Enterprise,"* came the reply, spoken in Romulan. "The *Syrinx* is no longer under your command."

"Have you lost your senses, Valak? What are you talking about?"

"You are not addressing Commander Valak, Lord Kazanak," said Picard. "Appearances can be deceiving, as I learned the hard way when I first came aboard your vessel. Look around you. Do you see any familiar faces?"

Kazanak looked from "Valak" to Picard and back again. Then the navigation officer turned around in his chair, and Kazanak found himself looking at his own face. His eyes bulged, and he gasped when he saw that the weapons and tactics officer standing behind his console had also turned into a double of himself. As he gazed wildly around the bridge, everywhere he looked, he saw his own face staring back at him.

"No!" he said. "No, this cannot *be!* It is not *possible!* It is a trick! How . . ." He sagged against one of the consoles, his voice trailing off as his senses reeled in the face of the unacceptable reality confronting him.

"Your mission has ended, Lord Kazanak," said Picard. "You have found what you were seeking. You have discovered the secret of Hermeticus Two."

La Forge stopped and held up in his hand. The others came to a halt behind him, crowding in as close as the narrow confines of the maintenance tube would permit. They had reached the hatchway that opened out into the corridor leading to Ten-Forward, where the Romulans were holding more of their fellow crew members.

"All right," La Forge said softly. "There will be guards out in the corridor and probably inside Ten-

Forward as well. We're going to take out the guards by the doors first, and we'll have to do it fast, before they can alert the ones inside. The second we step out of the hatch, they're bound to see us, so we've got to come out fast and come out shooting. Got it?"

The others nodded.

La Forge took a deep breath. "Okay. Phasers ready? Here goes."

He threw open the hatch and dived out into the corridor. He rolled and came up with his phaser, but just as he was about to fire, he froze. "What the hell . . . ?"

Lewis and the others had quickly followed him through the hatchway, but none of them had fired, either. There was nothing to shoot at. The Romulan guards were lying on the deck, motionless. Slowly, Geordi got up and exchanged puzzled glances with the others. They followed him as he cautiously approached the fallen guards.

"Cover me," he said softly as he knelt to check them.

"Arc they dead?" asked Lewis.

La Forge shook his head. "No. Just unconscious."

"What the hell happened?"

"I don't know." La Forge bit his lower lip nervously. "All right. We're going in. Watch yourselves."

The door to Ten-Forward slid open, and La Forge and the others came in fast, phasers held ready, but the Romulan guards inside were all unconscious on the floor, and their fellow crew members appeared to be unharmed.

"What in the name of . . . ?" La Forge's voice trailed off.

"There is no need for concern, Geordi," a familiar voice said. "Everything is under control."

"Deanna?" he said. He stared as Troi came toward him, smiling. Ro and Data were there, too, as were two strangers dressed in long black robes. He frowned, still holding his weapon uncertainly. "Who are they?"

Deanna turned and beckoned them forward. "Geordi, allow me to introduce Commander Morgan Llewellyn and Dr. Giorgi Vishinski, of the starship *Independence.*"

The flames from the burning shuttlecraft had been extinguished, but the mist from the fire-control system still hovered like a low fog over the deck of the shuttle bay, mingling with the smoke. Riker stood slightly bent over, breathing hard, blood streaming from his broken nose and one eye puffed almost completely shut. His entire upper body was battered and bruised from Korak's powerful blows, and it hurt when he breathed.

The Romulan wasn't in much better shape. He limped as he circled Riker warily, and his left wrist hung at a strange angle, broken where Riker had snapped it. Blood covered his mouth, bubbling as he breathed heavily, but Korak was not about to quit. He refused to allow himself to be bested by this human while his own people watched, and he wore a look of homicidal fury as he moved around unsteadily, watching for an opening.

The two combatants were almost evenly matched. Korak had the advantage in strength, and though Riker was quicker, the Romulan had easily been able to absorb most of his blows. Korak's blows, when they got through, had done more damage, and Riker was able to continue only by sheer force of will.

What saved Riker was his skill at aikido, which

enabled him to turn Korak's own considerable strength against him. The Romulan seemed baffled by the unfamiliar martial art, and though he had managed to land some damaging blows, Riker had tossed him around with motions that seemed deceptively simple and effortless, all the while taunting him and egging him on, knowing that Korak's greatest weakness was his temper. The Romulan was simply unable to accept that a human could be a match for him, and his frustration and fury at not being able to finish Riker off kept mounting until he was almost blind with rage.

The spectators on both sides watched silently and tensely. No one yelled encouragement. They all knew the battle was in deadly earnest, and they watched with rapt fascination as the two combatants fought, neither able to gain the upper hand. Even with his wrist broken, Korak kept on coming, pounding away with his one good arm and smashing at Riker with his left elbow and forearm. He seemed almost impervious to pain, but he was moving much more slowly now, hampered by his limp. Riker had snapped a kick into his leg that would have shattered a human kneecap, but amazingly, the Romulan was still on his feet.

"What's the matter, Korak?" Riker said, swallowing hard and breathing heavily as he fought exhaustion. "Getting tired?"

With a snarl of rage, Korak came at him again, and Riker caught hold of his right wrist, then sidestepped and made a tight circle, using Korak's own momentum to flip him over. He held on as Korak fell and was rewarded by the sharp sound of Korak's right wrist snapping. The Romulan cried out and landed hard. He tried to get back up, but collapsed when neither wrist would support him. He remained on his knees, arms crossed in front of his chest, unable to continue. He screamed with impotent rage.

"Shoot!" he shouted to his warriors, no longer caring if he was caught in their fire. "Kill him!"

Worf and the others quickly raised their weapons, but there was no response from the Romulans. The *Enterprise* crew could hardly see through the undulating mist and smoke.

"Shoot, curse your souls!" Korak screamed again. *"Kill him!"*

"There will be no more killing, Korak," said Picard, coming out of the swirling mist where the Romulans had stood.

"Captain!" said Riker, gazing at him with astonishment as Worf and the others came toward them, equally amazed to see him.

"I am all right, Number One," Picard said. "And so are all the others. The *Syrinx* has been neutralized, and the *Enterprise* is ours once more."

"But . . . how . . . ?"

"That, Number One, is going to take a good deal of explaining. And I do not yet possess all the answers. However, the first thing we need to do is get you to sickbay and let Dr. Crusher have a look at you." He glanced down at Korak, still on his knees and staring at him uncomprehendingly. "And him as well. Mr. Worf, assist Subcommander Korak to sickbay."

"With pleasure, sir." Worf glanced at Riker and nodded. "Well fought, Commander."

"Thanks," Riker said weakly.

"Come with me." Worf bent down to help Korak up.

"Take your filthy Klingon hands off me! Kill me and have done with it! I do not deserve to live!"

"You won't hear any argument from me," Worf said. "Now will you stand up, or must I carry you?"

Reluctantly Korak allowed Worf to help him to his feet and then moved off with him, his head bowed with shame.

As Picard led Riker and the others out of the shuttle bay, they saw the other Romulans sprawled out on the deck, motionless.

"Are they dead?" Riker asked.

"No," Picard replied. "Merely inactive."

Riker frowned. "Inactive?"

Picard smiled. "A borrowed term, Number One."

"Borrowed from whom?" asked Riker, now utterly confused.

"From a friend, Mr. Riker. From a friend."

They gathered around the conference table in the briefing room aboard the *Enterprise*. Riker, battered and bruised, with several fractured ribs, sat gingerly in his chair beside Deanna Troi, next to whom sat Ro Laren. On Laren's right was Data, with Geordi La Forge sitting next to him, and across from them sat Dr. Beverly Crusher, Worf, and Picard. Also at the table were the two men from the *Independence*, Llewellyn and Vishinski.

"Our friends from the ark asked that we proceed without them," said Llewellyn. "They sensed certain inhibitions among some of you, resulting from their being telepaths and felt that you would be able to ask your questions more freely in their absence."

The crew members of the *Enterprise* glanced around at one another.

"We have nothing to hide," Picard said. "And I was hoping that they would be present. I feel that we have a great deal to discuss."

Llewellyn smiled. "Forgive me, Captain, I did not mean to imply that any of you had anything to hide. It's just that living with us, they have learned that non-telepathic races feel a certain natural discomfort about others having complete access to all their thoughts. It took us many years to become accustomed to it ourselves. Counselor Troi, as an empath, perhaps you will understand. They sensed a quite understandable apprehension among many of you and felt that, at least initially, you would be more comfortable speaking with us."

"Who *are* they?" asked Riker.

"We call them ambimorphs," Vishinski said. "Their own name for themselves is unpronounceable. Even after all our years among them, none of us have learned to speak their language. They do not actually speak it among themselves, for that matter. They have a highly complex and symbolic written language, but their communication among themselves is totally nonverbal."

"Shape-changers," La Forge said. "And telepathic, too."

"If you are thinking that they would make formidable enemies," Llewellyn said, "you are quite correct. They would. If we had to go up against them, we wouldn't stand a chance."

"From what I have seen, I find that point difficult to argue," agreed Picard.

La Forge glanced at Llewellyn. "I . . . uh . . . see what you meant about those inhibitions." He hesitated. "Were you reading *my* mind?"

Llewellyn smiled. "No, Mr. La Forge, I am not telepathic, though living with the ambimorphs for as long as we have has increased our intuitive perceptions considerably. And if I may anticipate the next question, which you may or may not be able to bring yourselves to ask: no, I am not one of them masquerading as a human, though they could easily have accomplished that. You will have to take my word that I am who I claim to be, however. The ambimorphs' ability to transform themselves is such that even the most sophisticated medical scanners would be unable to detect them."

"Where do they come from?" asked Worf.

"We know only that they are from a distant star system," Vishinski replied. "As you have seen, their ship is multigenerational, and their life span is far greater than our own."

"The ark has been here for over thirty years, Commander," Picard said. "Exactly what do they want here?"

"Some of you already know part of the story," Llewellyn said, glancing at Ro, Troi, Data, and Crusher. "Their mission is essentially similar to yours." He smiled. "Perhaps I should say *ours*. After all this time I sometimes find it difficult to recall that I am still a Starfleet officer."

"So then they came in search of other intelligent beings?" Picard said.

"Yes," Lewellyn replied, "and they found several species at war with one another. When they first arrived in this sector, the Federation was still at war with the Klingon Empire and the Romulans were the wild card in the conflict. Now the Federation and the Klingons are allies, but the Romulans remain as warlike and unpredictable as ever. The situation was extremely unstable back then, and in many ways it still is. The ambimorphs had no idea what to make of it."

"They had long since evolved beyond the need for

violence," added Vishinski, "and they did not really understand what was going on or why. So instead of making contact with any of the warring species, they decided to wait until they learned more, primarily by monitoring communications at long range to get a better sense of the situation and the participants."

"Only you wound up making contact with them first," said Riker.

Llewellyn nodded. "We had discovered a small planetary body that wasn't on any of the charts, and when we investigated, our experience was much the same as yours. We discovered that it was not a small planet at all, but an interstellar ark, and we sent away teams down to investigate. That gave the ambimorphs their first opportunity to observe humans up close, and they proceeded cautiously. They tested us. They interfered with our communications, decoyed a number of other landing parties down, and watched us stumble around, trying to figure out what the hell was going on. All the time, they were around us, watching and waiting to see what we would do, how we would react to the situation. They particularly wanted to know if we would react violently."

"The sculptures," said Deanna. "I sensed something when I touched one of them, but it was only a vague impression, and then it was gone."

"Or telepathically blocked," Picard said. "So what we took to be artful arrangements of lights and sculptures were actually a number of them standing around among the streetlights and mimicking their form?"

"Actually the lights and sculptures *are* arranged in groups to create an aesthetic blend of light and shadow," said Vishinski. "However, it was a simple matter for the ambimorphs merely to 'add' a sculpture or two here and there, so they could monitor you from up close."

"Eventually they began to show themselves to us," Llewellyn said, "in humanoid form, though at a distance, again to see what we would do. And some of them came aboard our ship after posing as landing parties and getting themselves beamed up. Being telepaths, the deception was simple for them to carry off. All they required was proximity to an away team and a telepathic scan would do the rest. However, they never intended to take over our ship. I guess you might say they were just hedging their bets, placing themselves in position to neutralize us quickly if we suddenly turned hostile. And it also enabled them to make sure no messages were sent out to Starfleet."

"What happened to cause the entire crew to beam down, and why did four of your people attempt escape in a shuttlecraft?" Picard asked.

"We actually had no choice but to beam down the entire crew," replied Llewellyn. "When the ambimorphs finally made contact with us, after satisfying themselves that we weren't a savage species, they were warm and welcoming. Unfortunately, by that time, we had already been exposed."

"You see," Vishinski said, "with their ability to alter their own molecular structure, their bodies automatically compensated for any germs we might have carried that could threaten them. In essence, they have the most perfect immune systems in the universe. It never occurred to them that we were not so lucky."

"The crew of the *Independence* contracted a disease from the ambimorphs," said Dr. Crusher. "A virus caused by bacteria they apparently brought with them from their homeworld. They were naturally immune to it, but they were carriers."

"The virus spread with unbelievable speed," Vishinski said. "Our medical technology simply couldn't cope with it. We lost almost half our crew before the ambimorphs could put a stop to it."

"So then that's what the ambimorph meant when he said 'we killed them,'" said Picard.

Llewellyn nodded. "They were shocked and absolutely devastated," he said. "They still carry the guilt. It's a source of great pain to them, even though it was completely unintentional on their part."

"Then that explains the quarantine." Picard frowned. "So we've all been exposed?"

"No, you need have no worry on that count," replied Vishinski. "Once the ambimorphs realized what was happening, they were able to isolate the virus with my help and then destroy it within themselves."

"Unfortunately, they could do nothing for those who had already been infected," added Llewellyn, "and that included most of the crew. Many had already died, and some were hopelessly ill, but for the rest of us, they were able to come up with a treatment using antibodies they created for us in their own systems."

"It took time, however," said Vishinski. "I was charting virgin medical territory, and they were dealing with a completely alien morphology. The initial cell treatments killed the virus, but they also killed the members of our crew who volunteered to act as test subjects. Eventually the ambimorphs were able to manufacture antibodies that our systems could tolerate. The treatment does not constitute a cure, but it does hold the virus in stasis. However, we do require periodic treatments."

"So that's why none of you can ever leave," said Dr. Crusher. "Perhaps you no longer need to depend on the ambimorphs creating the cell lines for your treatments. In the past thirty years we've made significant advances in protein engineering. There's a chance we could duplicate the treatments."

"Perhaps, but that's not the only reason we stay here," said Llewellyn. "Our children all grew up aboard the ark, and many of them were born there. I even have grandchildren now who grew up with the ambimorphs. Except for us, the children have never known human society. Life aboard the ark is the only existence they know, and it's a good life. The ark is home for them, and they wouldn't want to leave. Even if they did, they'd never really fit in with human society. Aside from that, this has been a truly incredible opportunity for us. As the ambimorphs have studied us, so we have studied them. They're a unique species, highly advanced, and the most incredibly adaptable life-form we've ever encountered."

"Their ability to transform themselves, to alter their own molecular structure at will, makes them the ultimate survivors," said Vishinski. "It's fortunate for us that they are nonaggressive, for they could easily become the most dominant species in the universe. They have settled countless worlds, but always with an acute awareness of ecological balance. They look for a niche, then adapt themselves to fit in."

"Fascinating," said Picard. "However, one question remains unanswered. What of the shuttlecraft from the *Independence* that was found drifting in space with four dead men aboard?"

"That's right," said Troi. "You told us it was your captain and three of your fellow crew members."

Llewellyn nodded. "Yes, well, I must confess that I was less than honest with you about that, Counselor. You had a great deal to absorb, and I wanted to see how you would react to the rest of the story before I told you this part. You see, Captain Wiley, Lieutenant Commander Glener, Ensign Morris, and Chief Connors were among the first to succumb to the virus. The four so-called survivors found aboard the shuttlecraft were neither dead nor human. They were ambimorphs, posing as Captain Wiley, Commander Glener, Ensign Morris, and Chief Connors, men selected primarily because they had no families."

Picard frowned. "Selected for what purpose?"

"I think you already know the answer to that question, Captain," Llewellyn replied. "The ambimorphs' intention was to get to Earth and infiltrate Starfleet."

"Wait a minute. I thought you said the ambimorphs were nonaggressive," Riker said tensely.

Llewellyn raised his hand. "Hear me out," he said. "Their intentions *are* nonaggressive. But even after spending all those years with us, there is still much about us, our societies and cultures, that they do not know. They are not ready to make formal contact with the Federation, and they do not feel the Federation is ready for contact with them. At least not yet. Compared to them, we are primitive. They learned from us that planets could be quarantined and that the files relating to those planets could be classified. They wanted to make certain no other Federation ships came to the ark."

"Then the ambimorphs who escaped in the shuttle were responsible for the ark receiving the Hermeticus designation," said Picard. "But that was decades ago. What has happened to the four infiltrators since?"

"I can only surmise that they remained in their original cover identities," said Llewellyn. "As I said, their life span is much greater than ours. By now they could be anywhere. And they could be literally anyone."

"And you *cooperated* in this?" said Riker, aghast at the implications.

"Yes, but they could easily have done it without our cooperation," said Llewellyn. "They only wish to learn. And to keep tabs on us. We may not be as barbarous a species as we once were, but we do still have a propensity for violence." He glanced at Riker, who shifted in his seat uncomfortably. "My telling you this now will make no difference whatsoever. Feel free to make a complete report. You'll never find them, not in a million years. Not until they're ready to be found."

"You seem to be forgetting one thing," said Picard. "There is a classified file at Starfleet Command, containing the location coordinates for the ark. If we submit a complete report, other Federation ships may follow us. That decision will be out of our hands."

"It will make no difference, Captain Picard," said a voice they all heard in their minds. *"The ark will no longer be here."*

They looked up as two of the ambimorphs entered the briefing room. The shapeshifters had taken a roughly humanoid form, but their substance was protoplasmic. It was rather like looking at giant amoebas that had assumed a roughly human shape. The crew could see through them, and their internal structure appeared to be constantly shifting, flowing as they moved.

"This stage of our mission here is complete. We shall go home soon. We shall not live to see the completion of the voyage, but we have our work to occupy us, and our offspring will carry it on and deliver it to our homeworld."

"And what of the Romulans?" Picard asked.

"We will take them with us," the first ambimorph replied, telepathically. *"We want to study them and learn as much as possible about their species, as we have done with Commander Llewellyn and his people. What we have learned about your race, through them, has given us much cause for hope. Meaning no offense, we feel that the human race is not yet sufficiently evolved. However, we believe that in time, perhaps before a great many more of your years have passed, the situation will be more favorable for our races to establish formal contact. Those of us who are now among you have gone to prepare the way for that eventuality. Their mission is a peaceful one. They intend not to interfere, but to increase our knowledge of you and make discreet, informal contact with key individuals among your people, so that formal contact between our two races can eventually occur in a manner that will not disrupt your culture or your internal stability. But so long as the conflict continues between your people and the Romulans, we shall not become involved. We find violence barbaric and distasteful. There are more intelligent ways to resolve a conflict. When your people and the Romulans discover those methods, perhaps we can speak again."*

The other ambimorph moved toward the door and, as it opened, Valak entered, flanked by two *Enterprise* crewmen. He saw the ambimorphs in their natural state and recoiled from them. Then his gaze swept the crew of the *Enterprise* until it settled on Picard.

"What *are* these creatures?" he said.

"You will have plenty of opportunity to find that out," Picard replied. "It seems that you will remain with them."

Valak's eyes grew wide. "No! This is your ship, Picard! You cannot allow that!"

"The decision is not mine to make, Valak," Picard replied. "I warned you. You should have listened to me."

"What are they going to do with us?" Valak asked apprehensively.

"The crew of your vessel is being transferred to the ark as we speak," said the first ambimorph, still speaking to them all telepathically. *"Once the* Syrinx *has been vacated, it will be towed to a sector near the Romulan border of what you call the Neutral Zone, where it will be destroyed, along with the* Independence. *The debris will speak of a battle between two ships. A small group of Romulan survivors will be found drifting in a shuttlecraft. They will report an engagement in which a Federation vessel and their own ship were destroyed. They will also report that certain design flaws in the* Syrinx *rendered it vulnerable. Lord Kazanak, the designer of the vessel, will be among the survivors. He will pronounce his work a failure, and in time he will abandon the field of spacecraft engineering and assume a position of leadership in Romulan society."*

"You must be mad," said Valak. "You will never get away with this!"

The ambimorph turned toward him, and Valak gaped as he suddenly found himself looking at his own double, right down to the finest detail of his uniform, the insignia of the D'Kazanak class warbird.

"I believe we shall," the ambimorph replied in

Valak's own voice. "Your species is highly aggressive and extremely violent, much in need of guidance. In certain subtle ways, without interfering in your society, we may be able to provide such guidance. Perhaps not. In either case, we shall attempt to learn as much as possible about your race by moving among you, and as the rest of us depart on our long journey home, you and your crew will help us understand you better."

"No!" Valak tried to jerk away from the two crewmen who held him and suddenly found, to his astonishment, that he was being held by Talar and Korak. Shocked, he abruptly stopped struggling and turned back to Picard. "You cannot let them do this, Picard! You must *do* something!"

"Must I? You were going to take my ship back to Romulus as your prize of war," Picard replied. "You would have sold us in your slave markets or else killed us—even the children. Yet now you ask for my help?"

Valak swallowed hard and, struggling to control his emotions, drew himself up straight. "This is not over yet," he said, trying to keep his voice steady. "We shall fight and either regain our freedom or die like warriors in the attempt."

"Resistance will be pointless, Commander," said Vishinski. "The ambimorphs are telepathic, and they will know your plans even as you conceive them. Moreover, they can render you completely powerless with just a thought."

"Despite all that you have done," Picard said, "if I thought you and your crew would come to any harm, I would try to help you if I could. However, I cannot, and I am convinced the ambimorphs do not intend to harm any of you. If they had, they could have done so easily by now. You are a warrior, Valak, but you are also a scholar, and if you have any saving grace, it is that. As a scholar, you will have an unprecedented opportunity to do research that may one day be of great benefit to your people. I would seize that opportunity if I were you. I suspect you will find it offers much greater rewards than conquest."

Valak stared at him for a long moment, then nodded. "So then, the game is finished," he said resignedly. "And you have won."

"I would call it a draw," Picard replied, "because the ambimorphs intervened."

Valak shook his head. "No, Picard, you would have won in any case. The hostages escaped from the *Syrinx* on their own, and Riker bested Korak. He discovered weapons aboard the *Independence* that we should have found and confiscated, and once La Forge and his engineering crew had freed the others, they undoubtedly would have sabotaged our ship's systems. There would have been many casualties before it was all over, but to employ a metaphor from your game of chess, once your people took control of the board, the outcome was no longer in doubt. My compliments, Commander," he said, with a nod to Riker. "I warned Korak not to underestimate you. I had the superior vessel, I had the early advantage, and I believed I had the superior crew. On that last point I was wrong," he admitted wryly. "Perhaps it is just as well that I must stay on the ark. With my mission a failure, I would not have had much to look forward to when I returned to Romulus. At the very least, my career would have been finished."

"Your career as a warrior is over," his ambimorph double replied, "but your life as a scholar is only just beginning. I shall endeavor to pursue it for you on Romulus, and I hope you will pursue it with my people. You should find it . . . stimulating."

Valak smiled wryly. "Well . . . perhaps I shall. Good-bye, Picard. Meeting you has indeed been stimulating." He glanced at the ambimorphs. "I am ready."

They accompanied him out the door.

"He seems different from the others," Llewellyn said thoughtfully. "With more like him, who knows? Maybe there's hope for the Romulans, after all."

"There is always hope, Commander," said Picard. "Perhaps more now than before."

Epilogue

PICARD RETURNED TO THE BRIDGE after seeing Llewellyn and Vishinski off in the transporter room. It felt good to be back aboard his ship again and in control. The nightmare was over. The ship and his crew were safe. It was the closest they had ever come to complete disaster, but his crew had withstood the test, and with the help of the ambimorphs, they had pulled through. However, Picard had no doubt they would have done it on their own, anyway. Valak had been right in that regard. Perhaps he did not underestimate me, Picard thought, but he underestimated my crew.

"Have Llewellyn and Vishinski gone?" asked Riker.

Picard nodded. "Yes, they are back aboard the ark, Number One. And they have given me a complete log of their time with the ambimorphs. It should make fascinating reading."

Riker shook his head. "For thirty years, they've

been away from everything they knew, and they'll never be able to go back home again."

"On the contrary, Will," Picard said with a smile. "They *have* gone back home."

"Sir," said Data, "I am receiving a transmission from the ark. They are ready to get under way."

"Activate main viewer, Mr. Data."

The viewscreen came on, and they all watched as the huge ark began to move with a stately majesty, drifting away from them slowly at first, towing the *Independence* and the *Syrinx,* apparently holding them in some sort of forcefield as it gradually accelerated, then suddenly went to warp speed and disappeared.

"I can almost imagine how Valak must feel," Picard said. "He thought he had the *Enterprise.* Instead, he has lost his own ship, and now the ambimorphs have departed with their Romulan prize. Still, he may find it a valuable experience. Perhaps even a rewarding one."

"It's strange to think of ambimorphs posing as members of Starfleet," Riker said. "And a little frightening, too. You think we'll ever find out who they are?"

"They have had many years to establish themselves among us," Picard replied. "I suppose they could be anyone." He raised his eyebrows. "Even you, Number One."

"My ribs would argue that one," Riker said with a pained smile. "I can't will them to mend. And I think an ambimorph would have had more sense than to get into a brawl with a Romulan."

"I thought you would have had more sense, too," Picard said.

Riker nodded. "Well . . . it seemed like a good idea at the time."

"Right now I think it would be a good idea to get back to Federation space," Picard said with a smile. "Set course for Starbase Thirty-nine, Mr. Data, and prepare to get under way."

"Course set, sir, zero eight nine, mark nine five."

"Warp factor three, Mr. Data."

"Warp factor three, sir."

Picard leaned back in his chair and closed his eyes for a moment. He was tired, but it felt good to be back home. "Engage," he said.